Created with Vellum

GLOSSARY OF FOREIGN WORDS

Ancient Mer

Foniádes - Slayers
Apotreptikó - An inhospitable place
Dyás - Interval
Dyás Kyatára - Interval Curse
Álas Kyatára - Salt Curse

Polish

Nikt cię nie skrzwdzi. - Nobody will hurt you.
Jesteś wolny. - You are free

ALSO BY A.L. KNORR

The Elemental Origins Series

Born of Water

Born of Fire

Born of Earth

Born of Æther

Born of Air

The Elementals

Mira's Return Series

Returning

Falling

Surfacing

The Siren's Curse Trilogy

Salt & Stone

Salt & the Sovereign

Salt & the Sisters

Elemental Novellas

Pyro, A Fire Novella

Heat, A Fire Novella

The Kacy Chronicles

Descendant

Ascendant

Combatant

Transcendent

Join A.L. Knorr's VIP Reader List and she'll personally send you a reminder as soon as her next book is out. Visit www.alknorrbooks.com to sign up!

SALT & THE SOVEREIGN

THE SIREN'S CURSE, BOOK 2

A.L. KNORR

INTELLECTUALLY PROMISCUOUS PRESS

PROLOGUE

"I can't find him," Antoni said as he strode into the parlor and tossed his coat over the back of the couch nearest the door. "No one knows where he is."

My heart sank and I made eye contact with my daughter—Targa. I had wanted Jozef here with us when I began recounting my story, refusing my children's prompts to get started without him. Just the thought of seeing him again—now that my memories had returned to me—put me into a cold sweat of anxiety. Nerves were not something I normally suffered from, but in this case, under these circumstances...only a dead person wouldn't have butterflies.

Targa glanced from me to Antoni and back again. "How can that be? It's middle of the day on a Tuesday, he works for our salvage team. Shouldn't he be at work?"

"You might not believe this, but he gave his notice." Antoni sat down beside Targa, shooting a nod of hello at Emun, who was sitting beside me.

Targa goggled. "He *resigned*?"

I closed my eyes as guilt and remorse washed over me like a bucket of ice water. The last time I'd seen Jozef had been in the front yard, and I'd rejected his invitation to dinner. It was far from certain that he'd quit because I'd declined his offer, but I couldn't halt the notion that the two were somehow linked.

I opened my eyes and swallowed down the tears that wanted to come. It was too much all at once. "Do you know why?"

Antoni shook his head. "I talked to his boss—Lizster. Jozef didn't give a reason and he didn't give much notice either, only forty-eight hours. No forwarding address or number, and his apartment is up for rent already." Antoni's hazel eyes were full of sympathy. "I'm so sorry, Mira."

I had wanted to go searching for Jozef myself within hours of recovering my memory, but neither Targa nor Emun would allow me to leave the manor until they were sure I wasn't going to lose myself again. Shock went through our little circle in waves. Even Antoni—who was not related to me and not directly affected—hardly spoke for a few hours as he processed what had happened.

Truthfully, I had never felt so exhausted as I had in the days following Targa's calling me home, and Emun giving me the aquamarine which now sat at the base of my throat on a chain.

I had tried calling Jozef's cell but got a message saying the number had been disconnected. I'd sent him emails which went unanswered, and had finally begged Antoni to go find him for me.

"I'm truly sorry we're not able to find your friend, Mother." Emun shifted against the sofa for a better look at me. "But since he can't be found, and I think I could actually die of anticipation if we wait another minute, do you mind very much if we get started without him?"

His words were tentative, uncertain, and full of longing.

I looked at my son and reached for his hand. He grasped my fingers and squeezed. Emun had waited a very long time for this moment, and with or without Jozef, I didn't want him to wait any longer, either.

I cleared my throat and began, "I was born on March 4, 1810, and given the name Bel Grant..."

"Wait, Mom." Targa reached for her bag from the coffee table in front of her and dug inside. Retrieving her phone, she activated the screen and selected something. "Do you mind if I record you? This is way too important to relegate to something as infallible as human memory, let alone siren memory."

"Of course I don't mind," I told her. "It's a good idea. While it might not be as vivid as the memories provided by the Hall of Anamna, it's a lot more convenient."

The kids (I knew they weren't kids, but I couldn't help but think of them that way) glanced at one another.

"The Hall of Anamna?" Targa echoed. "What's that?"

"I'll explain, but first we have to go back to London, England. The war with France was over, but as I was just a young child, I had no interest in the war. My life revolved around my mother." My throat tightened as I thought about the last time I had seen her, and I shoved the awful scene aside. "She was like a god to me."

ONE

Everyone called my mother Polly. It was a name for sweet young girls, kind old ladies with knitting nestled on their laps, or clever feathered pets from tropical countries. I remembered thinking from a very young age how much the name did not suit the imposing character and visage of Polly Grant.

At six feet tall and with eyes so dark they appeared black, my mother was difficult to miss in a crowd. When she spoke, her words came out with an authority that convinced all those within hearing range that she was a woman not to be tested. She wore her long, dark hair in a high circular braid like a crown, which only added to her air of austere royalty.

I was five. Looking up at my mother was like looking up at a giant. Standing on the platform at a train station in London, she did not hold my hand, but instead rested her own heavy one on my shoulder. She was gazing off to the left, still as stone, her dark eyes trained on the tracks in the direction our train would arrive from. Her hand seemed to grow heavier by the moment. The suffocating weight and the heat of it made me feel like I was being slowly crushed into the earth. I wanted to push her hand off and take a deep breath, but I dared not. Polly was swift to quell rebellious behavior.

A short, elderly man in a black bowler stood a few feet away and to the right of me. Holding a newspaper in his hands, his face was not visible behind the pages. I could only see the gray tufts of hair curling out from under the brim of his hat. I stared at him, waiting for him to move the newspaper so I could see what he looked like. Waiting for trains was boring.

Sending my right foot out to the side, I slowly moved away from my mother, just enough to begin to slide out from under her oppressive grasp.

"Do not wander, Bel," she said quietly, not looking down at me. But she dropped her hand, and that was all I wanted. I took a deep inhale, relieved.

"No, Mama." Reaching into the pocket of my wool coat, I pulled out a piece of crinkled paper. "Just putting this wrapper in the bin."

She cast me a brief glance but didn't reply, and returned to her sentinel stance. I had learned to keep little bits of trash in my pocket for just this reason—small planned escapes of the kind only children reveled in.

Stepping back and turning, I scanned the station for a garbage receptacle. There were only a few passengers on the platform because it was just after lunch on a week day. I spotted the bin and made my way over, walking slowly and quietly, because only unruly and disobedient children ran and screamed on train platforms and on roads and in the parks.

Savoring my bit of freedom, I tossed the wrapper and watched it fall. When I returned to the platform, I made sure Polly could see where I was, but I didn't return to her right away. I stood to the side a little, watching the old man reading the paper.

Some sixth sense told him he was being watched. His gaze finally dropped to the little girl in the blue woolen coat—me. I was impressed with his thick white moustache. The moustache was curled up at the ends, like a small set of horns. We made eye contact. His moustache lifted and his pink cheeks rounded. The corners of his eyes crinkled.

I smiled too, drawn to his sparkling eyes and kind expression. The full-grown human male was captivating to me, since I'd interacted with so few of them. Not very many people looked at me the way he was looking at me—like he really *saw* me. Polly drew all attention to herself, and I didn't mind. Sometimes I felt like a small insect flying low to the ground, busy and invisible.

The old man glanced at my mother and back at me. "You must have gotten your eyes from your father," he said. "So blue. Like the sky, or a tropical sea."

I didn't know what to say to this. My father was not a part of my life and I had no memories of him. I knew other children had fathers, of course, but Polly was enough parent to fulfill the role of both, as she liked to remind me. I had never questioned the source of my eye color before that moment. The idea of getting some feature of mine from my father had never occurred to me. It was true, my eyes were very different from my mother's. We had the same dark hair, the same white skin, and we were both slender, but her eyes were dark and round, while mine were bright and tilted up a little at the outer corners. That my eyes were different from my mother's had never before been pointed out to me, and it was a moment that changed something. It was a moment of growing up, of questioning, of realization.

One's features were inherited, not given as if by magic, but bequeathed.

"Where are you going?" the kind man asked, and I liked his voice. It was gentle and soft, and he asked me this question as though he knew that if he said it too loudly it would alert Polly and our interaction would be over.

"To the seaside," I said, just as quietly. "Where are you going?"

"Bel," my mother said sharply, looking over. She snapped her gloved fingers and pointed at the ground beside her.

Slowly, a little sheepishly, I walked over to my place. My eyes closed as the weight of her hand descended on my shoulder once again. I opened my eyes to see the stranger watching my face. Somehow he knew better than to answer my question. But he watched us until my mother's gaze turned away again, returning to the tracks. A whistle sounded in the distance.

The old man released one hand from the newspaper, reached into his jacket pocket and pulled out a slip of paper. He held it between two fingers so I could see his train ticket. The letters spelled 'Cornwall' on the billet. He winked and his moustache lifted again. *Me too,* he mouthed.

I never saw the man again, but he'd given me something to ponder.

Some time later, as the train chugged its way across the rolling green moorlands, I was given a sandwich from Polly's bag. After I had eaten it, she took the kerchief it had been wrapped in, scattered the crumbs on the floor of the carriage, and put it back in her bag. She'd eaten as well and seemed relaxed, even relieved. It was as good a moment as I was going to get.

"Mama, why do we have different eyes?"

"Because you were born that way," she replied quickly.

I went back to staring out at the passing green, disappointed. But this was the best I was likely to get from Polly. It was not important for children to know why; that privilege was reserved for adults only. And I supposed, that one day when I got older, I would understand a lot more, too.

We arrived in Brighton to gray skies and drizzle. Stepping down from the train, I took as deep a breath of the sea air as I could hold in my little lungs. The salty humid air of the coast thrilled me to my very core. Though I knew better than to ask what we were doing here, I knew it had something to do with the ocean, and something to do with a recent event in my life that Polly referred to as my salt-birth.

Only a few weeks earlier, Polly had taken me to a place outside of London called Allhallows. It was an overnight trip, like the ones before it, and always to the same empty beach. I knew what to expect. Mama and I were to go swimming in the ocean together, under the cover of darkness, and away from the gas lamps of civilization. During these swims, Polly would lie in the shallow water of the beach, watching me play. I delighted in the way the water felt on my skin and the sand felt beneath my feet and between my toes. She simply watched me—calmly, patiently, and without explanation.

At Allhallows, I expected the same sort of delightful evening swim. These little outings had become my favorite thing, and though Polly never told me when she'd planned one for us, they'd become frequent. I learned that there was never a night swim that far away.

But something different happened at Allhallows—I transformed.

Though the transformation felt right and even good, I was frightened by what was happening to me. Polly had never shown me her true nature, so I didn't understand my own. But when she saw the way the muscles and bones of my legs were knitting together, the way the skin was changing to scales, she slid over in the water.

"Just relax, Bel," she whispered. "You're becoming what you were born to be."

It was then that she transformed beside me, allowing me to understand that this was normal, and this was what she'd been waiting for all along.

After Allhallows, life became a flurry of activity. I didn't understand the change in my mother's behaviors and routine, but I did understand that it had something to do with what had happened at Allhallows—that my salt-birth had triggered something in my mother's mind.

An aura of excitement radiated from Polly, and though I couldn't say her manner had changed, I sensed this new energy. She seemed happier, and eager for some objective to be met. She had meetings with people, people I understood she either had worked with or who had worked for her. These meetings seemed to have to do with getting ready to leave England.

Now, standing with my mother on an empty beach not far from Brighton, the night sky starless and flat with clouds, I understood that this was the moment she'd been preparing for.

"We're going to swim, Bel. For a long time. We have a long way to go." As she said this, she took off her dress, her petticoats, her shoes and stockings. She shed every last article of clothing and left them in a pile in the sea-grasses. She bade me do the same until we had no covering but the hair on our heads.

Walking into the water up to her knees, she held her hand out to me and beckoned. I ran to her, splashing in the water, my little heart pounding and my mind full of exploding stars.

"Where are we going?" I asked as we waded deeper.

Just before Polly dove into the waves, she answered, "We're going home."

WE SWAM with very little time to rest or explore, which—as a young and curious siren who had only recently had her salt-birth—was both emotionally painful and physically exhausting. Though I worked hard to keep up, it was far more difficult to swim through this new underwater universe and not be allowed to stop. There was so much to explore, so much to learn about. And we were so beautifully equipped to enjoy the environment that I couldn't understand how my mother was not drawn to every incredible feature we passed over and through.

We saw every kind of sea creature imaginable: huge masses of graceful rays, some individuals so large they were like underwater ships passing by, their strange square mouths double the length of Polly's entire body from one end to the other. We swam through forests of brightly colored seaweed, swaying gracefully and coated with fuzzy algae. Vivid orange and red fish sheltered there, peeking shyly from within the fronds. Large, prickly crustaceans crawled across curved pale landscapes. The terrain was caked with sand and spewed bubbles from cracks, around which small yellow crabs liked to cluster. But the natural wonders were only part of this striking realm, for we also passed over countless wrecks, not only of ships but also other strange, unidentified forms, alien shapes half buried in sand and crusted with coral.

Two underwater cities, distant and deep in the shadows, slid by as I followed my mother's long and powerful tail. How I gawked and begged to be allowed to go deep and explore.

"We've no time to lose, Bel," replied my mother, "even now, Okeanos is at risk."

"But how?"

Okeanos was a place, I now knew, and it was our home, but that was where my comprehension ended. The urgency I sensed in my mother had not been explained. I was just supposed to trust her.

"When you're older, you'll understand."

I had to be satisfied with telling myself that when I was grown and could go where I pleased, I would return this way and explore for as long as I liked. I wouldn't forget these cities. One had spindly, towering turrets with soft curves and arches. The other was all square edges, big brutal walls with huge stones fitted together tightly and almost seamlessly. Both were now home to millions of underwater species from microscopic algae, painted across the stones in bright colors, to huge eels poking their heads from crevices, the sizes of their toothy smiles mere hints at how long the attached bodies must be.

We stopped to catch a meal, and Polly paid particular attention to how much I ate, encouraging me to fill up. I should have known something was afoot for she didn't normally scrutinize my dining habits.

On we swam, and the terrain changed again. Rather than filling me with curiosity, the stark and barren topography here gave me a sense of foreboding. Suddenly, there seemed to be no life anywhere—no fish, no crustaceans, not even seaweed. When there was sand, it was black and gray; when there were rocks, they were as dark as ink and as sharp as razors. Even the texture and content of the water changed. It became a little more difficult to breathe, and tasted mildly acidic. I became conscious of my gills working to pull oxygen from the water.

"What is this place, mama?" I asked, trailing behind her and working harder, as always, my little tail burning and my heart pumping.

"It's the *apotreptikó*," she replied.

"What's that?"

She sighed audibly. "Just swim, Bel. We are getting close now."

And so I swam, and swam, and swam. I understood why she'd made me eat so much, because here there was no food. I began to grow hungry again, but knew better than to ask about hunting—there was nothing to hunt, and if there had been, Polly would not likely have allowed me to eat whatever could survive here in this oxygen-depleted and toxic place.

My focus lifted from the gloom and jagged edges below us to an increasing brightness on the horizon. I gladly picked up speed when Polly did, looking forward to leaving this strange and empty place.

Passing out of the *apotreptikó* was better than passing out of dark rain and shadow and into bright, strong sunlight. The world sprang to life, and the line between the *apotreptikó* and this abundant and beautiful jungle could not have been more distinct than if it had been drawn in ink.

I couldn't help but sigh with pleasure as the oxygen-rich water filled my gills and the smells of verdant green and rich minerals filled my senses.

Polly looked back when she heard me, giving me a rare smile. "Welcome to Okeanos."

My eyes widened. "*This* is our home?" I looked into the

horizon of this rich resource-filled land, but I saw no other sirens, nor any sign of places they might live.

"This is the outer reaches of it," Polly explained. "We still have far to swim, but we are in our territory now."

We hunted and fed, then slept for a time before moving on. Looking back over my shoulder at the blackness of the *apotreptikó* as it grew distant behind us, I let out a sigh of relief.

Sometime after that, more than two days of traveling I believe, though my memory for time is quite fuzzy, I witnessed something which was a foreshadowing of things to come. If I had been a little older and had been told a little more, I would have linked this event to the reason Polly was in such a hurry to get back to Okeanos. It wasn't until later that I put the two together.

Two creatures became visible as we swam over the top of a mountain of coral. Like everything else, the coral was rife with color, abundant with fish and sea-life, the water sparkling clean and delicious. My mother immediately redirected toward these two creatures, and I realized as she bore down on them that they were more human-like than we were.

One was clearly masculine, with a tapered waist and long limbs. The female was pale and slender. Both had long ropy hair, tangled masses of it, hopelessly matted. Polly would never have allowed my hair to become this way. During our rest breaks, Polly had taught me how to use my fingers to keep my hair relatively unknotted and free from algae-growth and my scalp and skin free from parasites. She told me a siren's grooming habits were equal to her health and vitality, and it was not a matter of vanity but hygiene. We allowed our nails to grow, but if they began to curve too much, or spiral, we cut them.

I stared at these two unusual beings with a mixture of horror and curiosity. They were too thin—gaunt, even—and were scouring the surface of the coral for sea vegetables with a desperation evident in their movements and frightened faces. There were fat gray parasites clinging to places on both of their skulls, and the whites of their eyes were tinged with yellow. They had the limbs, bodies, and faces of humans, but with webbing between their fingers and toes. Their feet were long and flexible, and reminded me of the fins of some kinds of fish I'd seen...less efficient than ours, but able to get around underwater with speed. Why were they in such poor health, I wondered. My stomach churned with pity for them.

They clung to one another, looking up with wide eyes as Polly thundered at them.

"What are you doing here?" she waved a hand back in the direction we came. "You are not permitted," she hissed. "Get out, quick, before I send our *Foniádes* after you."

They'd understood her, whether because they spoke our language or because no one could mistake the hostility in her tone and gestures, I didn't know. But they bolted back the way we'd come, heading for the *apotreptikó*.

Polly watched them go, a moue of disgust on her face. She muttered to herself. "Odenyalis, you've the heart of a traitor. It is worse than I thought."

"Mama," I asked, timidly, for her mutinous look was not one I had seen often. "What are they?"

"Atlanteans," she spat, before putting her back to the now-distant duo.

"Why can't they eat here? They look hungry and there is plenty of food." I might have added that they would most likely die before getting entirely past the extensive territory of the *apotreptikó*, but felt my mother would not appreciate me pointing out the obvious.

She shot a disgusted look at me.

"Isn't there?" I added, timidly, softening my tone to allow that I didn't know much, and could be wrong.

"It doesn't matter how much food—or anything else—we have, it's ours. It's not for those diseased scroungers. Now, move. We'll be at court by daybreak, but not nearly soon enough by the state of things."

Troubled, I worked to keep up with my mother as we grew ever closer to our final destination.

TWO

If I had thought the landscape beautiful once we'd passed out of the wasteland of the *apotreptikó*, it was nothing to the beauty that appeared below us as we crossed Okeanos. The best way to describe it was as a mountain range. And just as many of the largest mountain ranges of the earth's above-water surface are far-ranging and visually stunning, Okeanos was no different.

Seemingly endless peaks and valleys stretched out as far as the siren-eye could see. The tallest, most imposing peaks jutted upward to break the water's surface and stretch into the skies. Some valleys snaked tightly through steep canyon bottoms, while others stretched languidly wide and contained visible streams of fast-moving water—underwater highways fueled by varying temperatures and changing surfaces along the ocean floor. Every surface was busy and full of life. There appeared to be innumerable cracks in the rocks from which creatures emerged and into which they disappeared.

We were headed straight for the largest of these mountains. Polly said it was called Mount Califas and it was the heart of our territory.

I spotted the first sirens swimming among these valleys. My gaze consumed them hungrily, for the only other siren I'd seen at that point was my own mother. I even noticed a few young sirens, not much older than myself, swimming alongside their elders.

Polly did not greet these sirens, but something was communicated to them all the same. Whatever they were doing, they stopped and looked for her. Some seemed to share looks between them, while others watched as we swam by overhead before following at a distance.

I wanted desperately to ask who they were, why they were following us, and if I could talk to them, but there was something solemn and serious in my mother's face, and something even more foreboding in the faces of the others. So, I kept my mouth shut and trusted all would be revealed soon.

We swam for a long time and gathered sirens as we went, leading the migration to Mount Califas. We approached the imposing structure but my mother did not slow down. I watched as she swam into an inconspicuous crack in the rocks. I hesitated too long and sirens began to swim past me, following her inside. I realized I would lose my mother if I didn't join them, because she was not waiting for me.

As I slipped inside, the water temperature dropped and my eyes worked to adjust—the glow of bioluminescence in the tails of those around me being the only illumination. The crack became a tunnel, and the tunnel walls closed in and opened out before breaking off into other tunnels. Inside Mount Califas was a massive network of caves, pools, rivers, hallways, and caverns. I followed where the other sirens went, struggling to pass the ones in front of me in the narrow corridor.

The world began to brighten with shades of green and blue light. The sounds of water splashing and dripping, echoing against stone walls, reached my ears.

My head broke the surface and I found myself climbing out of the water along with the other sirens and into a huge arched cave speckled with light.

No one spoke as we stood on human legs and filtered through the enormous cave, our skin lit by the dim blue glow provided by glowworms and bioluminescent algae covering the walls.

I craned my neck to find my mother and saw her disappear through a large doorway illuminated with a soft white light. Someone had given her clothing, although I'd not seen who or when, for her body was covered with a simple robe tied at the waist with a ribbon. Her long hair lay dripping against her back and a circle of damp spread across her shoulder blades.

Indignation that the other sirens did not recognize that I was her daughter and let me pass rose inside me and I wanted to yell at them to let me through. But no one was speaking, and this moment held a grave silence that I was afraid to break.

One by one the sirens entered the doorway single file, and I took my turn. A stairway led us up and up and up and my young legs, unaccustomed to walking after the long time spent in my siren form, began to burn.

Daylight grew brighter as we ascended, but at no point did I see the sky. The long, silent climb gave me time to observe the strange surroundings. The play of illumination within this cave system was ever-changing and intriguing to watch. Slices of light shone from cracks in the rock, refracting and shooting into other cracks where it rebounded yet again.

The temperature rose, and we passed many rooms filled with color and pools and what looked at a glance like artwork. But there was no stopping because the siren parade moved at a constant pace.

When the soles of my bare feet finally touched the last step, those ahead of me had already spread out to form a semi-circle. Since it was impossible to see over the heads of the crowd, I pushed and elbowed my way indignantly toward the front. Something was happening that concerned my mother, and I was both out of my mind with curiosity and terrified to miss it.

I stopped when I reached the front row of sirens.

Many of the sirens in the room had procured clothing from somewhere, but just as many stood naked and dripping, watching with solemn eyes.

My heart was pounding and tiny minnows of anxiety swam circles in my belly.

That was when I saw *them*.

Not even the sight of my mother standing in a circle of bright sunlight pouring in through a hole in the ceiling could tear my eyes from the sight of *them*. And I instantly knew who they were: The *Foniádes*.

There were eight of them, and they were unlike any other siren I'd seen thus far, or could have dreamed up in my imagination.

They were taller than Polly, each of them broad and strong with muscular bodies. Feminine in shape and silhouette, and also positively predatory. Their pupils were large, even with the bright natural light in the room. Their irises were deep indigo blue and the small whites still visible were bright blue-white. When their eyes moved, it was to dart, watchfully, and because the irises were so large, it was difficult to pinpoint exactly where they were looking.

Their skin was not rosy and warm or in any human shade, but a cool, blue-gray color. Long arms ended in strong hands equipped with talons, and the parting of one's bluish lips revealed stark white teeth, a little too pointed to be friendly. They wore simple, tight sleeveless tunics that ended just below the pubic bone and matched the color of their skin. They all had high cheekbones and hair in shades of grays, blacks, and dark blues. For some it was shorn at the sides, and for others it was twisted into tight rows against the head and let to flow down the back. I noticed each wore a turquoise gem—at the throat of some, in the hair of others, on the wrist of yet another.

My mind was bursting with questions about these sirens—if that's what they were. That my mother had threatened the Atlanteans with sending the *Foniádes* after them had had such an instant effect made sense now. These creatures were intimidating merely standing and leaning against the stones the way they were now, I couldn't imagine what they could do when released against a foe.

Only when I'd looked my fill at these forbidding sirens did I notice that my mother stood in front of a throne made of bright blue stone, on which sat a queen wearing a crown and necklace of that same blue rock. The siren on the blue throne got to her feet. She took the steps down from her perch, slowly, with a soft, unsmiling expression. She was beautiful to look at, Odenyalis—I knew this was her name because my mother had spoken of her, though never with much regard. She wore a robe similar to the one Polly wore—simple, long-sleeved, and tied at the waist.

Odenyalis stood face to face with my mother, holding her hands out. Polly placed her hands on the offered palms.

Odenyalis kissed Polly once on each cheek before she lifted slender hands to the crown of blue gems and took it from her own head. Turning the crown around, she placed it on Polly's head, then she transferred the necklace and the ring on her finger.

Odenyalis kissed her again, but this time at the throat, in the hollow place between the collar bones. Odenyalis then pressed her first two fingers into this hollow place, closed her eyes and dropped her face down. A few moments passed before she lifted her gaze again, dropped her hand, and went to join the circle of sirens. I watched her face, and I thought she seemed happy, even relieved, but like she was working to keep her emotions hidden. A few sirens took Odenyalis by the hand and there were whispers, but I couldn't make out what was said. I know now that I couldn't make it out because it was in an ancient language that has now been lost, but the sirens were simply thanking Odenyalis for her service.

Polly turned to face the crowd. "I, Apollyona of Okeanos, humbly take up the coronation of the Salt, and serve you as Sovereign."

Apollyona? I thought. *That is her real name?* And somehow, it fell into place. This name suited her far better than Polly ever had. It struck me that she never thought enough of the few humans she'd had in her life to give them her real name. It was only later that I understood that all sirens have two names, the one they were born with, and the one the Salt gives to them sometime after puberty.

One by one, the sirens approached Apollyona and touched that space between her collarbones. Some kissed her cheeks, some didn't, but all touched the base of her neck.

I took my turn, hoping for something from my mother,

some word that she'd take me aside and explain everything later. But her eyes fell on me the same way they fell on any other. The only signal I got from her that I was any different from every other siren in the room was the smallest of smiles. She received the acknowledgement that I was giving her—she was now my Sovereign. I moved aside to let the next siren take her turn, including the *Foniádes*. It was then that I noticed that it was not only the *Foniádes* and the Sovereign who had these bright blue gems, but every siren in the room wore one, save those who—like me—had not yet passed through puberty.

I waited, hoping for something more from my mother, and as I stood back and watched, I noticed another siren dissimilar to the others in the room. But unlike the *Foniádes*, I noticed this one for her beauty and coloring rather than her height or intimidating features.

She was petite with long blue hair—big and puffy and fine—it moved as though she was standing in a breeze, but I thought it must just be light as silk. Her face was small and pointed, the outer corners of her eyes upturned. Her eyes seemed to change color, at one moment green, at another blue, and then gray. She was also dressed simply, but with more character, I thought. She wore a short blue shift dress with only one strap over her right shoulder. She was much shorter than Apollyona, and reached up to touch the new Sovereign's throat, but somehow, she seemed just as majestic as the new queen.

My gaze followed her as she made her way toward the steps leading down. She put a hand on the rock beside the stairway and paused for a moment, then she looked back over her shoulder and her eyes fell on my face. She smiled—a dazzling grin full of mischief, then turned and disappeared into the stairwell. It had happened so quickly that I thought I might have imagined it, but no, she'd smiled at me.

When the last of the sirens except the *Foniádes* had left the room, I stood up from the stone seat I'd found and gave my mother a hopeful look.

But she beckoned the *Foniádes* closer to listen to her.

"At the southeastern border," my mother said, her first words as the new Sovereign, "We found two Atlanteans stealing from Us. Enya allowed them to graze within our borders, but this will not do for Our reign. The new edict is that no Atlanteans are permitted to poach in Our territory. Find those two, for I am certain they will have returned by now. Bring them to me."

The *Foniádes* turned and left with that command. I fought the urge to shrink against the wall as they passed, but they took no notice of me.

Apollyona stood with her back to me, still, appearing to be lost in thought.

"Mother?" My voice seemed small and lost in that cave.

Apollyona looked over her shoulder then, as though only now remembering that she had a daughter. She squared her shoulders and beckoned. "What is it, Bel?"

I wanted to run to her, I wanted to throw my arms around her, and for some inexplicable reason, I wanted to let siren tears fall until I felt better. But Apollyona despised those kinds of 'displays of weakness,' as she'd called them, and what I wanted more than anything was to please my mother. So I approached with my hands clasped in front of me, slowly, outwardly calm.

"What is happening?" I asked.

She looked down at me, the jewels glittering from her head and the necklace at her throat giving her more of a queenly aura than any human queen I'd seen in paintings when we'd been on land, even though her robe was simple and her feet were bare.

"I'm your Sovereign," she replied. "Go and acquaint yourself with your new home. Stay out of trouble."

That was it? I blinked at her, confused.

She set a hand on my shoulder and her voice warmed a fraction. "You are too young to need a gem. Come and see me then." With that, she kissed the top of my head, the only bit of affection I'd received from her or anyone since entering Okeanos. "Now go and meet your sister sirens. I have things to do."

With that, she turned away and left the room through an archway behind the throne. I longed to go after her, to see what she had to do as Sovereign, to learn everything about my new home, about the *Foniádes*, and about the blue-haired siren. More than these things, I just wanted to be with her, as her daughter. My mother had never been perfect, and she had not educated me well, but she loved me in her way. She was my first love, and I felt I'd lost her at an age when I barely understood my own nature. I wanted Polly back.

But it was not to be the way it had been, and the most painful lesson of my young life was that everything changes, and once changed, will never go back to the way it was before, no matter how much one might want it.

I wished bitterly that I had paid more attention to everything Polly had ever said to me when it had just been the two of us. I wished I'd soaked up the moments spent with her, relished the sound of her voice when she'd spoken, listened to the sound of her heart on the rare moments when she'd held me. I lost something I thought I could never lose, and no one warned me it was coming—not even Polly.

In many ways it hit me like a death—Apollyona's ascension to Sovereignty. Polly was dead, and the siren sitting on the throne looked and sounded a lot like her in character, but was nothing like her in deed.

I became everyone's daughter, and no one's daughter—everyone's responsibility, and no one's responsibility—for the remainder of my childhood.

THREE

Life in Okeanos as a pre-pubescent siren was safe, easy, and protected. Years passed, and I approached the time when I would need to have my first mating cycle. Only after I'd completed one full cycle would I be given my gemstone.

I've since learned that sirens, even the ones who made their home in Okeanos, are nomadic by nature. The territory of Okeanos was massive, larger than most European countries, and sirens had the run of it. It was not unusual for a siren to disappear for months on end, reappearing to recount her adventures to her fellow sirens before disappearing again. Wandering and exploring was in our nature, and there were so few predators who might attack us that we roamed broadly and solitarily, afraid of nothing.

Even the large sharks of the ocean were unlikely to attack us, though I didn't learn why until much later in my life, and thanks to a certain oceanographer. The only predators we needed to fear were so rare that hardly any siren had ever seen either one—the giant squid and the kraken.

Exploring the underwater world of Okeanos was a never-ending source of joy and learning for me, but second to that was the exploration of the caves of Califas. They were an engineering marvel, for it was clear that the caves—while they might have begun as a natural phenomenon—had been developed and built out centuries, maybe even millennia, ago.

The cave network within the mountain range was vast: stretching outward to every corner of the world, but above and below it as well. Apollyona's throne room lay just beneath the highest peak of Califas, which jutted from the sea like a monstrous castle covered in verdant green life. Waterfalls streamed from its face, splashing into rocky pools and lagoons of crystal waters filled with every kind of food a siren could want. Beaches crusted some edges while large boulders lay upon others. From its highest cliff, one could see the surrounding islands and blue waters extending into what seemed like eternity.

I learned that crevices in the face of Califas had been excavated and installed with reflective tiles, working to pull the sunlight deep into the interior for hundreds of vertical feet— even beneath the waterline—before the reflective tiles petered out and all became darkness. In the deepest caverns, piles of these broken mirrors and pieces of colored tiles lay in mossy, slime-coated heaps. Decayed and brittle tiling and grouting tools lay scattered about, as though whoever had installed them had simply run out of energy or resources and had to abandon the project.

I was told that Okeanos was very, very old, and had existed like this for at least five thousand years. It had gone through periods of emptiness, where no one occupied its halls and caverns, and it had gone through periods of development, being undertaken—we surmised—by enterprising sirens with a vision. There were places under the mountains beyond Califas that had been mined and still had yellow dust and veins of a yellow glittery mineral threading through the stone. These mines lay abandoned and no one seemed interested in bringing them to life again, for all our doings were directed by Apollyona, and before her Odenyalis, neither of whom was interested in mining. Why should any siren have to mine anything? The Atlantic gave us all the food we needed and Okeanos was an underwater utopia. When a siren bound for land needed money to start a human life and search for a mate, Califas had treasure stored in its deep caves. When sirens found things of value on the ocean floor, they brought it to these caves. No one guarded it because no one needed to. Sirens did not have the kind of greed that plagued men—wanting more than they could ever use. The treasure of the ocean floors belonged to all of us, and we could take what we needed when we needed it.

I had heard stories of sirens using their voices to procure money from unfortunate humans who were so unlucky as to be in the way, but this activity had been discouraged by not only Odenyalis but Sovereigns before her. Apollyona did not speak of it specifically, so sirens continued for the most part to take treasure from the ocean rather than from humans.

The borders of Okeanos were patrolled by the *Foniádes* in shifts. There were not so many of these fearsome sirens—a few dozen at most—however, any siren roaming near the ends of Okeanos territory was required to keep an eye out for Atlantean trespassers.

For a time, I became obsessed with the *Foniádes*, and wished I had been born like them. They were so fierce, so different from the rest of us, and when I was young, I thought of them as superior. Their tails had gray backs, white bellies, sometimes with black tips on the ends of their fins—shark-like characteristics. They swam faster, and they were larger, stronger, and more aggressive than the rest of us. I wondered aloud why there were so few sirens born like this and was answered by a nearby mermaid who'd heard me.

"It's the law of the ocean. Humans call it the food chain," she said, approaching to converse about it. "There are multitudes of the smallest kinds of fish in the water, but have you ever noticed that the larger the species is, the fewer they are in number? It's why no one ever sees the kraken; it's the largest, and there must only be a few," she guessed. "Maybe even only one."

This concept seemed so clever to me at the time. My human education had halted when Apollyona had taken me back to Okeanos with her, although my siren education had begun. There were no classrooms or teachers. Instead, the ocean was my classroom and every older siren my teacher. The older, more experienced mermaids taught the younger ones what they had learned while they were last on land. The schooling of young sirens relied on the verbal sharing of stories. We were not organized, we were not industrious, we were not even particularly sociable, but somehow young sirens received a cobbled together education with the more intelligent ones curious enough to seek out knowledge, sometimes endlessly plaguing the older sirens with questions—I was among this number.

Just as there were rooms in Califas for treasure, so were there rooms for other oddities found on the ocean floor, less valuable but certainly not less interesting things. Things like books, maps, eating and drinking tools, sailing tools and equipment, sculptures and other pieces of art, parts of ships, bolts and bolts of fabric (some of which were used to make the simple robes worn by those who wished), vats of soggy food like salted beef and pork, and crates and crates of alcohol. Anything that had ever been transported by ship overhead, a portion of it inevitably ended up on the ocean floor. There were weapons, too, plenty of them and of all kinds—both of human origin and (as I learned later) Mer-made. There were spears, swords, tridents, and knives and cutlasses of all shapes and kinds. Most of them were rusted beyond usefulness, but I thought perhaps they told of how warlike the Mer must have been once. In the time of my youth, most Mer carried a small knife, which came in handy when hunting, salvaging, and eating. Only the *Foniádes* carried spears and tridents, but I'd never seen them actually use these weapons.

Curiosity meant that most sirens eventually found their way through all the nooks and crannies of Okeanos, drawing every last ounce of education offered.

As my puberty grew close, it was the coming and going of sirens—some returning with daughters—that captured my imagination next. I knew my time was coming and I felt a growing reluctance to face it. I made a study of the sirens who returned, picking up on what emotions I could and looking intently at them as they went into the simple ceremony of receiving their gem from Apollyona and being welcomed back to Okeanos. They seemed to me to have survived an ordeal. Some of them looked downright haggard, and took a long time to lose the weariness they returned with. Some of them seemed happy enough to return, and these sirens, I noticed, were of the simple-minded kind, the kind who did not appear to be as inquisitive as some...like me, like my mother, and like the blue-haired siren.

It seemed that the character and biological makeup of sirens could be as varied as those of the humans who lived above our heads and beyond our borders, perhaps even more so.

"THIS IS TRULY FASCINATING," said Emun, getting up from his seat and beginning to pace. "What you're describing is an entire Mer culture, an organized nation that existed beneath the waves."

He locked eyes with Targa and then cut to Antoni. He stopped pacing and began talking with his hands.

"What she's describing, it sounds just like where we were, where all the gems had been kept for God knows how long. It must have been Califas, not Atlantis, like we thought." He raked his hands through his hair. "I have so many questions, I don't even know where to begin."

"Yeah, like how come it was abandoned?" Targa shifted on the couch to sit cross-legged. "It looked like no one had been there in years."

"Decades, even," added Antoni.

"And who stashed the gems there? Were they forgotten?" Targa shrugged her shoulders up in bewilderment. "I mean, I know aquamarines aren't the most valuable of all the stones, but that was a lot of jewels just sitting deep underground, not being useful to anyone."

"And protected by some kind of magic, don't forget," added Antoni.

"I thought it was just a myth," Emun muttered quietly, speaking more to himself.

"So you had heard of Okeanos?" I had wondered what Emun knew of the place of my youth. He was, after all, a century and a half old. "But you'd never been there before."

"Well, to someone who doesn't know where it is you

could easily pass through those mountains and never know what was beneath them. The place is completely hidden unless you know to go underground. I've been around long enough to have heard the name in passing, but I thought it either wasn't real, had been destroyed long ago, or was just a ruin. Turns out, now I've actually been there, fought Atlanteans there!"

"So, what happened to the population that lived there?" Targa turned a concerned gaze on me. "It was your home once—our home. And all things considered, it wasn't that long ago that you actually lived there. Not even two hundred years since the events you've told us about so far. So, what went wrong?"

"That's what I'm trying to tell you," I said with a smile. "I haven't even gotten to the place where I've given birth to Emun yet. May I continue?"

"Sorry, please. Go ahead." Targa settled back against the couch and Emun made his way back to his chair.

"I explained that Apollyona dropped her mothering duties once she became Sovereign," I continued, jumping into the next important milestone in my history, "and so for a time I was left to figure things out on my own. But when I got a little older and was on the doorstep of puberty, a special siren came looking for me. It was as if she knew that there were gaps in my understanding, and had been waiting for the right moment to take me under her wing."

"Was it the one with the blue hair?" asked Targa, her expression hopeful. "You must have mentioned her for a reason."

I nodded. "Yes, it was the unusual one with the blue hair. You are right. Her name was Annikephoros..."

FOUR

"You are Polly's daughter, are you not?" The voice was soft and unfamiliar, but when I turned to see the speaker, I recognized her. This was Nike, and the only one of the Okeanos sirens I had ever heard refer to my mother by her human name. Sovereigns were respectfully referred to by their full name, which—as Apollyona had pointed out more than once—was given to her by that mysterious oceanic force we called simply 'the Salt.'

"Bel," I replied. "You're... Annikephoros." It took me a moment to recall her siren name, but I didn't want to make the mistake of calling her Nike, in case she had the same preferences as my mother. I had come to learn over the years that Nike was a sorceress, though I'd never seen her do anything magical. After the day of Apollyona's coronation, and the smile Nike had sent my way, she had never approached me to talk, and was even downright elusive. I believe now she was only biding her time until I had grown up.

She put my concerns to rest immediately. "Call me Nike."

She swam closer and I got my first close look at the only siren sorceress I knew of. She had unusual coloring, both on her upper human half and her siren half. Her hair was a most unusual shade of blue. Most siren hair was no different than human hair in color and texture, as far as I'd seen—browns, blacks, reds, golds and yellows. Nike's eyes shifted in color, but settled most often into a pale gray. Her skin appeared white in the sunlight but then seemed tan in the shadows, like it had some of the color-changing cells that other ocean-creatures had. I had seen some marvelous camouflaging properties on display by different kinds of fish and octopus, and I wondered if she could hide herself against any backdrop. Her hair and variable eyes—along with slightly more pointed ears—set Nike apart. She wore her aquamarine jewel at her throat, set in a thin metal claw and tied with a chain. It sat in the hollow of her neck, the place I was supposed to touch to show my deference.

I lifted a hand to reach forward, but she smiled and waved my gesture aside. "That's not necessary."

We swam side by side for a time, until I asked her what she was doing this far from Mount Califas. We were still within the borders of Okeanos, but we were approaching the kelp forests in the south, which marked the edges of the middle ring.

Okeanos, I was told by one of the *Foniádes*, was roughly circular and had three concentric rings. The outer ring was mostly flat and lay next to the *apotreptikó*, the middle ring was distinguished in parts by rolling hills and thick ropy forests of kelp which ran from sea floor all the way to the surface, and the center held the Califas range of mountains with Mt. Califas at the epicenter.

"I came looking for you, young Bel."

I was so startled that I came to a stop. "Me? Why?"

"I thought you might have...questions." Her gray eyes slid to mine as we resumed swimming.

I was surprised a second time. "Only about a thousand of them," I replied. "But no one has time for me."

"Least of all your mother," she added, gently.

I didn't reply to this stinging truth, only dropped my chin as my heart thudded painfully.

"My guess," continued Nike, fingering the thin fronds of young kelp trees reaching up from the ocean floor, "is that you don't understand your own mother's sovereignty, as she's never explained it to you."

"How do you know that?"

"Let's say, I've known Polly a very long time." Nike had a secret smile, and I sensed there was more to her answer but now was not the time to ask more. "Sovereignty is both simple and complicated. You know already, of course, about the *Dyás*?"

"The mating cycle?" This I thought I understood, for I'd seen sirens return from these cycles. Those who brought their siren offspring with them were celebrated. I was rapidly approaching the time for my own debut mating season.

"*Dyás* is a shortened name for this mating cycle which originates from the phrase *Dyás Kyatára*. Have you heard this before?" She gazed expectantly at me.

I shook my head. I hadn't.

She let out a sigh. "Polly's neglect of your education is worse than I feared."

I didn't know how to respond to this open criticism of my regal and powerful mother. I loved Apollyona, and my desire to please her had only grown since our return to Okeanos. But the goal seemed to grow more and more elusive as I approached the years of my sexual maturity, and

I didn't know why. I was sure it had to be something I had done, something that I had failed at. Failure was not something Apollyona allowed, but she also did not explain herself to anyone. As Sovereign, she didn't need to. But in my heart, I could not disagree with Nike's assessment. I was uneducated, seemingly the most uneducated young siren in the halls of Califas.

But Nike was going on, and I shoved these thoughts aside, fascinated and eager to hear her every word.

"*Dyás Kyatára* is translated from our ancient tongue, roughly meaning 'interval curse.' Some refer to it as the *Álas*, or the *Álas Kyatára*—the 'salt curse.' This season is not something you should look forward to, my sweet Bel."

"It's a curse? But it's how we procreate. How can it be a curse?"

Her elegant fingers went to the stone at her throat. "Because we need these to be protected from it. You don't need one at your age, since you are too young, but you'll know what I mean when it comes time for your first cycle. The power the *Dyás* will have over you once you cross the threshold into maturity is fierce and irresistible. I mean that quite literally. Without your gemstone, you will be unable to resist it. It will rule you."

My head was whirling. No one had explained the sirens' mating cycle to me this way before; it was always simply a fact of our lives, just the way things were. It had never occurred to me that there was anything unnatural or even malignant about it. I opened my mouth to ask her more questions about the *Dyás,* but she was asking me a question.

"What is it that the mating cycle gives a siren, aside from hopefully a daughter?"

I thought about this, about how young sirens who had yet to undertake their first cycle wanted to be around those who had just returned, if only to hear them talk about their experience.

"Experience? Knowledge about the world beyond Okeanos?"

Nike nodded.

"So, the *Dyás* makes sirens smart?"

Nike agreed, but fleshed out this idea more fully. "The cycles can be very painful. They give sirens the experience of love and loss and they cause emotional scarring. That, combined with her experience of life in the ocean, can lend itself to great wisdom. Life on land is much harder than it is down here. Here we rule, there is none to oppose us, and even the large predators of the ocean rarely move against a siren. They recognize us as their rulers and fear us."

This part I knew as well. We were carnivorous and some of us were excellent hunters. Of course the animals of the oceans feared us.

"The gems mean we do not need to take on any more of these seasons on land than we have to. When Odenyalis ruled, she required us to have enough *Dyás* as it took to produce two siren offspring: one to replace ourselves and one to grow our numbers. After that, no siren was forced to undertake additional cycles unless they wanted to. Under Apollyona's rule, we are required to go on at least one. She's more lenient with us than Odenyalis or previous Sovereigns were in the past."

I went quiet as I digested this. I was no longer paying attention to our surroundings, as there was too much going on in my head.

"So, without our gems, the Salt controls us."

Nike nodded. "The Salt for us could be likened to a deity. We don't fully understand how it works, but the fact that the Sovereign is gifted with power cannot be denied.

There is something real there, and whether it has consciousness or not has long been a matter of debate among the more academic among us."

"An academic siren?" I had to laugh. "I haven't run across many of those."

Nike smiled as she drifted along beside me, passing through the fronds of the kelp. "Well, now you have. And though your mother has not shared much of herself with you, she is an academic at heart as well." Nike's smile turned wry. "And a politician."

"I don't know this word."

"You will. You'll learn it on your first *Dyás* and then you'll understand what it means much better than if I explained it to you."

This might have annoyed me if I had not had so many other questions.

In Califas, there were halls and caves filled with mosaic paintings, images of history, cracked and broken in many places, crumbling and neglected in others. But as far as I knew, there was no recording of how many mating seasons each siren citizen of Okeanos had endured.

"How do we know how many cycles a siren has been through? Is that why everyone followed my m—Apollyona when we arrived here for the first time?"

"We don't track it simply because it is in our blood, the magic that links us all. Being Sovereign comes with certain advantages," Nike explained. "When your mother became our Sovereign, she inherited these powers from Odenyalis—her predecessor."

"Enya," I said, which was the name Odenyalis was now known by. "What are these powers?"

"To those who have never been in the Sovereign's seat, it is something of a mystery," Nike said with a grim smile.

"We know these powers exist because we can feel them, ebbing and flowing from Apollyona. Can you not feel them?"

I nodded, but this explanation was an understatement. Apollyona had been terrifying even before we returned to Okeanos. When she became Sovereign, she had become deified in my mind and in my physical reaction to her.

"So, besides the feeling that she could crush you at any given moment," I said, "no one actually knows how powerful the Sovereign really is...except for past Sovereigns?"

"Some say even those past Sovereigns come to forget what those powers are, and in this way the natural order is maintained."

"Do you think that's true?"

Nike shrugged and her expression became veiled and far away.

"It's impossible to say. I have questioned Enya about it, but she either genuinely forgets or she feigns forgetfulness." She wrinkled her nose. "It's very annoying. I suspect Sovereigns become aware of a great many things, and they like to keep this knowledge a secret because it adds to the respect they are given."

I was quietly astounded at the way Nike was discussing this so blithely. I had never heard other sirens speak this way about the Sovereign, or speculate about the nature of the Sovereignty. Apollyona was to be respected and obeyed, otherwise, what would separate us from the other creatures of the oceans? This was our civilization and it worked for us. We had the wealth and resources of all the Atlantic at our fingertips, we were unchallenged in our rule, and we were impenetrable, protected from harm at all times.

I watched Nike's face, wondering what made her think this way.

"You don't like it?" I asked, hesitantly.

Her eyes sharpened. "What makes you say that?"

"I've never heard anyone else talk this way. Everyone else is respectful, even awed."

The corners of Nike's mouth lifted momentarily. "She gestured to her sharper than normal ear-tips, her pointed features, and blue hair. "Yes, well. I'm not your average siren, now, am I?"

I shook my head. "Why are you different?"

"I suspect my mother dabbled in some pool she was not meant to," Nike replied with an impish grin.

"She never told you?"

"I never knew her. I was cared for by my father before making my way to Okeanos on my own. I suspect the Sovereign at the time really didn't know what to make of me." Nike shrugged again, and the elegant motion was becoming familiar to me. "She welcomed me warmly enough in the end."

"Because of your magic?"

Her eyes glittered with mirth and mischief. "How do you know I have magic? Have you ever seen it?"

"I hear... talk."

"The rumors, you mean."

"But it's true, isn't it? You can do things that none of us can do. They call you the siren sorceress."

"Do they?" She feigned surprise, her blue hair cascading from her head as she shook it in artificial wonder.

"You're not behaving any differently than the Sovereigns," I said, cheekily, pointing at her. "Hiding your abilities from the rest of us."

Some of her mirth vanished and I thought she flashed

me a look of respect. "You're cleverer than your mother gives you credit for."

It was as though someone had sent a thin, white-hot blade through my chest, for these words precisely framed my most ardent desire—some recognition from my own mother.

Nike did not miss the pain flashing across my face.

"She makes another error in this," she said quietly. Her eyes were drawn downward and beyond us. "But, look. We have a friend in trouble."

Following where Nike had pointed, I picked out a large, slow moving sea turtle in the distance.

"Shall we see if we can help her?"

Nike swam toward the creature and I followed, still swallowing down the pain she had so swiftly been able to resurrect.

Approaching the sea turtle revealed what Nike had instinctively known—this was a creature not only in trouble, but in pain. As we came alongside the slow-moving animal, I forgot about my own pain in lieu of hers.

Ropes—wrapped around her shell and between her front legs and her neck—had been there so long that her body had grown around them. She'd suffered this way for a very long time, but it appeared now she was close to the end of her suffering, for the rope across her neck was embedded in her flesh deep enough to affect her ability to swallow.

I reached for the small knife at my hip, which I wore in a light holster strapped around my waist when I went out exploring.

Nike stopped me. "You can't cut it away with a knife, Bel. It will kill her to remove it, look how deep its buried. She got wrapped up in these ropes when she was just a young turtle."

Nike reached for a dangling end of one of the ropes. As she held it up, I saw the rudimentary but sharp metal hook still fastened to the end.

"Atlantean fishing equipment." Nike frowned. "Probably poachers."

"You don't know that," I replied. "She could have come from anywhere, even from the Pacific. You said she's been like this for years."

We swam alongside the turtle for a while. She ignored us, her beak opening and closing slowly.

"We can't just leave her to die," I said, finally.

"We're not going to." Nike's expression switched from thoughtful to resolute and she gave me a serious look. "You wanted to see some of my magic? Today is your day. Do not speak of what you see to anyone. Promise me?"

I agreed.

Nike's hands began to work over and under the turtle's form, never touching her but dancing around her, fingers fluttering as though weaving with some invisible cloth.

At first nothing seemed to change, but then I noticed the turtle's colors fading, turning white. Looking closer, I realized the turtle wasn't fading, but was being wrapped in a white caul. The membrane thickened and became pearlescent, and soon the turtle was no longer visible at all. What remained was a softly pulsating sac.

"Can I touch it?"

"Sure."

I softly brushed the membrane with my fingertips. Jerking my hand back in surprise, I looked up at Nike. "It's warm! It feels like flesh."

She smiled and we watched as the large sac began to drift slowly toward the ocean floor. "Like a uterus," she said quietly.

"What does it do?" The cleverness of the sac was apparent; how the turtle would be assisted was not yet so obvious.

"It helps her in the only way it knows how," was the cryptic reply.

It was weeks later when I finally had the chance to see the result of this magic.

"SO, WHAT WAS IT?" Targa interrupted, putting a hand on my arm to stop me in my tracks. "What did she do?"

The four of us had gone for a walk to stretch our legs and get out of the manor after lunch. Emun and Antoni stopped also and stepped closer to hear me answer over the wind.

"I did not forget what I had seen Nike do to the turtle, and though I asked her to explain, she only told me that if I had enough curiosity, I would find out for myself." I turned my back on the wind so they could hear me better before continuing.

"I returned to the place where we'd left the turtle. I watched it, day in and day out. The sac seemed to age and lose its fullness as time went by, until one day it was a strange pale thing draped over the dark, jagged rocks. Deflated like an old balloon..."

DESCENDING TO THE DEPTHS, my pupils expanding wide to adjust to the near zero sunlight penetration, I approached what looked like a canvas sail, wrinkled and misshapen. But before I lost interest and moved on, I realized it lacked the texture of canvas and instead had a spongy, less porous character.

Then it *moved.*

Not the whole thing, just a very small part of it. Close enough now to touch it, I reached out and ran my hand along its surface. It was warmer than the water, and it seemed to respond to my touch in a crawling, shying-away motion, the way a horse's skin can move in only one place, sliding over the musculature.

A small, rounded lump moved beneath it near my hand, and I touched that as well, feeling the hard dome shaped thing.

It came to me suddenly, and I couldn't stop myself from saying, "You clever sorceress," aloud. Arresting the urge to help the lump free itself from the now empty sac, I put my hands behind my back and watched, captivated, as a young sea turtle emerged from its now far-too-large casing.

"Bet you're wondering what in the world just happened," I said to the turtle as it flapped tiny flippers and worked to ascend. As it drifted past my face, I saw that it had similar distinct shell markings of the adult we'd come across, but no longer was it scarred and dying, with ropes digging into its flesh. It was perfect, as new and pristine as it had been in its youth.

I watched the sea turtle disappear overhead, smiling to myself and shaking my head.

Then I moved on, and forgot all about it.

EMUN, Antoni, and Targa were silent for a long time after this anecdote, so we finished our beach walk with only the sound of the waves as our backdrop.

Sera and Adalbert wanted to clean the parlor we'd been using, so we went up to what Targa still referred to as Martinius's office on the third floor where Adalbert had lit a fire for us. Sera had prepared hot tea and brought it up to us just as rain began to spatter against the old glass of the windows.

"So that's really the secret then, that is the only thing that explains how you could be my mother, and Targa's mother as well," said Emun, settling into one of the plush chairs and picking up his mug of hot tea. "Sometime after the events of *The Sybellen*, you returned to Okeanos..."

"Or at least to wherever Nike was at the time," Antoni added.

"She was in Okeanos," I confirmed. "And yes, that was where I went after Gdansk."

"And," Emun continued where he'd left off, "Nike used this same magic on you, to reverse your age." My son raised his eyes to mine. "But *why*?"

"The why will take some time to answer, and I want to do it properly." My heart softened as I gazed at my children. "You both deserve that, but especially you, Emun. You who were deprived of so much, and who had to survive all on your own."

My voice tightened up when I thought of my young son, my young triton, left to fend for himself, not even understanding his true nature when his salt-birth finally occurred. He'd likely been surrounded by drowned sailors. I wondered if he'd found Mattis's body and I shoved the unpleasant question to the side.

I took a breath to refocus. "So, you understand what Nike was capable of. The next important milestone in this story occurred years after this event. After I had gone on three mating cycles and returned each time to Okeanos without a daughter."

All three of them stared at me. Targa's mouth dropped open. "Before Poland? You'd already been on *three* of these *Dyás* thingies?"

"Where did you go?" Emun asked.

"What was your first mating cycle like?" Targa asked right after.

"Did you have only sons?" Antoni interjected.

I raised my hands, laughing. "I want to keep this story on track, so in short I'll tell you that on my first *Dyás* I ended up on the coast of Portugal and it was a short and disastrous experience from which I eagerly returned to claim my gem. That cycle resulted in a miscarriage, and there had been no love in the relationship."

Targa made a sound of sympathy.

I rubbed my hands over my face at the memory of that time. "It was so long ago now, please do not feel sorry for me. I never think of that time, and it's not important for the story." I looked at Antoni next. "To answer your question—yes, the following two mating cycles resulted in sons and me returning empty-handed to Okeanos yet again."

Emun put a hand over his lips and his eyes drifted shut. "How difficult it must have been for you to have given birth to twin boys at your next *Dyás*."

"It was difficult, but it has come to result in the greatest gifts I could ever desire." I looked from Emun to Targa and back again. "The two of you."

"But why did you continue to torture yourself if you didn't have to? You said that under Apollyona's rule, every siren was only required to go on one cycle, but now this is four cycles you've been through."

"The second and third I undertook because I felt like a

failure. Those sirens who returned to Okeanos with daughters had something wonderful I knew nothing about. They also had a lighter burden to bear, knowing that they'd contributed something to Okeanos." I took a deep inhale, preparing to relive the next part of my history. "The fourth I undertook because of an overinflated sense of justice, and perhaps ego had something to do with it. Let me explain..."

FIVE

A bright summer sun sent its powerful rays down on Mount Califas where the sirens of Okeanos had gathered. The mountain was so steep, it was more like a collection of huge natural pillars reaching from the teal sea to the azure sky, encrusted with lush green plant life clinging to every surface. Cascades poured from low open mouths in the rock, filling the air at the base of the mountain with moisture. Rainbows arched over every waterfall while birds fluttered and swooped around the pools filled with flashing fish.

Looking down from the very top of Califas was a dizzying experience, and a little unsettling. Being high on a mountaintop was the very antithesis of a mermaid's natural habitat, but it was there that sirens who had returned home from their *Dyás* were presented with the gems which would protect them from the siren's curse. The location allowed the returning siren to see her home stretched out before her like a gift, and to bathe in the sun's life-giving rays.

Apollyona, resplendent in a yellow robe, stood before a returning siren named Lia. Apollyona's aquamarine crown and necklace flashed in the sun—just as they had when she first gave me my gem. The gem ceremony was held only once, when a siren returned from her first *Dyás*. After that, if a siren chose to take on a second, she could leave her gem with the Sovereign and have it returned to her privately afterward. Smiles were on every face because Lia had returned with a daughter, an eight-year-old siren. Lia had completed a successful first mating cycle, which would bolster our ranks.

Nike stood at my shoulder, commentating on the simple ceremony. Sirens were not extravagant with these events, and Apollyona herself was the most ceremonious feature.

Lia stood before our Sovereign with her daughter. The child held her mother's hand and looked around in awe the same way I had when I had first arrived in Okeanos.

We stood on a rock at the back of the crowd where we had a good view of the proceedings and where Nike's whispered words wouldn't disturb anyone.

"When Odenyalis ruled, the ceremony was different. It was longer, and additional *Dyás* were greatly encouraged," Nike whispered in my ear as we watched. "Odenyalis used to give a long speech about how the cycles made for a larger and wiser population, that they were needed to secure the future of Okeanos."

My eyes darted to where the former Sovereign stood near the back row directly opposite us, watching the proceedings.

"Apollyona doesn't say anything about the *Dyás*, encouraging or not," Nike pointed out.

"Why do you think that is?" I whispered back.

"Well it's a cruel thing for a mermaid, is it not?" Nike rested her chin on my shoulder. "Mating cycles are hard on us, even successful ones. Perhaps Apollyona is just being kind."

Though she was whispering, I thought I detected a note of irony in Nike's words. The sorceress did not really believe that Apollyona would do anything purely for kindness, and neither did I.

My eyes fell on a mousy-haired siren standing just behind Apollyona and holding a small wooden box with brass hinges. She never took her eyes from the proceedings and seemed emotionally wrapped up in the presentation of the gem. The announcement of the returning siren's name and her daughter's name was the only welcome from Apollyona. She turned to the mousy-haired siren, who presented the box to the Sovereign—with its top flipped open—so that Apollyona could pluck an aquamarine from it and present it to Lia.

"That's Trina," Nike answered my unasked question, "Apollyona's newest handmaiden."

I watched as Trina wiped a tear from the corner of her eye and gazed adoringly at Apollyona as the Sovereign lay the aquamarine in the palm of Lia's hand. Then Apollyona lifted her own chin so Lia could touch her fingers to the Sovereign's throat.

"She's very invested," I whispered. "Trina, I mean."

I felt Nike nod. "Why do you think Apollyona chose her? She's obedient, and won't question Apollyona's decisions."

A stab of jealousy in my heart surprised me and I wondered why Apollyona hadn't offered me a position at her side. Perhaps I shouldn't have been surprised, for Apollyona did not treat me any differently than any other siren under her rule. But sometimes, often unexpectedly, the rejection still hurt.

With the gem given, and Lia and her daughter welcomed, the siren ceremony came to an end. Some sirens disappeared through an archway leading into the mountain, where steps led down into the interior. Others navigated a set of treacherous curved steps leading to the pools below, and still others lingered at the mountaintop, talking and enjoying the view.

Nike and I made to descend the outer steps when one of the *Foniádes* appeared at the archway and approached Apollyona.

The taller siren touched the Sovereign's throat with a bowed head and said, "We've taken four more Atlanteans found well inside our borders. We've brought them to you, as requested."

Nike and I shared a look. Nothing had been heard about Atlanteans for years, not since Apollyona had laid down her decree when she'd first taken the throne.

Apollyona thanked the *Foniádes* and disappeared into the mountain. Trina kept a close step behind the Sovereign.

Curious, Nike and I followed.

Apollyona made her way down to the throne room but did not stop there. She descended further into the belly of Califas. Nike and I kept our distance. We appeared to be the only sirens who'd overheard the exchange above—or at least we were the only ones curious about the Atlanteans. Sirens bathing in the freshwater pools inside the art-lined caves watched us pass without comment.

Apollyona entered a huge, arched cavern lit with slanting reflections of sunlight and littered with many pools of dark water. Some of the pools were small and shallow, warm and sparkling with minerals, while others were deep and led to underground rivers, some so long and winding they exited into the Atlantic beyond the borders of Okeanos.

Nike and I came up short at the scene that met us inside the cave. Three more *Foniádes* flanked four kneeling Atlanteans. Pitiful creatures they were, thin and unkempt with haunted eyes and patches of hair missing because of the sea lice that had invaded their scalps.

Apollyona stopped before them, then suddenly turned to look directly at Nike and me.

"Leave us," she commanded, her voice loud and ringing.

Nike and I looked at one another in surprise. It had not been in the nature of Apollyona, or the rule of any Sovereign before her, to do things in secret. Her command only served to deepen my desire to stay and witness how she was going to deal with these Atlanteans.

I opened my mouth to protest, but Trina stepped closer, the expression on her face fierce with righteous anger.

"Did you not hear your Sovereign?" she snapped, pointing to the stairway we'd just descended. "Out. Now!"

Rebellion surged through me like a hot rushing river and I made to argue when I felt Nike's hand hook my elbow.

"Come on," she said quietly. "We'd better go."

For a moment I locked eyes with my mother and glared at her, but what I saw there unnerved me—it was like she didn't recognize who I was. She looked at me as though I was a stranger. That look was like a physical blow to my gut.

I stepped into the dark pool nearest us, one I knew to be deep and to lead into open water far from Califas. Exiting this way when Trina was pointing to the stairwell was more a way to be rebellious than anything else, to show her that I would not bend entirely. Trina was just a siren, with no Salt-given power over any other.

Nike followed me into the pool.

Trina spat, "Doesn't matter which way you leave, just go. And don't ever hesitate at the command of your Sovereign again."

We slipped under the water's surface and our legs melded into tails. As Nike and I made our winding, convoluted way through the bowels of Califas, anger seethed. I was more determined than ever to find out what Apollyona had planned for those sad Atlanteans.

Nike let me fume in silence until, by the time we were ejected from a crack in the rocky coral beyond Califas, I was feeling a little less irate.

"What do you think she's going to do about them?" I asked as we swam on, not really noticing or caring where we were headed.

"Inform them sternly of our laws?" Nike ventured, but with more humor than seriousness in her tone.

I grunted and became lost in my own wonderings again until Nike interrupted me.

"Look," she said, tugging on my elbow.

Following her gaze, I saw the *Foniádes* escorting the four Atlanteans away from Califas.

"You see, nothing to worry about. They'll be taken to the borders of Okeanos with a warning and sent away."

"If that's the case," I chewed my lip, still feeling that something wasn't right, "then why did Apollyona not let us witness it?"

"I'm sure she had her reasons." But even Nike sounded doubtful.

The next day, Nike and I were exploring a wreck when I saw one of the *Foniádes* in the distance. Without a second thought, I took off toward her.

"Where are you..." Nike began, but saw the siren in the distance and followed.

Asking her to wait, I caught up to her. "What happened with the Atlanteans yesterday?"

"Executed," she replied simply, almost as though I was stupid for thinking anything else would have happened to them. "Except for one."

Shock stole my voice and my jaw dropped in horror.

"Except for one?" Nike asked as she approached.

The *Foniádes* gave a nod. "She was to watch and then was sent to warn her kind what would happen to them if they ever ventured inside Okeanos territory."

A chill ran up my spine as I stared at the siren. Apollyona had had her *Foniádes* slay those poor creatures and forced one of them to watch the executions. My gaze fell to the spear in her hand.

"That's wrong," I choked out. "Can't you see that?"

The *Foniádes* regarded me coolly. "It's the Sovereign who decides what is right or wrong. She has been deemed worthy by the Salt to do so. You know this."

Clearly not wanting to discuss the matter further, she swam away.

I stared at Nike, horrified. "She can't do this. It's not right, it's not how the laws of the ocean work. That's a human law she's enforcing. We are not humans."

"The Salt made her our Sovereign, Bel," replied Nike. "The Salt is the only law we know, and she's the Salt's representative. There are greater forces at work here than we understand."

I shook my head, putting a hand on my stomach and swallowing down the rising bile at the thought of what my mother had done. "It's murder. The Salt has made a mistake."

"I don't think the Salt *can* make mistakes," she said, gently. "If we thought that, our whole way of being would simply fall apart, descend into chaos. We need some kind of transcendent—"

"How does the Salt decide who is to rule us?" I interrupted.

A slow smile crossed Nike's face, and the smile surprised and unnerved me. "Now you're asking the right question, Bel."

"What do you mean?" All my focus was on the siren sorceress in front of me now. "What do you know?"

"We sirens leave it to the Salt to decide who our ruler is to be, thinking it to be a kind of magic that cannot be influenced. But it *can*."

My heart began to pound. "How?"

"Think about what you have seen already in your lifetime. You saw Odenyalis step down from Sovereignty and hand it willingly over to Apollyona. You also know now that Odenyalis encouraged sirens to take on more mating cycles, but that Apollyona does not. Apollyona focuses our *Foniádes* on keeping Okeanos safe from outsiders offensively."

"While Odenyalis' strategy was to bolster our numbers by encouraging us to go through more mating cycles and bring home more than one daughter."

Nike nodded. "Odenyalis did not relish the power of the Sovereignty, though the Salt deemed her worthy."

My mother's eagerness to return to Okeanos rose in my memory. It was as if she had known the throne was waiting for her. But how could she have known the Salt was going to choose her, unless she had done something to make it happen?

Nike was watching me intently. My mind raced, and I

felt as though I was on the edge of some paradigm shift. My gaze met Nike's, and realization lit my thoughts up like fireworks.

"It's the cycles," I said, breathlessly. "Isn't it?"

My mother had never told me about the results of any of her past cycles, let alone that she'd ever had more than one.

I continued, "More cycles trigger the Salt to pass the Sovereignty on?"

Nike didn't nod, but her expression told me she thought I was right and was pleased I'd figured it out.

"If you disagree with how Apollyona is treating the Atlanteans, you are not helpless to change it," Nike said quietly.

I kept my voice low in case there were sirens nearby, though I thought all sirens should know this was how Sovereignty was achieved. "Why is it a secret?"

"Why do you think?"

We began to swim toward the sunny pools at the base of Mount Califas, our favorite place to eat.

"Apollyona doesn't want anyone to know, at least, not the *wrong* sirens," I ventured, wrestling with my anger boiling just under the surface at this discovery. "How did you find out?"

"I just looked around and figured it out. I've been here a long time, Bel. I know how many daughters Apollyona has."

"Why didn't you tell anyone?"

She didn't answer, but her eyes implored me to figure it out on my own.

"Apollyona made you vow not to tell?" Again, from the look on her face, I knew I was right. "Or what?"

"What do I hate more than anything?"

"Life on land." I had understood this about Nike immediately, and she was the only one of the sirens who did not have to go on a mating cycle. There was something different about Nike, not just in how she looked, her abilities, and her coloring, but something in her nature as well.

"When I hit puberty, I did not feel the urge to find a mate the way the rest of the sirens do," she said. "I waited and waited, but it never came. The Sovereign of my youth was Xantiaset, known before her reign as Tia. Tia began to watch me. All sirens are connected to their Sovereign, and the Sovereign is connected to her sirens. She could feel something was different about me, though no other sirens made comments about it or seemed to care."

We reached the surface. Our tails split and transformed into human skin, bone, and muscle as we left the ocean. My first breath of oxygen worked to clear my thinking, like wiping condensation away from a window inside a greenhouse.

We climbed to one of the lowest pools, a sparkling warm pond fed by a stream of water trickling over mossy rocks. Orange, yellow and blue fish caught the bugs skating along the surface.

Nike slipped into the pool and her tail returned, but I kept my human form and let my feet dangle in the water while we resumed our conversation.

"Tia pulled me aside one day to ask me how I was feeling. I had been dreading the day," Nike explained as she lay back against a stone and trailed a finger along the backs of the fish swimming near her. "I thought for sure she would send me away, force me to go on a mating cycle my body clearly didn't want."

"Did she?"

Nike smiled at me, and her light gray eyes shone with unshed tears. She shook her head. "Remarkable Sovereign, Xantiaset. She didn't send me away, but she did suggest that

I leave for a while and come back in a few months—if not years—just to make it appear as though I'd gone on a mating cycle. She wanted to avoid the questions that would arise if it didn't at least *look* like I'd gone on a cycle."

"But the other sirens weren't interested, you said. They didn't care that you hadn't appeared to reach puberty yet."

"They didn't, but someone might have eventually. Tia just wanted to avoid anyone bringing attention to me. I think she wanted to avoid sending me away officially." Nike shrugged. "Anyway, I left Okeanos for a while, but I didn't go on land. I went to the Pacific. I learned a lot and it was like a wonderful holiday. When I returned to Okeanos, Xantiaset welcomed me back and gave me this." Nike's slender tapered fingers fluttered to her throat where her gemstone sat.

"So you've never been on a mating cycle?"

"No, and I've been wearing the gem for so long I don't know what would happen if I gave it up."

"And no one has ever asked you about it?"

"Not until Apollyona." Nike frowned. "She knows."

"You know about how Sovereignty is achieved," I mused, "and she's threatening to send you on a mating cycle if you give away the secret."

Nike gazed at me, her lips upturned in a mild smile that told me I was right in my assumption. But my sorceress friend took it a step further. In a whisper, she said, "She's afraid of you, Bel."

"Me?" I shook my head and laughed at the ridiculous idea, but Nike looked serious. At her expression, my laughter died. "Why?"

"You're different. You ask more questions, and you have a different moral compass than most sirens. Your reaction to the way she treated those Atlanteans is proof of that."

"You're different too, though."

"Yes, but I have no interest in going on a mating cycle, and that's what it would require if I wanted power. Which I don't." She shuddered. "I'm not suited to lead."

"Neither is Apollyona." I said this without hesitation.

"Do you think you could do a better job?" Nike asked.

"I *know* I could. The Atlanteans do not deserve to be murdered. All they're doing is looking for food, and we've plenty of that."

Nike stared at me then, the challenge clear in her eyes.

I looked away, internally withering at what I now understood. Mating cycles were hard, and my gem meant I was no longer required to do one again. Odenyalis had decreed that all sirens would receive a gem when they'd successfully produced two daughters, but Apollyona only required that a siren complete one mating cycle. While daughters were celebrated, it was ultimately of no consequence to Apollyona—she would give the siren her gem and she could live out the rest of her days free from the curse. The sirens lived underwater and under her rule, never really understanding how she had been given the Sovereignty in the first place, or how they could attain it themselves if they were so ambitious.

But was I that ambitious? I thought about the Atlanteans we had first run across when returning to Okeanos. I remembered the disgust and intolerance Apollyona had shown. My stomach soured with distaste. Even when I'd been small, I had known there was something wrong with it. Okeanos was vast and so full of resources that the sirens couldn't use it up in thousands of years, even if the population grew exponentially.

My mind then turned to the Atlanteans recently caught, and to the only remaining Atlantean sent away to tell the story of the fearsome Apollyona, Sovereign of Okeanos, as a warning to stay away. It would be effective because it was so harsh, so cruel, so heartless.

And no other sirens seemed to care, if they were even aware, that Apollyona was doing this.

I wasn't particularly interested in power, but I was interested in living compassionately with all the creatures of the oceans, and I was interested in justice and fairness. How could I live with myself knowing this was happening and I had the ability to do something about it? I thought of a quote I'd learned while I was living through a mating cycle on land—'The only thing necessary for the triumph of evil is for good men to do nothing.' It was no different in any civilization or species anywhere on earth or in the world's deep oceans.

"It could take years," I said softly. The task ahead of me stretched out like a very long journey.

"Sirens have nothing but years," Nike replied. "Apollyona has nothing but years in power ahead of her, if you do nothing."

My eyes cut sharply to Nike's fine-featured face. "But you won't do it."

"My place is not on land, Bel."

She was right. Nike was different; she was not suited to life on land. If her body had not given her the urgency to find a mate, then why should she force it? She might end up suffering worse than any other siren who ever suffered through a mating cycle. At least the *Dyás* had some kind of mercy. We forgot things, we forgot our siren lives as we focused on the mating cycle and on our child. It wasn't until the cycle had run its course that the Salt returned to call us—sometimes cruelly—back to the sea. Beckoning at first, but that beckoning, if ignored, soon turned to an irresistible need.

I touched my gemstone where it sat between my collarbones. Slowly, I reached back and undid the clasp.

Nike's eyes widened as I handed it to her, but she took it. "Just like that? You're not going to give it to Apollyona?"

Sirens who elected to go on a mating cycle, few and far between though they were, gave their gemstone to the Sovereign for safe-keeping. But giving the stone to the Sovereign was not a decree; it was just what was done, and everything in me bristled against giving it to Apollyona. I'd rather slip away unnoticed. Months of my absence could pass before she'd even notice and inquire about me.

"Will you keep it safe for me?"

"You know I will." Nike took the gem and wrapped its chain around her wrist three times, turning it into a bracelet.

My decision made, all that was left to do was wait. Swim in the salty waters and let the briny deep do its work.

Over the course of the next few months, my mind and body changed. The power of the gem's absence triggered the start of a cycle, and the desire to leave the water and find a mate grew stronger and stronger. My mind refocused on the task ahead. I began to roam farther and farther from Mount Califas and the center of life in Okeanos. I began to spend more time alone.

And one day, I ventured as far as I had ventured since my last mating cycle, and just... kept going.

"THAT CYCLE, as you know, I went to South America. I bore a son and left not long after he was weaned. I returned to Okeanos to recuperate—I don't know if Apollyona even noticed that I'd been gone. A few years later, I repeated the process, that time going back to England for the first time since I was a child."

I refilled my tea and continued, "The time I met Mattis was more eventful..."

SIX

It had been days since I'd left Califas when I thought I heard Nike's voice calling my name. Thinking I was just imagining it. It was Nike whom I would miss the most on this next *Dyás*. She alone knew the significance.

"Bel, wait!"

I turned, realizing that she was catching up to me, her blue hair flying behind her as she swam rapidly, bright scales gleaming against the gloom.

"Miss me already?" I turned to face the sorceress. I adjusted the strap of the bag I was carrying, heavy with bit of gold and gems I'd taken from the caves.

She gave me a smile tinged with sadness. She stopped in front of me and her hair made a fantastic cloud which drifted around her head.

"I made you something."

She held out her open palm. On it was a simple chain with a ring attached made of a bright yellow metal, similar to that which I had seen used to make settings for Apollyona's gemstones and jewelry. This metal was called orichalcum, a substance nearly as valuable as gold, and though I had never come across this metal in any of my human lives, the caves of Okeanos were rich with it. It always fetched a handsome price and some uncomfortable questions when traded.

Picking up the ring and chain, I inspected them. The chain was simple, but the ring was a thick sturdy band. Welded perpendicular to it was a little cylinder made of the same metal. Markings engraved into the side of the cylinder and the inside of the band were so shallow they could barely be seen. On the topside of the cylinder was a thin, tight seam, as though it had a cap.

I glanced at her, wary. "Please tell me there is not an aquamarine inside this."

She shook her head and her eye had that mischievous glint I had come to love. "That would undermine your efforts to unseat Apollyona."

"Then what's in here?" I pointed at the cylinder, knowing it was hollow and that Nike would not be giving me this trinket unless it had some value beyond the intrinsic.

A dimple appeared. "During the rule of Odenyalis, I took four gems and hid them in or near the world's major bodies of water. As you know, I abhorred the idea of mating cycles, but I believed I would eventually be forced to take my turn. I rebelled against the idea and wanted to make a safety net for myself. No matter how far from home I got, I wanted to know there was a gem not so far away that I couldn't retrieve it before the Salt overtook me." She touched the cylinder. "Inside are four maps, each leading to one gem. I think the risk of me being forced to take a *Dyás* has passed, so I want you to have it."

I gave a delighted laugh. Nike never failed to amaze me. "You crammed four maps inside this tiny little thing?"

"Not paper maps. It's a kind of spell." She put her hand over mine and wrapped my fingers around the ring and chain. "I hope you won't need them, but just in case."

"If I ever become Sovereign," I grinned at my impish friend, "I can see I'll have to keep an extra close eye on you—rulebreaker."

She did not smile but returned my look with a solemn one of her own. "*When* you become Sovereign. Endure, and you will succeed."

I unclasped the chain and fastened it around my neck. "Thank you."

"And one more thing." She grasped my forearm gently. "Do not use your siren voice on your next mate. Let it happen naturally, don't force it or deceive him in any way."

"Why not?"

"Because, when nature is allowed to take its own course without manipulation, astonishing and magnificent things happen. Things that would not otherwise happen if we change a human's way of thinking over to our own by force." Her hand tightened but her touch remained gentle. She touched her other palm to my forehead. "You will be sorely tempted. You may forget a great many things, but you will never forget this: do not deceive your beloved."

A pulse went through my forehead from her palm and I closed my eyes as it passed through the back of my head like a wave of warm water. Opening my eyes, I met her gaze. "Did you just put a spell on me?"

She shook her head and took both of my hands in hers. "Not a spell, just a calling. We forget so easily without our gems. It's part of our curse. This is too important, both for you and for the future of Okeanos."

I didn't realize it at the time, but what Nike had done in that moment was fix her advice in my mind forever.

We said goodbye and parted again. I looked over my shoulder a few times as the distance between us widened, until I could no longer see her distinct thatch of blue hair.

I didn't look back again.

JUST PAST the borders of the *apotreptikó* came the sensation that someone was watching me—not just watching, but following. At first, I wondered if Nike was tailing me, but I dismissed the notion—she knew I wouldn't turn back.

Skimming along the ocean floor in an area where sunlight pierced the shadows with flickering beams of light, illuminating motes and flashing on the backs of small silver fish, I paused over a bed of coral and watched with my peripheral vision for a time.

A distant figure darted behind the coral and I realized it wasn't even a mermaid. The flash I'd seen had revealed legs and long webbed feet.

"I won't hurt you," I called.

After several long moments of waiting, I almost gave up and continued on my way. Then the long-webbed fingers of an Atlantean female appeared over the golden coral wall, then drifting matted hair, then a face with large, haunted eyes.

I tried to give her a smile but the corners of my mouth wavered as she came forward, revealing all of her pitiful self.

Gaunt-faced, and poorly nourished, just like the Atlanteans Apollyona had so heartlessly executed, her face was human but difficult to look at. Large, dark irises took me in almost hungrily. She wore colorless, algae-coated clothing tied at the waist with ropes she'd likely taken off a shipwreck. I shuddered when I thought she may well have taken the rags from a corpse as well. Her elbows and knees were knobs of bone, and her skin had a gray cast. Dark hair, matted close to the scalp, floated in a cloud around her head like so much seaweed. Her high brow and cheekbones suggested that were she healthy, she might have been beautiful.

"Why are you following me?" I asked gently.

She drew close, cautiously, her gaze never leaving me but cutting from my face to my neck where sat the ring with the small metal cylinder Nike had given me. It occurred to me that she was either extremely curious about this object or she was hoping to steal it.

Then she spoke and the sound of her voice startled me, for it was dry as paper and deep as a man's.

"Is that your gemstone, then? Inside there?" She gestured at the ring and my attention was drawn to her hand, where her nails were so long, they'd become talons and had just begun to spiral.

"How do you know about our gemstones?"

"All of us know," she husked. Her haunted eyes darted from the ring to my face again. "Well?"

"No, it's not. It's just a gift from a friend."

She was drifting closer. I could make out more of her ghastly details—the dark splotches in her irises from parasites in her guts, the horrible stench of rot coming from her mouth.

I could not fear such a creature, but there was an unsettling and strange greedy air about her, probably to do more with starving than anything else.

"Do not drift, accidentally or purposefully, into the territory of Okeanos." I warned her. "It's not safe for you right now."

At the reference to Okeanos, her lip curled ever so slightly, revealing gray teeth.

"Never has been," she rasped, her covetous eyes taking me in like I was a meal, and still casting to the ring.

"I hope to change that," I said softly.

"Evil queen you have now, don't you?" But she wasn't looking for confirmation, as she already believed this. "Evil and long-living."

Her hand drifted to her side, where I noticed a short-handled blade with a broken handle strapped to her leg. She did not touch the weapon. She'd be foolish to do so and she knew it.

"We might have long lives," I replied, "but our Sovereigns can be unseated before their deaths."

"Unseat the Sovereign," she echoed, in a way that made me wonder if she hadn't realized she'd spoken out loud.

"I hope to change things. Our people should be able to share the realm of Okeanos peacefully. There are more than enough resources for everyone."

She was taken with a violent cough, but when it did not stop, I realized that the cough was what passed for a laugh. She curled her taloned hand in front of her mouth, her shoulders shook, her eyes crinkled and her brow drew together—her entire being reflected disbelief and disdain for the idea of sharing Okeanos.

"You must be very young. Beautiful and fat with health, but young and stupid."

I was so shocked at this speech that my mouth opened, but I found I had no words.

"Have not your wise sirens told you? Are you really so ignorant of our history? Too much bad blood. We shall never be comrades. Never." A light appeared in her eyes, one tinged with lunacy. Something about her expression sent a shiver down my spine. "While a single Atlantean remains alive, Mer will never be safe, and while the evil queen rules your halls, we will never be safe."

I wanted to ask what she thought sirens had to fear from Atlanteans, but felt it would be pointless to ask. This Atlantean seemed on the brink of reason. I began to swim away.

"Atlantis will rise again," she called, following after me, her voice like the groan of an old nail in water-logged wood. "We will rise again. We will vanquish our enemies. We will kill your unrighteous Sovereign and scatter your people to the dark places of the oceans."

I put on more speed and she fell behind.

"You will know, you will know what it's like to be wanderers! You'll be next. It's your turn. Your turn is coming!"

Her voice was fading fast now, even for my siren ears.

"...strangers in a strange land, feeble outcasts..."

She continued to call after me, but distance swallowed up her half-crazed curses.

I swam on. As the Salt plied at my thoughts and emotions with soft fingers and the days turned into months, she was relegated to that shadowy territory whose borders soon stretch wide for a siren without her gem. She became blotted out—forgotten, just like the ring at my neck.

I HAD ALREADY LOST track of time before I became trapped in the old wreck along the shores of that hot, tropical place. The Salt had done its work, seasons had passed. Years could have passed for all I was aware of it. Okeanos was like a distant dream I'd had before, just moments of something I'd once experienced slipping through my fingers whenever I tried to lay hold of it, see it more clearly. Sometimes I would break the surface for a look around, and at these moments, accompanying the influx of fresh oxygen into my human lungs, my memory would return. It would dissolve again soon after, pitted by the Salt in much the same way as a limestone statue from one of the great Greek collections which had found its way to the bottom of the deep.

But even more distant was the thing I had left Okeanos to do. I was left with the perplexed notion that I'd forgotten something important, but whatever it was had been shunted to the side by a more pressing desire—that of locating human men and beginning my search for a mate in earnest.

The feeling was a slow-growing coral in the groves of my heart. The waters around me became bright and clear, full of fast and shiny fish, more colorful and varied than the flowers found in botanical gardens or the rainforests of South America. These fish were an endless source of pleasure for my eyes and food for my stomach. I instinctively knew which would be easier to catch, which might cause me digestive distress, which had impossibly inconvenient bone-structures...riddled with deadly spines on the inside, and which might outright kill me. If I were to distill these survival instincts into one piece of wisdom for the wayfaring siren, it would be this: don't touch anything in the world's oceans that is either very pretty or very ugly. Luckily, my favorite foods were sardines, roe, a very dark-green species of kelp, blue-green algae which sparkled with minerals and gathered in warmer seas, and the occasional sea bass—all of which were in abundance.

The drive to find a mate brought me first to shallower seas, then to beaches. On one of these beautiful, warm, tropic beaches, I was drawn to a shipwreck laying mostly upside down and mostly underwater. The hull was intact and not overly large, nor was it outfitted for battle, as there were no gun ports speckling its sides. Both of its masts protruded from their original places in the ship's deck, but lay at terrible angles, giving the sad impression of defeat. The sound of water inside sloshing against the hull with the movement of the waves drew me near, and peeking curiously through the cracks in its hull revealed a school of fat sardines. Mouth watering, I wriggled my way inside by way of the broken hatch cover.

Feasting on these omega-rich fish, I explored the dark interior of the ship and became captivated by the play of sunlight coming in as sharp lines and illuminating the inside in an interesting way.

Satiated, I soon fell asleep, nestled in a bed of seaweed.

The distant sound of voices woke me and drew me to a crack where I witnessed the evidence—though not the ship itself—of a much larger vessel sailing past. I watched the shadow of it passing, ears perked to the sound of humans laughing and water sliding along the expansive hull and carried underwater to me.

When the wake hit my wreck repeatedly and the ship groaned as it shifted, I barely noticed. I feasted on another serving of sardines, and when I had grown bored of the interior of my little wreck, I looked for a way out.

Only now, there was none.

SEVEN

To this day, I could not tell you how much time passed as I swam back and forth, slept, and lived in the hold of that old wreck. But I'll never forget the day I was discovered by humans who'd come into my territory (for by that time, I thought of the tiny space as 'my territory'). Looking back—once I'd been freed and returned to myself again—this feeling of territorialism helped me understand Apollyona's determination to keep the Atlanteans from sharing our resources, for if any creature—human or otherwise—made an attempt to fish near my wreck, I was overcome by a fierce desire to protect my food source.

I heard them before I saw them.

Men's voices. They sounded relaxed—laughter and levity in their tones. I retreated to the darkest shadow of the wreck and became still, the sharp stones and coral of the reef pressing into my back. Seaweed cradled me, swaying gently to cover me. I listened, my gills moving minimally as I drew water through them.

When the voices drew close and the splashing sound of

feet wading through the rocky shallows told me they were drawing nearer to my hiding place, my heartbeat accelerated. The pace of my breathing increased and my hands tightened into fists, the now long and sharp nails of my fingers cutting into my palms. I could see nothing but shadows moving across the cracks in the hull. I was afraid, but also curious, and these two battled inside me, for I wanted to get a look at my enemy, to determine whether they were larger and stronger than me.

Staying in the darkest shadows, I inched my way along the hull to peek through a crack, my head breaking the surface. Between the soggy wooden slats, fuzzy with years of algae growth, I saw a pair of ankles. The voices had grown conversational. They seemed curious about the wreck—my wreck.

One of them dropped something into one of the larger cracks on the other end of the broken old ship. Silver flashed in the sun, passing through a small shoal of fish. Some part of my brain recognized the hook shaped metal. They were after my food!

Darting forward, my desire to stay hidden completely forgotten, I grasped the line and yanked. The shoal of fish darted in every direction and there was a cry of surprise from above as a rough wooden rod was pulled from its owner's hands. The fishing rod flew toward the wreck, became wedged in the crack and snapped in two as I pulled the rest of the fishing kit into the water with a snarl.

Splashing sounds approached as the man who'd cried out called to his friends in excited tones. Three heads blocked out the sun at various points in the hull. There was silence as they squinted in at me, then hushed and excited chatter.

Nothing about their language was familiar to me, and their features and faces were barely visible with the morning sun at their backs.

I retreated to the seaweed-riddled shadows again, my fear returning.

One of the men left, but the other two continued to look in at me at intervals. As the sun moved across the sky, more faces appeared, followed by more excited talking. But the energy seemed to change when a man with a very large head—he blocked out much more of the light—arrived. Then there was a lot of movement: splashing footsteps around the shallowest parts, the coming and going of shadows and voices, the sounds of work being done.

I hissed, startled when they dumped a bucket of water between the planks and it splashed overhead. It was the first of many. Confused and frightened, I pressed against the furthest depths of the hull as the splashes became frequent and steady. Bucket after bucket was deposited into the wreck.

Soon the water began to change. I sensed it with my tail first, then my gills. Slowly the texture, taste and tone of the water I was breathing was being transformed.

My fear began to dissipate, and I wondered what they were doing. Curiosity drew me from the depths to taste and smell the water.

Sweet water, tasting of cold stones and minerals, had begun to permeate the briny seawater. A current moved through my wreck, driven by the repeated pouring of water into the top, which brushed over my skin and tail and slowly pressed the saltwater out through the cracks in the wreck's frame.

The intrusion of sweet water continued. Men came and

went, the voices changed as they took turns at this chore, talking amongst themselves and stepping carefully with bare feet among the sharp rocks.

I became conscious of my own thoughts again and a panic that I'd been seen by humans in my siren form rose. But as the freshwater wore away the animal instinct, I recognized that there was nothing to be done about being discovered, and these men were actually rescuing me. Further to this deduction, I realized with no small amount of exasperation that I had had the power to free myself from the wreck the entire time. I had only been lacking the human intelligence required to conceive of a plan and execute it. At high tide, there was no air in the wreck at all, but at low tide there was a small amount of space above the waterline. If I had had enough intelligence to stick my face above water and take a few breaths, I could have solved my own problem.

Another startlingly logical question struck my mind. *How* did these men know that sweet water would save me? They had to be aware of the existence of mermaids already. Could it be that our world was not as secret as we thought it was?

Drifting in that empty and ruined hull, as more and more human thoughts and emotions forming in my psyche, a whispered name came from all around, pressing in on me like a blanket.

Bel.

Startled, my head jerked up and my ears perked. Had I imagined it? My name passed by my ears again like a warm current.

Bel.

"Yes?" It took me a moment to realize the ocean was speaking to me. No, not speaking to me. *Naming* me.

Sybellen.

My siren name settled over my shoulders like a cloak, familiar and special. Mine. I became so excited I began to swim in loops and figure-eights, tight ones, which I realize now probably made it appear to my rescuers as though I was having a panic attack. Grinning from ear to ear and full of grateful joy that I had finally acquired my siren name, the desire to share it with someone, anyone, overcame me.

I broke the surface and said my name aloud, it bounced off the hull and echoed around me, and for the first time since I had become trapped in that wreck, my human lungs filled with oxygen. In an aching and violent reaction, I began to cough. The tickling in my throat and the pain as my lungs expanded seized control of my body.

Alarmed, the men reacted.

A great cracking noise startled me back underwater. The coughing ceased and the pain in my chest eased as I breathed through my gills again, but by then the oxygen in my lungs had returned me to a near fully human mind.

I watched with curiosity as one of the men pried lose several planks from the hull, making a hole large enough for me to pass through. The crack and groan of soggy wood and rusty nails giving way filled my hollow. Fear was nonsensical. These men were freeing me, and even if they had some malignant ulterior motive for doing so, I did not need to be frightened of them. I could make them do whatever I wished with my siren voice.

The man with the large head peered into the hole and then reached in a hand.

"Nikt cię nie skrzwdzi," he said. He smiled and his eyes crinkled, transforming his face into something beautiful. The sun passed behind his hat, giving his whole countenance a corona of warm yellow light.

My heart rang like a bell and the vibration ran along my spine and to the very ends of my fingertips and tail. I had no idea what he said, but it didn't matter. He was to be my mate.

My face broke the surface and I looked up into the eyes of the man who owned the voice. I realized his large head only looked so because of the hat he wore. None of the other men wore hats. Somehow, this man was set apart from them.

"Jesteś wolny." He continued to smile and beckon to me. My heart felt as though it had tripled in size and become soft and juicy, like ripe summer fruit.

"Sybellen," I croaked from a raw throat.

His brows drew together momentarily in confusion. "Sybellen?"

"My name," I clarified. "It is Sybellen."

He didn't say anything at first, and I didn't know if it was because he was startled that I'd spoken, or startled that I'd introduced myself. I actually hadn't meant to, I had only been reacting to my oceanic christening, but it must have seemed like an introduction to him. Given the choice, I would have given him my human name, but it was too late for that.

Then he gave a delighted laugh. In a richly accented voice, he said, "You speak English! My great-uncle was right."

I didn't properly process the latter phrase—which was so oddly out of place—because my eyes were taking in his features hungrily. The attraction I felt to him was steadily warming my body, right through my soul. His proportions, symmetry, frame, features, kind expression—his every detail screamed that he was perfect for fathering my child.

I reached up a hand, and even though help was now the

last thing I needed, I allowed him to pull me from the wreck. As I passed out of the water, I shed my mermaid's tail and crawled from the wreck with long, pale legs. Naked as the day I was born, and about as slimy, I got to my feet.

Only then did I see the crowd of men who had gathered to watch.

The man in the hat spoke to one of them in his foreign tongue. The fellow produced a lump of dingy white cloth, which was taken and then handed to me.

Standing there in the shallows with the sharp stones cutting into the soles of my newly formed feet, I stared at the cloth stupidly.

"It's all we have on short notice," the man in the hat said, shifting from one leg to the other to move between me and the staring crowd.

I looked into his face, quizzically.

"Here, let me help you." His voice was so gentle, and it made my insides vibrate in a way nothing else had (at least that I could remember at the time).

He shook out the cloth and looped it over my head. It was a shirt to cover my naked body, and reminded me that humans were ashamed to be naked. I put my arms through the billowy sleeves. The shirt, smelling of sweat and beer, fell to just above my knees. The gaping collar fell over one shoulder, and the man in the hat laced up the thong at the chest to tighten it. His fingers brushed my skin and nearly set it to flaming.

My recent state of affairs—trapped in the wreck, salt-flush, living on instinct alone—was not really something I felt the need to process any further. All of my concentration was now centered around this man, and I had already begun to think of him as mine.

THE OBJECT OF MY AFFECTION, as you know, was Mattis Novak—shipping magnate and ambitious businessman. He took me to the rooms he'd rented at a tavern in a nearby port town, and sourced me a dress that fit. But before I was allowed to put it on, I was offered a bath to wash the salt from my body and hair. The soap I was given—stinking potently of artificial perfume—I declined, but the bath I gratefully accepted.

As I washed myself and soaked in the sweet, rapidly cooling bathwater, an excitement to begin the next phase of my life infiltrated every fiber of my being. This time would be different. This time, I'd found someone really special, someone I would stay with until death parted us. Let the woes of the Atlanteans and the sirens of Okeanos sort itself out, I had found someone I believed would make me deliciously happy. This time I also had Nike's enlightenment that avoiding the use of my siren voice would allow wonderful things to happen. And after three failed *Dyás*, I needed any wonderful things nature might see fit to give me.

Mattis was a man who had the ability to get things done, to motivate others and to make them like him at the same time. The clothing, the bath, and a room on the top floor were all taken care of within a matter of minutes. This was a quality of his which may not seem directly important to the story, but I am certain that if Mattis had been a less ambitious, less organized, or less driven type of person, my story and his would have turned out very differently.

"Are you hungry?" he asked as I entered his room on the top floor—the quietest and least bothered by the smells of cooking, hops, and the unwashed patrons in the tavern below. He gestured that I should take one of the chairs near the small fireplace. "I can't imagine you wouldn't be. How long were you trapped inside that ship?"

"I don't know, and yes, I am hungry." Point of fact, I had smelled the savory scents of fried fish and potatoes (mingled with everything else I chose to ignore) when we'd entered the tavern, and it had set my mouth to watering furiously. The intervening time for the bath had only heightened that hunger.

Mattis pulled on a thin rope hanging near the door and distantly, in some lower floor of the building, a bell tinkled.

"I suppose you had no ways of marking the days." He sat across from me. "Not that you were in any mind to be making sums."

"How do you know this about us? How do you know," I amended, "about us at all?"

"Your kind is legendary among my kind."

"Your kind?"

"Sailors." He smiled as he pulled off his knee-high leather boots and wriggled his toes. His eyes rolled up in his head as though in some kind of ecstasy. "It feels so good to be released from those boots." He shot the offending footwear a distasteful look. "I had them made when I was in London last. I think I'll keep the shoemaker I have in Gdansk."

"Is that where you're from?"

He nodded. "But we are getting off track."

A knock at the door interrupted us. Mattis sprang to his feet and opened it to greet a server from the tavern. "Bring us two plates from the kitchens, whatever you have that smells so wonderful. Two pints of light ale, please."

The server answered back in a different language and they conversed for a moment in a friendly way. The server peered in at me under Mattis's armpit and I caught a flash of dark, curious eyes. He departed with Mattis's request and Mattis closed the door and returned to me.

"Many seafaring men believe you to be creatures of myth, but there are a surprising number of them who watch for you diligently while sailing. My great-uncle Gerhard told me stories when I was but a young boy." He eyes swept over me, sparkling. "Kept me hanging on his every word, so he did. According to him, his brother had a mermaid for a wife."

Another knock preceded the same servant entering with two dripping mugs of ale, which he set on the small round table between us. His eyes lingered on me as he and Mattis spoke in the local language again. He backed out of the room, never once showing me his back.

"That is until she disappeared one day, taking some family jewels and gold with her."

"Did you believe him?"

"Only when I was a small boy, but when I grew up, I realized he was having fun with me."

"He was," I agreed. "Mermaids do not need to take treasure from men. We have enough riches." I pinched my lips shut, realizing I was saying too much. No one was supposed to know about my kind, and here I was confirming everything and adding to his knowledge. If I had been my mother, I would have befuddled Mattis with my voice there and then, followed by systematically erasing the memory of every man who'd worked on the freshwater line to save me.

"Those men, the ones who helped put freshwater into my wreck, do they all work for you?"

"Most of them. Some of them are sailors, and others work at the dock here in St. Croix. A few were villagers who got caught up in the effort to free you."

"But it was you who knew what to do?"

Mattis took a long swig of the ale, leaving a thick foam moustache on his upper lip. He wiped it away against his sleeve. I watched the gesture with a hungry gaze, my eyes lingering on his full red lips and white teeth.

"Uncle Gerhard told me that saltwater makes mermaids unfriendly." Mattis seemed to choose his words carefully. "And freshwater does the opposite. I didn't know if it was a bit of fabrication, but I thought it worth trying to help a beautiful creature such as yourself. Men do not so often get to see mermaids close up."

"But you are not afraid?"

His brows drew together. "What should I be afraid of?"

"This Gerhard did not warn you of our mystical powers?"

"That you can change from human to mermaid and back again at will? Certainly. That you have the most beautiful voices ever heard by men and that your singing has been known to lure men to their doom?" He waved a hand and his blue eyes caught mine. "If you were going to do such a thing, you would have done it by now."

So, he was not aware of the power of my voice, then. If he had been, perhaps he would not have rescued me, for fear I would have swindled him out of his sense and his belongings.

We were presented with large plates of food heaping with simple fried fish, boiled potatoes, a fat slice of ham, and something that looked like a fat banana and tasted like potato, chopped up and pan-fried. I ate ravenously as Mattis chattered between bites about the look on his man's face when he'd come running into the tavern to tell Mattis of their find. His efforts to hide the fact that they'd discovered something incredible were poor indeed. Mattis laughed heartily as he described how the fellow, by the name of Swigg, came bolting into the tavern, red-faced and nearly foaming at the mouth with excitement. He then came to a stiff and immediate halt just inside the tavern door, for Mattis had taught them, as well as he could, to be gentlemen.

Swigg had spied Mattis working on his ledgers in a corner table, and had high-stepped awkwardly across the tavern in a clear effort to slow down and take his time when it was obvious what he really wanted to do was bolt. His parody of a man who 'knew-nothing-very-much-at-all, thank-you-good-sirs, nice-to-see-you, I've-no-news-whatsoever' caught Mattis's eye immediately, not to mention almost every other eye in the place.

Naturally, his news was enough to make Mattis put away his things and hastily join the men on the stony beach to see if their tale was true.

"When I first laid eyes on you," Mattis said through a mouthful of potato, "I thought I'd never seen anything so beautiful."

I swallowed down the last bit of fish and stared at him. "Me too."

Mattis stopped chewing and stared at me, the whites of his eyes visible all around. It seemed a long time before he swallowed his mouthful, and I could follow its progress down the column of his throat.

"No human woman has ever called me beautiful," he finally said. "Women of the sort of breeding my mother would like me to associate with do not say such things out loud."

"They think it, though." I took another bite of the banana-potato, and chased it with a large gulp of beer.

"I believe they assign me descriptors such as 'eligible,' and 'good prospect.'" His tone sounded almost sour. "Before my company began to prosper, these same women would not look at me in the street, for I was the son of a carpenter and not a man to pay attention to. How quickly they changed their minds as the winds of fortune blew my way."

His tone of disgust pleased me. I said, "So you are not beholden to any of them?"

He blinked that same startled expression at me again, before bellowing laughter. "You do not mince words, mermaid."

"Why should I?"

"That's an excellent question," he put up a finger, "and had I the time of a wealthy philosopher, I would spend many an evening dissecting it." Mattis then went on, as we finished our meal and our ale, about the complications of gallant life, mentioning at least once that though I looked like a woman, my attitudes were very different, for no self-respecting woman would take a private meal with him in his rooms let alone stand naked and completely shameless in front of a crowd of gawking men.

I did not pay so much attention to his words as I enjoyed the warming effect his voice had on my body.

It wasn't until he asked me, "What will you do now that you are free?" that I gave him my own startled look. That he should even ask the question seemed so unexpected, it astonished me back into my brain.

"I'll come with you and be your wife," I replied, setting my now empty plate aside.

Mattis choked on his last piece of fish and began to cough and hack.

Alarmed, I got up and hit him between the shoulder blades, a bit too hard, probably. He wheezed, and his face turned red and tears streamed down his cheeks. I handed him his mug of half-finished ale and he took it, gratefully taking big gulps and breathing loudly through his nose.

"You should never make such jokes while a man has food in his mouth," he wheezed, coughing into his fist again and then thumping it against his chest. "Or ever, in places where my mother might like to socialize."

"I wasn't joking." I returned to my seat. "Are you all right?"

He'd gone quiet again, wide-eyed and watching me. "My God, you're serious?"

I didn't need to reply, because he could see my intent in my face. Why should I not let this human male know that I wanted him? It was better than using my voice on him. He liked me, I could feel it. The way he spoke about the women in his hometown told me enough.

Though Okeanos was not forgotten, my goal of returning to its caves and glittering pools to restore balance, respectability, and peace had already begun to lose meaning for me. A new desire took root, one which exceeded all others—make Mattis my mate, produce a child, and be with the man I had already fallen in love with.

You see, part of the siren's curse—the most insidious part, if you ask me—is its ability to play with a mermaid's wants and goals. In the absence of a gem, a siren is under the thumb of the *Dyás*. She is as subject to the effects of salt on her system as the seedling of a young tree is to the sun and the weather. A bee flies from flower to flower, never settling on just one for very long, but while it is on the flower under its feet, no other nectar ever tasted quite as sweet, indeed none of the flowers nearby or in the distance can distract the bee from its work on the current blossom, until that blossom has given up all it has.

Only then will the bee raise its head and move on to the next.

EIGHT

We were married in a simple ceremony on St. Croix, surrounded by Mattis's men, people from the port village, and natives who made their life on the island. It was a happy affair, with everyone contributing something to the evening feast.

"Do you not want to be married at home, where your family can be part of it?" I asked Mattis a few days before the wedding ceremony was to take place.

"I would like that very much, but after I leave St. Croix, I am destined for South Carolina, and after that Boston, and after that Belfast. It will be autumn before I am home again." He touched my cheek and gazed at me affectionately. "I don't know about you, but I don't want to wait that long, and my men are a little shy of having a woman onboard who is not my wife."

I had accepted this easily. Sirens didn't expect their relatives to attend. A mating cycle was a lonely affair, and we ourselves forgot it was a cycle that could not be ignored while we were in it. And so, at the time, I was deeply in love with Mattis, and fully intended to stay with him on land. I was happy, I was beginning a new life, and the power of the Salt was distant and unthreatening.

I journeyed to many places with Mattis and his crew, sharing his quarters and getting to know the men in his employ. They treated me with the utmost respect and deference and they let me practice speaking Polish with them while not asking me too many questions.

Unlike Mattis's mother.

When we finally made it home to Poland, we were greeted at the dock by Mattis's parents—who'd been alerted to our arrival while we were still distant on the horizon—Aleksandra and Emun. Aleksandra was a petite woman in a homespun dress of muted colors and a bonnet covering her silvery gray hair. Her hands were rough from a life of hard work. Mattis had told me she worked as a laundrywoman until his shipping business was making enough money for her to stop working. Emun was an older, bent version of Mattis and a man of few words. I felt accepted by him immediately.

Aleksandra, though she pulled me into an embrace and took my two hands in hers to squeeze them when Mattis told them I was now their daughter-in-law, had an uncomfortably probing gaze. She was not cold nor unkind, but neither did her scrutinous gaze or her investigative questions relent until Mattis told her to let me be.

"But what of her family? Will we not meet your in-laws?" Aleksandra asked as she squeezed Mattis's elbow. We made our way off the docks toward a waiting carriage.

"She has no family, Mama," Mattis responded, flicking his fingers absentmindedly at one of his men and giving some order only that man could understand.

"No family at all?" Aleksandra's gaze softened and filled with pity. She turned to me. "You poor dear. What happened to your parents? Have you no siblings, no aunts or uncles, no cousins?"

"We are her family now, Mama," Mattis answered.

"And what of her last name?"

"Her name is Novak, Mama," Mattis answered patiently as we arrived at the carriage. A man came running up with a sheaf of papers and handed them to Mattis.

"Of course," Aleksandra laughed, "but what was her maiden name?"

"It was Grant," I replied, giving her the surname I had been born under.

"Grant," Aleksandra said. "How English sounding. Are you English? Where did you learn Polish? How did you find yourself in St. Croix?"

"She was shipwrecked," my new husband answered the last question with a quirk.

Aleksandra's eyes widened to the size of saucers. "Shipwrecked! You poor dear!" She patted my hand as I looked over her head at Mattis, unsure of whether to laugh or to glare at him. "You must have been through a dreadful thing, simply dreadful."

"She has, Mama."

Mattis handed the sheaf of papers to a man in uniform passing by and then turned to help his mother up into the carriage.

"And what she needs," he continued, as Aleksandra put a foot on the step and pulled herself up, "is some peace and quiet."

Aleksandra sat on the navy upholstery in the carriage and smiled at her son. Putting a finger to the side of her nose, she winked. "I understand, my son."

Mattis put his hands on my waist and helped me into

the carriage. His father stepped up and settled in the seat across from me and Aleksandra.

"You're not coming?" I asked, noting the dark circles under my husband's eyes.

Mattis shook his head. "Not yet. Give me a few hours while I help the men with the cargo and check in at the office. I'll see you at the house tonight for dinner."

As the carriage door shut and we began to roll down the cobbled streets away from the port, I was blissfully unaware that goodbyes would become all too frequent and extended during our marriage.

Early in the new year, I announced my pregnancy to Mattis and his family. While it was cause for celebration in the Novak house (a small, drafty house outside of the city limits), it did not keep Mattis closer to home. His business seemed to grow faster than the twins in my belly.

EARLY ONE MORNING, after having fed Emun and Michal, I returned to bed where Mattis was drowsing. He watched me through mostly closed lids as I crawled between the sheets. Lifting a finger, he gestured at the ring hanging at my throat.

"Why don't you wear that on your finger?"

Shrugging, I flopped down on the pillow on my side, looking at his face. "I suppose I've gotten used to it there. Feels strange when I take it off, and it would probably feel strange if I wore it somewhere different."

"May I see it? It's a curious thing, isn't it?"

I crooked up on my elbow and unlatched the chain, handing him the ring and chain.

"What's it made of? Looks a lot like gold, but there's

something a little off in the color. Too yellow, maybe." He took the ring and inspected it. "Interesting markings."

I frowned. "I think I knew what the metal was at one time, but now I've forgotten. I don't think its gold though, something starting with...O."

"What language is this?" He squinted at it. "It's not one I've ever seen before, and I've traveled more than most."

My frown deepened. "I've forgotten that, too. But it'll be a language most humans wouldn't know. That ring was given to me by a friend." I hadn't thought of Nike in a long time and the image of her mischievous grin and floating cloud of blue hair filled my mind. "She gave it to me for emergencies."

"Like the emergency of being trapped inside a wreck and not having sense enough to get yourself out?" He cocked an eyebrow over the ring between us. "Didn't do you much good, did it?"

I smiled. "I guess not for that kind of emergency."

Mattis slid it over his finger but the ring wouldn't go over his knuckle. He pulled it off and switched to his pinky, where it fit at the base perfectly.

A rainbow of light filled the space above the bed and we both gasped and looked up, eyes wide.

Mattis cursed, but his expression was amazed rather than upset.

"What is this?" His voice was hushed.

We sat up and leaned against the headboard to get a better look at the light streaming from the top of the cylinder.

A confusion of colored lines, bright with angles and curves, each of them—sprayed outward from the tiny opening. Four colors traced lines and shapes in a three-dimensional mess of indiscernible imagery.

Mattis got it before I did. Squinting at the magical hologram floating above our heads, and holding the ring now very still between his fingers, he exclaimed, "Maps!"

He was right, and the word shook something loose from my memory. Maps to gemstones.

If I trained my eye on one color only, I could make out the distinct shape of markings which could only belong to a map. "But how are you supposed to read them? It's too difficult to make out." My eye fell on the tiny hole at the top of the cylinder. "May I see it?"

The maps jostled and jumped around in the air as Mattis handed me the ring. Placing my thumbnail over three-quarters of the tiny hole I was able to shut out three colors almost completely. Shifting my nail just a fraction made the yellow, blue, and red maps completely disappear.

Mattis and I looked up at the now much more distinct green map. Mattis laughed. "You are fully within your wits, my love! What do you suppose it leads to?"

He reached a hand through the projection and pointed to its center, marked by a small green circle with a ring around it—like a bullseye.

"Gems," I answered, marveling again at Nike's magic. "Clever siren."

"A siren made this?"

I nodded. "Not just any siren, a sorceress who likes to keep her powers a secret. She gave it to me when I left..."

My words faded away as I searched through a foggy past for images of where I'd come from. All I could conjure up was a mountain jutting from the ocean and reaching high into the sky.

"For what emergency?" Mattis asked.

"In case I should be close to salt-flush and too far from

home to save myself. She planted these gems for herself but gave me the means to find them."

"What's salt-flush?"

Although Mattis had found me in a salt-flush state and was well acquainted with what salt-flush looked like, we'd never actually talked about in specific terms. He listened quietly as I explained the role of salt in a siren's life. His expression, understandably, grew worried when I haltingly explained that many sirens experienced a drive to return to the ocean.

I kissed him, wanting to erase the concern. "I won't leave you and the boys if that's what you're thinking."

"How do you know?" He turned his hazel eyes to me, clouded and disturbed.

"I just won't," I said, stoutly, confident in the control I had over my emotions. I was determined not to be like 'weaker' sirens. Mattis and I had a love that was strong and true and I felt good here on land. I hadn't had a girl child, and while initially this had upset me, I had rationalized it into joy. I would stay with my human husband and my human boys until the end of my life or theirs, whichever came first.

How foolish we sirens are when we are in love. All sirens are deceived while at the height of their mating cycle, with their child in infancy and the love they feel for their mate at its most powerful, their human logic and reason the strongest it will ever be.

The curse makes fools of us all.

Nevertheless, I felt resolute. I kissed away Mattis's concern and we continued to talk languidly that morning. We bonded with Michal and Emun Jr, our tiny beautiful twins, and we bonded with one another. For me, it was the apex of happiness in terms of what I could remember of my life at that time.

EMUN, Targa, and Antoni were listening quietly with dark expressions now, for they all knew how this particular part of the story ended.

My gaze fell on my son, the remaining twin and the precious gift that had somehow been returned to me. He was the reminder of Mattis and the love I had for him, and the joy we'd shared when the twins were born. But in Emun's face, nothing of Mattis could be seen. He had all of his features and coloring from me, even his gestures and movements were Mer, in the same way Targa had very little of her father in her.

"But you bring in a piece of the story at this time, don't you?" I said quietly to Emun. "It wasn't until a few years later that Nike's gift went missing. You were growing up and had passed the point at which most female children have their salt-birth... and I was descending into madness in my efforts to fight the Salt. In my previous *Dyás*, I had given in to the pull of the ocean quickly, and didn't know the difficulty that lay ahead."

Emun rubbed a palm over his face but he couldn't wipe away the troubled look in his eyes, the regret.

"Poor Papa," he said, his voice a little hoarse. "It was such a close thing."

Antoni spoke up from where he and Targa were seated together on the couch closest the fireplace. "What am I missing?"

"Mattis took the ring and gave it to Rainer Veigel," Targa explained. "He commissioned him to find the gems."

"Or at least one," Emun added. "One is all that was needed. Given the complexity of finding such a small thing—even with a magical map—who knows how long it took Rainer to find it. I don't know when father made the commission."

"It would have been when you were three or so," I surmised. "That was around the time the ring went missing." My brow creased. "Although I was so lost in my own suffering that it could have disappeared earlier."

"So, years," Targa said, scooting closer to Antoni, who lifted an arm and put it over the back of the sofa behind her. "It took him years to find it."

"Of course. It would have, especially in those days." Emun stood up and began to pace, raking his fingers through his long black hair and mussing it up. "He would have gone by ship..."

"Knowing Nike," I said, watching my son pace, "the hiding places would have been on remote places in the middle of the world's oceans."

"Hidden somewhere a siren would be able to find them when she needs them," Targa added. "She'd only need them if she was too far from Okeanos to get back in time before she lost all her human reason."

I nodded. "I'm sure Rainer had to travel to what seemed like the ends of the earth to retrieve one of those stones. He may have even had to go underwater."

"You don't remember the detail of the maps? Where they led?" Antoni asked me.

I shook my head. "It was so long ago."

"Did you know father took the ring?" Emun asked.

"Not at first, which shows you just how much the curse changes us. I went from not feeling right if it wasn't around my neck, to not even noticing it was gone because all I wanted to do was bathe in the ocean and let the salt ease my pain. Eventually, Mattis did tell me he'd taken it, and that help was on the way in the form of Rainer. None of his family knew any of this, of course." I looked at Emun. "Your grandparents should have been told. It would have helped them to cope with what was going on. It was surely making no sense to them."

Targa was nodding at this. She'd read Aleksandra's diary and knew very well what Mattis's parents had gone through.

"But you swore Father to secrecy?" Emun asked.

"Actually, I didn't have to. Once we'd returned to Poland from St. Croix, Mattis changed all of the crew who had been on the St. Croix trip with him. Anyone who knew what I was left Gdansk—sent to far outposts, maybe even fired for all I knew. Mattis believed as much as I did that my true nature had to be kept a secret. He was terrified that if anyone found out, the worst of 'anyone' being those in the church, that we'd be separated. I'd be driven out, possibly captured, or even killed."

Emun nodded. He knew what the people of that time were like. Superstitious, religious, fearful, and sometimes irrational in their beliefs. He understood better than Targa or Antoni because he'd lived through it.

"But you didn't know how long it would take Rainer to find one of the gems..."

"Or *if* he would even be successful," Antoni added. "You must have felt completely helpless."

"Father would have," Emun said, and then he turned his intense blue gaze on me. "But Mama, you were so lost in your affliction that you probably barely remembered the name Rainer most of the time." His eyes darkened at the pain of whatever he was recalling. "I remember how much you changed, how much you were hurting, because I could feel it, too."

My throat closed up as I looked at my long-lost son. "You were always the one who seemed to understand me the best, and now I know why." My voice cracked, and regret filled my belly with vinegar. "Triton."

I could say no more than this without the possibility of opening the faucet on a flood of siren tears, and there was so much more still to tell. I took a deep breath.

"There is a reason it is called a curse," I went on. "Curses are cruel things. I didn't know that Mattis and the sailors on *The Sybellen* lost their lives that night, and I certainly didn't know that he'd taken you with him. I might not have believed it if I had been told. It was extremely reckless of Mattis to take you out when a storm was coming."

The corners of Emun's mouth turned down. "He knew we were connected, and even though he didn't know the extent of it, he thought that if you heard my voice calling you over the waves that night, you would come to us."

But I hadn't heard Emun calling, I had gone too far and too deep by then to hear anything. Even if I had heard him, I don't know if I'd have had the will to return against the power of the curse.

"I went to sea that night thinking I'd never see my husband and children again, thinking that I'd failed again, thinking how I hadn't been strong enough to fight the curse the way I promised Mattis I would. The Salt seemed to punish me for fighting it for so long. I intended to go home to Okeanos, but instead I lost years of my life lying dormant on the bottom of the ocean."

"Dormant?" Targa straightened. "What do you mean

dormant? Like how a bear goes into hibernation for the winter?"

"Diapause," Emun said.

Antoni's gaze went from me to Emun. "Dia-what?"

"It's deeper than hibernation. Animals hibernate over the winter season and come out of it in the spring to mate and feed. Dormancy is more serious than that. All metabolic activity grinds to a crawl." His gaze met mine. "It's a sleeping death."

I nodded, my eyes locked with his as a moment of understanding passed between us. "You know because you've done it."

Targa and Antoni's eyes cut to Emun, both filled with curiosity.

"Is that true?" Targa asked.

Emun sat down in his chair again. "Yes. It's true. After periods of great trauma, all you want to do is descend into peace and darkness. The weight of the miles of water over your head, the diminished oxygen, it's comforting. It erases memory. Humans don't realize this, but sleep erases their memory, too, just on a much smaller scale."

Antoni said, "You are right about sleep erasing memory. I read a study about it in university for my marketing class. Scientists used to think that memories were transferred to the neocortex during sleep, but newer studies revealed that the hippocampus acts as a temporary storage system that is cleared overnight to make room for new memories. It takes repetition in order for something to be recalled."

Targa's voice was tinged with laughter. "Why exactly did you need to know that for marketing?"

"Because," Antoni answered, "when you're buying advertising you have to understand that people need repetitive exposure in order for your message to stick. That's why radio jingles are so effective. A short, repetitive song about whatever it is you want people to remember, no matter how inane and annoying."

Antoni slowed down, becoming aware that Emun, Targa, and I were all watching him. He squirmed in his seat.

"It makes the ad stick in the neocortex." He cleared his throat and laced his fingers in his lap. "Sorry. Please go on."

Targa kissed him on the cheek and he gave her a bashful smile. They returned their attention to Emun.

"So, you descend to find relief, tranquility," Emun went on, raising his hands in a 'there you go' gesture. "And you fall asleep."

"For how long?" Antoni asked, his look of suppressed alarm returning.

"Years," Emun and I answered together. I smiled at my son. "What was this great trauma you suffered?"

He gave a secretive, close-mouthed smile. "This is not time for my stories."

"How do you not go completely salt-flush while you're lying dormant on the ocean floor for years?" asked Targa.

"Because your metabolism almost stops," explained Emun, leaning back against his chair and reaching for the mug of tea on the table beside him. "It's like time stops. You're no closer to salt-flush when you wake than you were when you went to sleep."

"Oh. That makes sense." Targa leaned forward and picked up her own mug of tea. She turned her bright teal eyes on me. "Okay, so you went dormant. What happened next?"

NINE

As the miles increased between me and my family, I felt as though I could not swim far enough nor fast enough to get away from the sorrow. The salt is always a comfort, but I was so starved for it that I headed for the saltiest and deepest of water. I stayed near the ocean floor, choosing the downward path whenever there was an option. It seemed the more weight there was on top of me, the less I felt the pain and sorrow of my tragic *Dyás*.

As I descended, I moved more and more slowly, I ate less, and I was less curious and more tired. I don't actually recall coming to a halt or falling asleep, but when I woke, I had to find my way out of a crack in the earth where only the strangest bioluminescent creatures lived. Some of this deep-sea life was like something from a human's worst nightmare, but to me they were beautiful.

When my body told me it was time to surface, I found myself quite changed. I remembered nothing of my life in Gdansk—it had been erased completely. I made my way toward the rays of the sun, moving very slowly. When I looked down at myself, I could see every rib, the details of my musculature, and even veins, which are almost never visible on mermaids. So, the first thing I did was hunt. I felt a calling to return home, and my memories of home were as clear as any memory can be. Okeanos called me as strongly as the desire to find a mate had called me previously. I turned southwest, the direction of Okeanos from where I had lain, and hunted as I swam.

I had not expected anything in particular when I returned, other than to get my gem back from Nike's keeping and to return to life in Okeanos. The fiery concern I had once had about improving our fraught relationship with the Atlanteans was distant in my mind. I did not think of the reason I left Okeanos in the first place, for the Salt and the curse had done its work. I was like a new creature, a recently born siren with no past.

As I passed through the *apotreptikó* and made my way to Califas, a strange thing began to happen. Every mermaid I saw—even the distant ones—I felt connected to by an invisible tether. It was almost as though I could hear their heartbeats, pick up on the subtle play of their emotions, taste their feelings like they were drops of blood in the water. They followed me, just the way all of the sirens had followed Apollyona when she returned as Sovereign. At some point, I realized why they were following me, and though I did not say anything or reveal my own thoughts to my sirens—which was how I suddenly thought of them—I had a moment of thunderous revelation.

I was their new Sovereign. The Salt was what deemed a siren worthy of Sovereignty, and my connection to my people could be felt from both sides.

Apollyona would know I was coming, because she'd be able to feel it. I mused about this as I walked the steps to the throne room to accept my fate. I was numb, not fully accepting of it, though my body knew exactly what was taking place and could not deny it—as a girl cannot deny her first period.

Ascending the last step, naked and still dripping—though if I'd wished for a robe, I knew that someone would procure one without me needing to ask, as Apollyona had when she'd ascended—I stepped in front of the throne and my mother.

Though she'd had time to process my approach, she could not fully hide her shock. Whether this was at having lost the Sovereignty so quickly, or that she'd never believed me capable or worthy of taking our most superior position, I'll never know. But she was not as gracious as Odenyalis had been when she passed the crown to her successor.

She was breathing slowly but heavily, the cords on her neck standing out and her chest and shoulders rising and falling as she fought for control. I was her superior now in every way; the Salt decreed it and there would be no contesting it from any of the sirens in Okeanos, least of all the former Sovereign.

She and I stared at one another, our eyes locked in a way that felt near impossible to break. Her glare was ice-cold. Her jaw muscles worked as she ground her teeth and prepared herself for what had to be done.

The room was full of sirens and the *Foniádes*, who stood either side of the aquamarine throne.

Apollyona stared at me for a long time. Only when the time had grown a little too long did she rise and walk down the steps. She came to stand in front of me but she did not kiss my cheeks. The battle over her emotions was visceral to me, and a wave of pity passed through me. I am sure my flinty expression softened, for her own expression returned a glimmer of respect.

I had done what she had never expected me to do, and the Salt said I'd done it fairly and rightly.

"My name is Sybellen." My name echoed off the cave walls.

Apollyona gave a curt nod, as though she'd finally reached acceptance. She removed the aquamarine crown and placed it on my own head. The necklace followed, and only after it was resting on my collarbones and several more moments had passed, did she reach out and place her fingers at my throat, dropping her eyes as she did so.

But I was having my own moment of wrestling with emotion, for when the gemstones touched my head, a rush of memories invaded my mind and I nearly staggered under the suddenness of it.

Mattis, Emun, and Michal, and all the people from my life in Poland were there—like a dream I had a long time ago. I felt no pain, only acceptance. I was a siren, and this was the way of things. There was no use bemoaning what is or what is no longer. I was Sovereign, and it was the sacrifice of my human family that had allowed it to be.

The passing of the Sovereignty is not a moment for chatter. It was done. I turned to the assembled sirens and pledged, "I, Sybellen of Okeanos, humbly take up the coronation of the Salt, and serve you as Sovereign."

Unwittingly, I had succeeded at my original goal, in spite of how convinced I had been of failure.

I had become the reigning Sovereign of Okeanos.

AFTER THE SIRENS of Okeanos had paid their respects and left the throne room, only the *Foniádes*, Polly, and Nike remained. I called the *Foniádes* close. My new decree had to start with these sirens and spread from there.

"You are not to harm Atlanteans who come within our borders," I said.

Polly visibly stiffened and she moved closer. "Sybellen. I beg of you not to be hasty. Please," she put up a hand and gestured to the archway behind the throne, "visit the Hall of Anamna before you change anything concerning the Atlanteans."

"Hall of Anamna?" This was the first I had heard the term.

"Anamna means memories," Nike said quietly. "It is one of the gifts of the Sovereign alone." Her eyes canted accusingly to Polly. "One of the many things your mother did not inform you of when you were little."

Polly had the grace to cast her eyes down in shame, but it lasted only a moment before she lifted them again. "I did not want to bother you with such things..."

"Such things, as you believed I would never need to know," I interrupted, feeling disappointment curdle in my gut. "Your plans for Okeanos were only ever your own, Mother. If you had prepared me the way a mother should..."

"I only wanted to protect you, Sybellen."

"That is only part of the job, *Polly*." I spoke harshly and regretted it a moment later. This woman had made mistakes, but she had still loved me in her imperfect way, perhaps the only way she herself had ever been shown.

My tone softened. "I have learned that the job of a mother is to prepare, protect, and provide for her child..."

I stopped as the hypocrisy of my words cut too sharply for me to continue. I swallowed hard.

Sirens were caring of their siren offspring, but what of the sweet human males left behind? How could I preach to

Polly about what motherhood means, when I had failed repeatedly at it myself?

"It is right that you call me Polly now," my mother said, surprising me with both the humility of her statement and the acceptance in her tone. "I was wrong to misjudge you, to keep you ignorant. Maybe one day you will forgive me."

This was so out of character for our former ruler that Nike and I shared a suspicious look. Sovereign or not, Polly was regal, queenly, and never admitted to being wrong.

"But, having been under that crown before you, I beseech you to take advantage of all of its gifts. Know our legacy before you dismantle the protections I sacrificed so much to put in place." She gestured again toward the archway behind the throne.

I turned toward it and took the steps up. With a glance, I invited Nike to join me. We passed through to the Hall of Anamna together.

"What is this place?" My voice echoed in the darkness, hinting at the emptiness and vastness of the cavern beyond.

The sound of a stone grinding against stone made me turn. Nike had her hands against a boulder set on a shelf on the wall inside the doorway, shoving it aside. Sunlight poured through a crack in the wall behind the boulder. I gasped at the result.

The light zigzagged through the Hall, finding the reflective surfaces engineered for that purpose and illuminating the Hall of Anamna fully. I began to walk the Hall, my bare feet silent on the cold, uneven floor.

"The Sovereign inherits the memories of all the Sovereigns before her," Nike said as she walked just behind me.

Along the uneven cave walls were mosaics. Constructed with a variety of reflective and non-reflective tiles, stones and gems, were portraits of sirens—possibly hundreds of them. The Hall ahead turned corners and wound its way through the rock, with uneven stairs here and there, and no straight lines in sight. The artwork too had been done without any straight lines; everything was organic, asymmetrical, colorful, and very beautiful.

The portraits were as varied as no doubt the sirens whom they depicted had been. Some of them wore clothing, others were naked. Some were in mermaid form, others sat or stood on human legs. Some portraits were busts only, showing only the neck and head, others were full-body and included backgrounds of seascapes or landscapes behind them.

"Who made these?" I asked breathlessly, as I walked the Hall slowly, stopping to take in the portraits on either side of me.

"Who else? Sirens," Nike replied. "When the reign of a Sovereign comes to an end, the art appears soon afterward created by whoever is moved to do it by the Salt. Someone who has the talent to do it well. The Salt knows."

"The Salt knows," I echoed. I reached out a hand to touch the mosaic before me, but hesitated, feeling that to touch it meant something bigger than simply feeling the cold stone beneath my skin.

The Sovereign depicted wore a bright azure robe of flowing fabric. She stood against a background of a green and brown mountainside. Pillars and rooftops were visible behind her. Sparkling brown and orange tiles were used to depict her eyes, while the rest of her face was done in flat colored ceramic. The effect made her eyes appear alive, multi-dimensional. They seemed as though they followed me wherever I moved.

"How did they achieve this?" I was unable to tear my own eyes away from the face of the Sovereign on the wall.

"What, exactly?"

"The eyes, they move."

Nike chuckled softly. "They don't move, at least not to anyone but you. Within these portraits lies the history and knowledge of your Sovereign ancestors. Whatever they knew, whatever they experienced, it's yours now."

"How?"

"The Salt knows. It's magic." Nike laughed, but then her smile faltered. "It's part of our curse. No one can tell you *how*, but I think if you touch it, you'll discover it personally."

I stepped back, wanting to keep walking and see more portraits.

I walked the rest of the Hall with Nike, taking in the faces and forms of the mermaids who'd ruled our abundant lands before me. Every face had an expression, and the eyes always moved and came alive. None of the mosaics had birth years or death years, but every portrait did have a siren name—their Sovereign name.

When I reached the end, Odenyalis's portrait, the Hall just ended with a plain, pitted wall of stone. Putting my hand against it, I realized that there was no room for Apollyona's portrait yet, and whoever came to create it would have to remove the stone and go deeper into the rock.

Putting my back to the rock, I faced the Hall of Anamna. "Polly begged me to come here to learn about the Atlanteans, but she didn't tell me where to start."

"She didn't need to. There is one Sovereign who must be beckoning you more than the others."

I nodded, thinking of the Sovereign in the blue robes. "There is."

"Then she is where you should start."

I walked the long Hall back to the Sovereign near the

entrance. She was among the oldest. Yes, her eyes were glimmering, warm and beckoning. I hadn't noticed her name before, but it was there in thin black tiles and a cursive script.

Sisinyxa.

I reached toward her portrait, hesitating only a moment before looking up at those glittery eyes again.

"What do you have to show me, Sisinyxa?" I whispered as my hand touched the stone.

TEN

The world became a gray blur. Vertigo and nausea swept over me as I lost sensation of my body. Slowly, my vision settled and color returned to the world. I was someone else, but I was simply a passenger, with no ability to control the body in which I now found myself—no matter how much I desired to. I was riding behind her eyes, her thoughts, and I surrendered to the education I was about to receive.

SISINYXA TOOK stone steps up to a terrace and passed through massive pillars holding up a circular ceiling. The sounds of music, laughter and chatter filled her ears, while the scent of roasted meat and wine made her mouth water.

Passing a mirror, Sisinyxa glanced at her reflection and stopped for a moment to tuck a stray curl into her golden headband. I was taken aback by a detail I noticed about her ears. The small fleshy bit in front of her ear canal—the bit called the tragus—was larger than normal. Aside from this, Sisinyxa looked much like her image in the Hall of

Anamna, only more beautiful. Her skin was olive-toned and rosy. Her chocolate brown hair had been curled and partially pinned to the top of her head, held there with a disc of yellow metal. The rest of her hair fell down around her shoulders and cascaded to her waist. She wore a bosom-revealing blue bodice with only one shoulder strap, the skin of her taut belly visible between the tight sleeveless vest, and a slim-fitting skirt made of what seemed like miles of fabric. Leather sandals clad her feet, and she could feel the thongs laced up her calves to just under her knees. Her body was petite and compact, curvy, yet athletic, and she had calluses on her right palm. I learned later how she'd come by these calluses—swordplay. Sisinyxa was an exceptional soldier as well as a cunning Sovereign.

Nowhere on her person did I spot an aquamarine gemstone. I searched her mind for the blue stone, but it was not in her thoughts. She was not on a *Dyás*, for I understood that searching for a mate had not brought her to this place. Puzzled, I set these wonderings aside and settled in to watch and experience Sisinyxa's memories. The image had chosen to show me this, so it was my duty to figure out why.

Sisinyxa passed by the mirrors and into a large space over which an open oculus in the domed ceiling revealed the blue sky above. It was hot, and everyone in the room gleamed with a layer of sweat. Most of them were being fanned by servants with simple white clothing garbing their hips, even the women, who walked about bare-breasted, carrying trays of fruit and wine.

She passed by luxurious couches and tables bountiful with food, where dozens of people sat and talked. Most of those present were men, though there were a few elegant and richly dressed (much like Sisinyxa herself) women among them. I understood from Sisinyxa's memory that these were aristocrats. Some were royal, and many were politically active. It crossed my mind how interesting it was that I could access her memories and understanding of a situation like this.

Sisinyxa stopped at a fountain to chat with someone who was of no consequence to her, only well-positioned for her to listen in on a conversation happening between a couple of men lounging around a low table bearing jeweled wine goblets. I was able to tell, from her memories, that their names were Renlaus and Nestor. Sisinyxa homed in on their conversation while she made small talk with the woman at the fountain.

"You see the woman there in the blue robes?" Nestor muttered quietly to the other.

"How could I miss her? I noticed her the moment she appeared," the second man, Renlaus, bent low to answer. "You know her? Of what family is she?"

Nestor laughed, low and throaty and full of love for his own voice. "My dear Renlaus, she is of a family which you've never heard. Her home, I'm told, is a place so full of resources it would put Atlantis to shame."

Renlaus gave a small, disbelieving gasp. "This is not possible. We are the world's wealthiest. We own everything of value for thousands of miles...unless," he hesitated, "... unless she is from the mystical far East? Is that where she is from, dear Nestor?"

The other did not answer, and Sisinyxa pictured him shaking his head, bidding the other man to continue guessing with his eyes. Sisinyxa was enjoying this conversation because she knew that Renlaus knew perfectly well who she was and was playing a little joke on Nestor.

"Tell me at least that she is no human," Renlaus said. "A

woman so beautiful and powerful must at the very least be one of us."

Again, a pregnant silence, and Renlaus gasped again. "What then? Come, you have me on my knees with curiosity!"

"She is the Queen of Okeanos, my friend." Nestor pitched his voice lower. "And she is Mer."

"Okeanos." Renlaus, sounded puzzled by this. "I have never heard of it."

"And you will not, but remember the name, my friend, for it is a very great secret."

"Where is it?"

"That," Nestor replied, leaning back against the couch heavily, "is what I am trying to learn."

Sisinyxa eavesdropped with great humor burbling in her chest. Renlaus knew exactly where Okeanos was, and all about its resources and its citizens. Renlaus was a well-paid Atlantean, an exceptional sailor, and the captain of his own ship. Renlaus had been delivering shipments from Atlantis to Okeanos for years—goods the Mer could not acquire from salvaging the ocean floors: textiles and bolts of fine cloth, colored tiles, mirrors, tools for mining and tiling and working with stone. He and his Atlantean sailors delivered whatever Sisinyxa had bartered for and helped deliver it to their store caves under Mount Califas.

"Where did you get this, my friend?" Nestor asked.

Sisinyxa turned her head to catch the two men in her peripheral vision. Nestor was fingering a bright yellow-gold ring on Renlaus's pinky finger—a gift from Sisinyxa herself. A down payment, in fact, on Renlaus's next delivery.

"Bought it at market last year," Renlaus answered smoothly. "It is simple, but I like simple, and besides I plan to give it to Adria upon our engagement after I've found the right stone for it."

"Which market?" Nestor prodded further. "The one in Narisse?"

"The very same," Renlaus replied, snappily. "More wine?"

Sisinyxa, sensing the dangerous territory Renlaus was treading, took that moment to leave the fountain and join Nestor and Renlaus.

Both men got to their feet when they saw her coming, their eyes devouring her in different ways—Renlaus for her beauty, and Nestor with a kind of greedy hunger that had more to do with ambition than lust.

"Sisinyxa." Nestor inclined his head and took her hand, lifting her hand to his lips to kiss it so his eyes never had to leave her face. "Always a pleasure."

"Nestor." She dipped her chin. She kept her face a serene mask of beauty and grace, but I could sense her caution around this man—her wariness of him was a low thrum in her gut. Her gaze shifted to Renlaus and the two of them shared a conspiratorial smile. "Renlaus."

Nestor gave a small gasp and looked from one to the other with surprise as he realized they knew one another.

"My lady." Renlaus kissed her hand after Nestor and gestured to their couches. "Won't you join us?"

"But for a moment, thank you." She sank gracefully to the plush lounge chair and shook her head at a passing servant offering her a drink.

The men sat down with her.

"I only came to see if you might have changed your mind," she said to Nestor, taking a grape from the bowl on the table and popping it into her mouth.

Nestor gave a low but unsettled laugh and brushed a

hand across his brow. A ring bearing his crest caught the light—a lion with six legs. "About the council's position on women in power? Of course not. As much as I want to make an arrangement with you for as much orichalcum as you can bring me, I am not able to work miracles, my dear. Women have never, nor will they ever, have a seat in the government of Atlantis."

Liar, thought Sisinyxa. She had a strong trade position, owing to the rich mines of Okeanos, full of this old world's most precious metal—mountain copper, otherwise known as orichalcum. And though she had many opportunities to trade it with the various merchants of Atlantis, only one man—she believed—had the ability to give her what she wanted most: a say in Atlantean law.

Nestor continued, "We do not even allow Atlantean women a voice in the house. They serve best where their skills shine—raising our sons and daughters, working in our schools, and cooking in our kitchens. So why would we ever allow the Mer a seat in our house?"

"You allow Carthaginians, Lemurians, and Agarthans a seat in your house because they are valuable trade partners," Sisinyxa replied without hesitation or thought. "If you will not allow a woman, at least consider my husband."

Nestor frowned thoughtfully. "As you say, the Council of Atlantis has diverse representation from many important nations." He tilted his head toward her, peering at her from under his brows. "But at least we know where those lands are. We know how to get to them, how many citizens and soldiers they have, and many other important statistics, which they allow us to collect. About you?"

He picked up his goblet. Lifting it to his lips, he paused. "We know very little about your nation, not even its location. All we know is that it's somewhere out there." He gestured widely to the blue horizon where the wind lifted small whitecaps to sparkle under the summer sun. "Allow us to visit."

Sisinyxa smiled but her thoughts went something like: *over my dead body*.

Nestor took a languid sip of wine and put his goblet down again. "Perhaps then we can find a way to allow Ajak a seat at the table, second tier, among the other foreigners. But do not forget that such an honor would never be bestowed without the promise of a steady supply of mountain copper from your mines."

Sisinyxa had opened her mouth to reply when she felt a large, warm hand on her shoulder. Looking up, she smiled into the face of a broad and striking man. He slid onto the seat beside her, dropping a kiss on her cheekbone. Her heart immediately surged toward him, everything in her yearning to please him, to love him. This was Ajak, her partner and husband.

Ajak was Mer. The realization jarred me like the earth had moved under my feet.

I could only take him in so far as Sisinyxa allowed her eyes to rest on him, but what I saw was a male figure and presence very much like the human and Atlantean men around him, and yet different also. He had a thick solidity, a capable squareness about his shoulders and limbs which left an unmistakable impression of great strength. And yet he lacked the muscular striations and vascularity of strong human and Atlantean men. His skin was smooth, opaque, and flawless, and without freckle, blemish, bruise, or asymmetry. He was dressed in a simple sleeveless white robe which ended just above the knee. The fabric was loose and draped wide at the neck and arms. His legs, arms, and chest were hairless, while a dark shadow spread across his cheeks and down his neck, telling of the ability to grow a thick nest of a beard if he so chose. His eyes were a light crystal brown, like honey, and seemed almost to glow as though lit from within by a candle. Curiously, he lacked the oversize flap of flesh in front of the ear canal which Sisinyxa had, and seemed in form and stature like the perfect male specimen. In short, he was spectacular.

The men around the small table greeted one another warmly enough. Ajak took Sisinyxa's hand, so small inside his own. The hard calluses on Ajak's hands made Sisinyxa's own rough palms seem soft.

"Still resistant to the benefits of having the viewpoints of the fairer sex in your hallowed halls?" Ajak's voice flowed from his mouth, sounding of rain and distant thunder. I felt sure that should he have wished to be better heard above the din of the surrounding party he could easily have done so.

"Perhaps if we had more women like Sisinyxa, it would be easier to drum up confidence that such a move would be anything but a disaster," Nestor replied, his tone oily.

"We have had female Sovereigns for many years," Ajak said, "and I daresay we have reaped the rewards."

Nestor's eyebrows shot up. "I thought you, as Sisinyxa's husband, were King. It is not so?" He was evidently caught off guard by this information, and hadn't known Sisinyxa to be the head.

"No, I am the Sovereign's mate—husband in your terms —nothing more. The Sovereign has gifts unique among the Mer. We are all connected to one another, but so is one Sovereign to the next," Ajak said in that warm voice. "This moment will be recorded for a future Sovereign, that she may better understand where her people came from. Unfortunately," Ajak glanced down at his lover and his eyes sparkled, "this gift is not inherited by the male of our kind. We have other...gifts."

Sisinyxa gave Ajak a subtle warning look; she was concerned that he was giving away too much. Ajak pressed his lips together and gave her the smallest apologetic nod.

"Recorded?" Renlaus said, his voice filled with astonishment, which mirrored the shock on Nestor's face as well. "How is this accomplished?"

"It is a gift of the gods," Sisinyxa said, meaning *gift of the Salt*, but she did not clarify this for the Atlanteans. She did not fully understand herself how the memories were passed from one Sovereign to another, nor did she care. To avoid any more secrets being spilled, she continued briskly, "If we cannot budge your position today then let us move quickly to our other business. Have you readied our latest order?"

"Ah yes," Nestor replied, growing immediately bored. "Your never-ending desire for textiles, tiles, mirrors, grout, and other such mundane materials. We will supply them for as long as your orichalcum remains the high quality is has thus far proven to be." He lifted his goblet once again. "Your order awaits transfer to your ships in the harbor. Godspeed."

And with that, he downed the rest of his wine, got up, bade them good day, and moved toward another table filled with drinking men.

"I am sorry we continue to fail in your ambition," Renlaus said with what appeared to be genuine regret. "Atlanteans are stubborn."

"No matter," Sisinyxa said, rising from the couch. Ajak stood as well and lay a comforting hand on her lower back. "We are patient. Governments change hands, those in power pass away, making way for new and progressive thought-leaders. That which made Atlantis what it is today will not achieve its goals for tomorrow. You'll see. Atlantis needs us. It just doesn't know it yet."

Renlaus looked doubtful but did not disagree.

No more was said between the three but goodbye, but I understood that Sisinyxa and Ajak expected to see Renlaus on the shores of Mount Califas with their shipment by the next full moon. Sisinyxa was as determined as ever to achieve a position in Atlantean government, and believed wholeheartedly that it was only a matter of time.

As I was to see in the next memory, her goal would never be realized.

ELEVEN

The world blurred into a million shades of gray, flying by like a sandstorm. All suddenly halted and the particles settled to form an image of a place I recognized—the top of Mount Califas. Color bled slowly into the scene before it then sprang into life.

Sisinyxa stood looking out over Okeanos. She was trembling, and though Ajak stood behind her with his long arms wrapped around her torso, pulling her into his chest, she was cold and fearful.

The sound of thunder rumbling in the east was constant, and a dark shadow grew on the horizon, bleeding out to the north and south like ink spilling from an overturned pot.

Mer citizens rustled and talked in hushed tones behind Sisinyxa.

"Come, my love," Ajak whispered into her hair. "We'd best get our people inside. Whatever kind of storm this is, it cannot hurt us when we're deep underwater or within the belly of Califas. See how it grows? It's coming our way, probably faster than we realize."

"The gods must be very angry. It's coming from the direction of Atlantis," Sisinyxa said, turning to peer up at Ajak. His strong jaw cut sharp angles against the still bright blue sky of the west. "Do you think they are all right?"

Ajak frowned. "I should say not. Perhaps the fools finally killed themselves with their avarice. Come." He took her by the hand.

Ajak and Sisinyxa ushered the crowd of watching Mer into the cracks within the mountain, descending until they were deep within the rock. Some stayed within the caves, while others went out through the tunnels to the sea floor to watch from the bottom. Down this far, they were still well protected. Whatever was happening overhead, the Mer would wait it out.

As Sisinyxa followed her people down, I was overwhelmed by the sheer numbers of her citizens, and not just the total number of Mer but the number of tritons. Sirens and tritons in equal number, children of both genders—swinging between their parents as they descended, or clinging onto their parents' backs. There were babies also, and it began to dawn on me that these children had been born here. That meant they had Mer fathers.

The crowds dispersed into their underwater life, under orders from Sisinyxa not to surface until she gave them permission. She did not even send a scout to climb to the top of Califas for a full twenty-four hours, for fear of the power of the storm they'd seen approaching. There was a moment where even deep within Okeanos, a roaring sound like a great angry dragon belching fire had passed overhead. All the water shifted, sucking those Mer along the ocean floor at first toward the east then back to the west, like it couldn't make up its mind which direction it wanted to go. It did this multiple times, at first with increasing power, which alarmed the Mer. But just when the citizens began to mumble among themselves about these waves passing through their territory, the frequency and power of the shifting waters began to ease, until they stopped altogether.

The world went blurry again, this time coming into focus on a beach on Mount Califas.

Sisinyxa stood on the beach, watching a dozen bobbing heads approach in the water. They looked at first like seals, just the tops of their heads visible. As their feet struck bottom they stood and waded onto the beach. Atlanteans, their gills just closing up and smoothing over as they took in the fresh air. The webbing between their fingers retracted until the flesh between each digit was no different from that of humans. Their feet were already in full human form by the time they were kneeling on the sand in front of Sisinyxa and Ajak.

Nestor was among them, as was Renlaus. Sisinyxa narrowed her eyes at Renlaus, who had clearly given away the secret of Okeanos's location to his fellow Atlanteans. She felt deeply betrayed and foolish for having trusted Renlaus, but she could not have accomplished what she wished to inside Mount Califas without an Atlantean partner, so she'd been forced to trust someone.

Renlaus bowed his head in shame and would not look her in the eye. There were bruises across his ribs on one side and his lower lip was cracked and swollen. She wondered if Renlaus had felt he had no other choice, given the catastrophe that must have befallen Atlantis, or if he had been coerced.

"My Queen," Nestor said, bowing his head so low to the beach that when he lifted it to look up at her, his forehead was coated with sand. "Oh, my Queen. A great calamity has befallen us! Atlantis is no more. In one day, the gods wiped out our great city, angry with the people for their dens of iniquity, their greed, and their war-mongering ways. I tried to warn them! We did not partake. We are the innocent and in need of your mercy and grace. Surely the gods wish for you to bestow your hospitality upon us!"

Sisinyxa's skin crawled at this display. She felt no leader should ever embarrass himself in this way at any time, allowing himself to appear so weak in front of his inferiors.

Nestor continued to wail with great drama and fervor, tears streaming down his face. He remained on his knees and lifted his hands into the air as though worshipping Sisinyxa. "Only you can save us, we beg you. Give us a safe haven, allow us into the safety of your bosom. Sanctuary, Mistress, sanctuary!" he cried, and the other Atlanteans began to take up the call.

"Silence!" Sisinyxa shouted, and I could feel the rising repulsion in her breast at the approach these Atlanteans had taken. With all her heart she wished for them to stand and speak to her like normal, respectable men and women. She might even have ordered food to be brought to the beach and requested them to tell the story of Atlantis's destruction.

Nestor did not fall silent, and following his lead with gusto, neither did the other Atlanteans.

"Disaster, oh disaster!" Nestor wailed, bowing down to the sand yet again. "We are homeless, we have lost everything. Tens of thousands of Atlanteans have been lost. Only we remain. Only we have survived."

Sisinyxa's patience was wearing thin and she began to back away from the group of survivors, uncertain how to treat these people who appeared to be on the edge of hysteria. The Atlanteans' expressions were haggard, tormented. Their eyes rolled, and some had foam at the corners of their mouths. Their appearance seemed somehow intended to be unsettling, and that was exactly how Sisinyxa felt.

As she backed up, Nestor crawled forward on the sand, wailing ever louder, followed by the Atlanteans, who did exactly as he was doing, including Renlaus.

"Restrain them," Sisinyxa shouted to the Mer.

Immediately, fifteen of her people jumped forward, both *Foniádes* and tritons, some wielding spears. A line of spears and forks were stabbed into the ground in front of the Atlanteans to stop them from advancing, and behind the spears, a line of tritons and *Foniádes* stood tense, awaiting orders from their Sovereign.

Sisinyxa was breathing heavily. Her face was hot with fury, both at the betrayal of Renlaus and the behavior of the Atlanteans.

"My love." Ajak came to her side and took her hand, pulling her away from the crowd. "Say the word and we will send them away, but remember the storm. If we could feel it at the very depths of the ocean, imagine what it was like for them."

"They did not come here with peace in their hearts," Sisinyxa hissed. "Yes, they are desperate, I can see that. But Nestor is humiliating himself with his desperation. Look at his eyes. He has not lost his wits, he's an opportunist to the bitter end. Look at Renlaus, do you not see the abuse he endured? I know what is happening here. They mean to prey on my goodwill and sympathy, to be allowed entry. But I know that man." Her fiery gaze cut to Nestor, still whimpering and begging behind her line of defense. "He will stop at nothing when he sees what we have. It is already too much that he knows where we are. I should have him killed, along with Renlaus and the rest of them."

At this, Ajak paled. Nevertheless, all he said was, "Give your order, Sovereign. We will obey."

Sisinyxa stood there on the beach, her fists clenched, her heart in a rage. Even the Atlanteans began to grow quiet as they realized that their begging and crying and show of trauma had not immediately gotten them what they wanted.

Nestor came close to the spears then, wrapping his fingers around two of them, sliding around the metal the way a python slides around its victim before squeezing the life out of it.

"Sisinyxa" he whispered acidly, "after all I've done for you..."

He got no further, for Sisinyxa marched forward on the sand.

"You are not welcome here," she shouted. "You are hereby banished from these islands and these waters. Go! Depart with our wishes that you make a new home elsewhere in the world's vast oceans and coastlines, and prosper."

Inside Sisinyxa, a battle raged of woman versus Sovereign. She wanted to tell them that she was sorry for whatever they had been through, truly sorry for the loss of their city and their families. But she could not show any weakness. Certainly, she could not show Nestor any crack in her ultimate purpose of keeping Okeanos safe.

"If you are not gone from our mountains by nightfall tomorrow, you will be hunted down and executed. You may hunt for food on your way out, but you may never return upon pain of death. Now, go!"

At first, the Atlanteans did not respond; they seemed frozen as Sisinyxa's words died out. Nestor's expression went from pale shock to a cold rage. He snorted deep in his throat and spat a gob of saliva between the prongs of the spears before turning and straightening in front of his people.

The Atlanteans took on the expressions of those whose game was up. Gone were their tears and wailing, gone was their bowing and scraping. Gone was the display that now was so obviously pure theater. They returned to the water's edge and waded into the waves.

Nestor, the last to enter the water, looked back over his shoulder at where Sisinyxa still stood on the beach, surrounded by Mer. His last words before he sank into the Atlantic were said so softly that only the ears of a Mer could have possibly heard them.

"You'll regret this."

TWELVE

The images blurred again and settled with Sisinyxa on one of the lower, broader peaks of Mount Califas. Sisinyxa and several of her *Foniádes* had been drawn from the interior of Mount Califas by screams in the distance. Her heart was thrumming in her chest and a low tide of panic edged beneath her calm. Ajak and many of the tritons had gone to the south to quell a skirmish with a surprisingly large Atlantean force.

A storm to the North had left the Mer in Califas feeling somewhat protected, but it had been an error in judgement. Even Sisinyxa, who knew Nestor's ire might never die, had allowed herself to lower her guard just a little. After all, it had been years since the confrontation on the beach.

Ships emerged from the belly of the storm like a vengeful spear cast by the gods. The lead ship drove through the waves, the deadly point plunging toward Mount Califas, followed shortly by a dozen more. They were coming, dark hulls cutting like blades, organized, deadly. Flying from the lead ship's towering mast was a crest Sisinyxa recognized—a lion with six legs—Nestor's crest.

"So, he has finally returned," one of the *Foniádes* flanking Sisinyxa said, her tone sharp. "You were right to make us train harder than we have ever trained before, Sovereign."

Sisinyxa might have smiled at her loyal *Foniádes*, who even in the face of death believed in her Queen. Instead, she barked, "Send two of your fastest for Ajak. Now!"

The sirens in their prime were equipped to fight, and the *Foniádes* were fiercer than ever before, but against the army and weapons Nestor had somehow mustered over the years, they would need all the tritons. It was clear now that the Atlantean incursion to the south had been a diversion to draw their best fighting force away from Califas.

Nestor's ship was already nearing the spit of land that formed the shore of Mount Califas. Sisinyxa couldn't see Nestor himself amongst the ranks of Atlantean warriors leaping from the ship, but she knew he was there. She raised her gaze from the lead ship to the dozens more spreading across the islets like a black, barbed net.

Sirens were caught in that net, outnumbered and outmaneuvered. Even so, they fought. She snatched up a spear and her palm found the handle of the blade at her side.

"Sovereign, to the caves!" someone called behind her, but she was already making for the cliff face. Leaping from the ledge—feeling the wind whistle across her face—she dove into the lagoon below.

The Atlanteans had a foothold on the beach before she even emerged from the water. Forming a rough battle line, they stood shoulder to shoulder with spears at the ready. Their voices raised in a chanting call, setting the tempo for their advance. They trudged forward in unison as a trio of sirens turned for a last stand, claws flexed and teeth bared, two wielding spears and one a short, two-edged sword. The brave Mer pounced, but before they could even reach their enemies, spear thrusts drove them to the sand, dead or dying.

The bronze points gleamed red in the sun as Sisinyxa pulled her own blade and charged, *Foniádes* falling in behind. Despite the furious haze threatening to swallow her, a plan was forming in her mind. It was desperate and reckless, but it was all she had against the sudden onslaught.

"Drive through them and into the water!" Sisinyxa screamed to be heard over their battle chants.

The Atlanteans braced their spears to be leaped upon in the manner of other Mer who had already fallen. Instead, Sisinyxa darted in low, zig-zagging beneath their confused thrusts, to stab with spear and then hack with sword. Close packed as they were, their spear shafts cracked and rattled against each other as they fought to bring the long weapons to bear. The *Foniádes*, following her example, found the confused knot of warriors easy to dispatch.

Sisinyxa struck out with her blade, parting a haft in one stroke, and then drove her heel into the Atlantean's chest. He crashed into his comrades with bone-snapping force. Now she had a clear line to the sea.

"Move!" she roared and raced over the wet sand.

One look over her shoulder confirmed her remaining *Foniádes* were following. Dozens of Atlanteans would never rise, but at least four of her guard had joined them on the red sand.

Then she was leaping the crest of a wave and plunging into the welcome cool of the sea. Her transformation ripped across her body almost painfully, her tail powering her through the rolling riptides. Her own strength thrummed and pulsed as she took her aquatic form and she felt something like hope.

She intended to turn her *Foniádes* to strike the Atlantean line along the rear. Like a darning needle they would weave in and out, breaking the Atlanteans. She hoped to rout the invaders before Ajak and his tritons even returned.

Then she looked beyond the receding slope of the beach and her heart clenched in her chest.

Hundreds more Atlantean warriors filled the incoming tide, ranging out like murderous schools of fish. No sirens dared fight them here, instead they used their greater underwater speed to escape. The Atlanteans moved with coordinated effort, cutting off and herding those they could not catch. Outmaneuvered and outflanked, the sirens fell to a flurry of thrusts and cuts that darkened the seas with clouds of red. The shallow water was a churning, boiling mass of froth and foam. Those Atlanteans not dispatching the sirens were advancing toward the beach to reinforce their allies on the land.

Her plan to perforate the Atlantean line was pointless now. After the next charge, the enemy would be too well placed.

She faced her *Foniádes* and saw them straining against the desire to rush out and fight. The blood in the water called to them, and their bodies answered back. Their eyes were a solid, hungry black, and their lips peeled back to reveal teeth grown into nests of jagged fangs. Their skin reflected a dull gray tone in the wave-filtered sunlight, as long, powerful tails swept side to side to hold their bodies steady.

One of them gestured sharply toward a dark cleft in the

rocky shelf that flanked the shallow beach area. She wanted Sisinyxa to retreat. Shaking her head, Sisinyxa powered toward the Atlanteans moving to encircle fleeing Mer, her spear outstretched. The *Foniádes* followed.

The Atlanteans were now coming from below, their course meant to cut down the Mer as they dove, heading toward the mouths pitting Mount Califas. Left unchecked, the Atlanteans would rise among the sirens and slaughter them before they even knew what had happened. Sisinyxa and her *Foniádes* descended on the hunters and returned the favor.

Fighting underwater made slashes and hacks with a weapon ineffectual, but the piercing point of a weapon, especially driven by a Mer moving at full speed, was absolutely lethal. The *Foniádes* fought like blood-mad terrors, venting their wrath in explosions of violence that left Atlanteans maimed or dying wherever they went. The Atlantean hunting pack dissolved into a few stragglers desperately swimming in any direction to escape their shark-skinned destroyers. None of them made it very far.

The group of sirens had just cleared the carnage when a hard, metallic clank sounded through the water and a rush of something hurtled toward Sisinyxa. A glinting missile sailed inches from Sisinyxa's face.

Tracing the trail of bubbles, she saw three pairs of Atlanteans each holding a strange tube of metal between them. A third Atlantean drove what looked like a spiked mallet into the tube and the same series of sounds heralded another trio of harpoons streaking toward them. Two passed harmlessly between them, but one gouged a nasty line across the scalp of one of the *Foniádes*.

They needed to make for the caves, now.

She signaled the retreat and the Mer dove for the cave

entrance as more harpoons began to hurtle between them. Slipping inside one after the other, they swam single-file through the narrow veins, hoping that the disorienting network would swallow the Atlanteans who—not knowing where they were going—would be lost for hours. After she emerged in a large cavern into which Mer were pouring from two other doorways, Sisinyxa's tail rent again and she climbed from the water.

"Report," she called as more *Foniádes* and sirens emerged from the entry pool to the chamber chosen for this purpose. This cave had fewer entry points than most of the caverns of Califas—there were only three ways in or out. Sisinyxa strode over to a table where several sirens stood looking at maps which displayed Okeanos both above and below.

"We managed to seal most entrances," answered one of the *Foniádes*. The silver hair running along the ridge of her shaved skull was tinted pink with blood. "But not all of them. Atlanteans seized several and even now they are pouring into the tunnels and subterranean river networks."

Sisinyxa frowned and chewed her lip with nervous energy. The interconnected waterways and passages, while long and convoluted, offered countless way to strike at the heart of Califas. If the attackers had been fewer in number, she could send *Foniádes* and her fiercest sirens out to meet and stop the Atlantean penetration. But there were so many. It was dizzying, the force Nestor had gathered.

"What about the surface?" Sisinyxa asked, processing the terrible possibilities of so many Atlanteans in the caves, like an invading colony of ants.

"The Atlanteans are not pressing their advantage," answered another, this one with a topknot and features as sharp as her eyeteeth. "The tritons who did not accompany

Ajak to the south are pushing them back in places, but it seems the greatest portion of their effort is to press into the caves."

"Why the caves?" someone asked, but Sisinyxa was too busy staring at the maps and thinking to notice who. "They must know that once the tritons come down here, they'll be trapped face to face with them, with no way out."

Sisinyxa did not say what she thought in response: Not before they've slaughtered the bulk of us, and *if* the rest of the tritons made it back to Mount Califas in time.

"That must be why they attacked the south and the surface," the sharp-featured one observed, black eyes flashing. "They wanted to draw the tritons away..."

"But with the thousands they brought, fighting in narrow passages and caves means their numbers are wasted," the dark-crested one pointed out.

Multiple voices began to talk and argue, but then Sisinyxa remembered the sight of Nestor's flag on the lead ship. It was a bold, even reckless, move to lead an invasion. Even the most impetuous leaders would not risk it, but Nestor had. She suddenly understood, as she remembered his face and whispered promise that day on the beach.

"This is vengeance as much as conquest." Sisinyxa raised her voice to quiet the babble. "Nestor leads this attack and he knows, thanks to Renlaus, that the caves and their waters run through Califas like blood through a body. Even if one in ten of his warriors finds their way deeper, we will have hundreds of Atlanteans attacking us across so many fronts that there is no way we will be able to stop them all."

That sobering reality quieted every mouth and drew every eye to her. She felt the enormity of their combined gaze, but squared her shoulders.

"Our only hope is stop them here in this chamber. They'll go with the natural flows of the water, wanting to conserve energy, and they'll be guessing that's what we did as well. This cavern," her finger fell to the underground maps and traced a line across a series of nexus chambers that hung like knots among a web passages and subterranean streams, "is the hub they'll be led to. There is no better opportunity to halt their progress than here. If we hold this, we might buy enough time for the tritons to return. We need to act quickly. Hold your ground. This our only chance, understood?"

One look at the dark, fierce eyes around her gave her all the answer she needed. Breaking at Sisinyxa's order, the sirens and *Foniádes* spread to the entrances leading from the cavern, hiding themselves in the dark crevasses.

A sleek, slip of a siren sprang from an entry pool.

"They're coming!" she said with a forceful whisper.

Tension crackled through the air at the news.

Quickly, Sisinyxa rose from behind the makeshift barricade the Mer had previously constructed, and waved her blade in two quick strokes. Dozens of feet above the entry pool, among balconies and walkways, another sword flashed in acknowledgment. They were ready and waiting.

"Hold," she hissed as those around her pressed toward the barricade.

Nestor and his forces had caught them unawares and they'd paid dearly for it. If everyone could hold their nerves, they might turn the tables. The blood of her murdered people called out to her, but she wanted victory, not vengeance. Preserving the people left would be victory enough.

The first Atlanteans emerged quickly and quietly from the broadest entry pool, eyes darting around the darkened chamber. Atlanteans saw better in the strange glimmering dark than mere humans, but they were no Mer.

The scouts ranged around the chamber, closer and closer to the barricades where the Mer lay hidden. Silently, Sisinyxa willed every warrior to remain patient. Finally, the scout signaled and several Atlanteans leapt back into the water to give the all-clear to the waiting forces.

It was just as well, because no sooner had the messengers departed than an Atlantean mounted the barricade and saw the mass of waiting Mer. Before he could scream, he was pulled down and dealt with. The remaining scouts soon noticed one of their number missing. Several of them clambered over the barricade as the full Atlantean force began to pour into the chamber. Most died without ever realizing what had happened, while a few turned to run and were dragged back to die screaming in the dark behind the barricade.

In the rush of water and clamor of weapons that came with the Atlantean forces entering the chamber, the screams were mostly lost. Soon enough, the Atlanteans were marching forward, forming a battle line on the rough floor of the cavern as they squinted into the darkness. Many of them had emerged from the pool when Sisinyxa leapt onto the barricade and leveled her spear condemningly at them.

"Now!" she barked.

A storm of rock, broken masonry, and jagged shale fell down on the heads of the Atlanteans. Men ducked and dove in frantic attempts to avoid being crushed and maimed by the avalanche of debris, clogging up the pool with their splashing, screaming efforts. The Atlantean battle line, fearing an attack upon their rear, spun round to launch spear and arrow, along with hateful curses, at those hidden among the gantries over the entry pool. Most of the sirens found refuge in the rails and crenellations, but here and there a Mer would fall alongside the rain of stones.

Without another word, Sisinyxa leapt over the barricade, her warriors hot on her heels, and pounced on the exposed backs of the Atlanteans. They fell on them like a stabbing, slashing whirlwind, their voices a screaming vengeful gale. The Atlanteans gave ground, pressed step by bloody step back toward the pool where so many of their comrades were still trying to avoid being crushed. Packed as close as they were, their spear formations were struggling to do anything but die as the Mer moved among them.

Every blow Sisinyxa struck felt like an avenging stroke, righting another wrong, appeasing the blood of the innocents still floating on the shores beyond these caves. In that instant, victory and vengeance were one, and she reveled in the strength it gave her.

The Mer would be victorious and Nestor would pay for what he'd done.

But the mass of warriors pressing into the entry pool was more than the Mer bargained for, and more Atlanteans, living and dead, were driven into the cavern by those pressing from behind. Soon there was not enough rubble to suppress them all. The floundering line of Atlantean warriors began to thicken, and then stopped giving ground. Those fresh to the fight reached over the sagging shoulders of the ones in front to jab and rake with their spears.

Sisinyxa was forced backward to avoid two separate thrusts. The Mer were being driven back as more Atlanteans pressed into the cavern. Then they took up their chant once more. Step by step, they moved as a single stabbing, advancing creature, and the Mer had to give way or fall.

"To the barricade!" Sisinyxa shouted, and the command was taken up by the Mer who'd heard her.

Warily as they could, the Mer drew back to the barricade and the deeper darkness that lay on that side of the chamber, where the thin refracting light did not reach. What light there was suddenly dimmed further as—most likely—clouds outside moved across the sun.

The Atlanteans pursued, but soon found the way made treacherous by darkness and the deep hidden pools. Their group began to fracture. Here and there, *Foniádes* exploded from the black opaque water of a pool to snatch an Atlantean and drag him underwater where she was stronger than he.

"Where are the tritons?" Sisinyxa hissed at the *Foniádes* at her shoulder. "Ajak should be here by now."

The whites of her eyes were visible. "They're coming, Sovereign."

Sisinyxa snarled with enough ferocity that the *Foniádes* stepped back. Rage, hot and intoxicating, rushed through her veins, and without warning she vaulted on top of the barricade.

"Where is Nestor?" she screamed at the encroaching phalanx of Atlanteans. "Where is he?"

For a moment, the Atlanteans kept chanting their battle march, but she screamed louder still, her siren voice blasting like brass instruments. Finally, they began to quiet. A moment later, a band of figures pushed to the front of the battle line.

"Here," came the familiar voice.

She looked down to see Nestor standing among his retainers. All of them were armed with fine weapons and armor. Even though he stood below her, in full battle dress, Nestor seemed larger and more imposing than he'd ever appeared in his robes at the parties from those long-ago days before Atlantis had fallen.

"So, this is your answer?" she demanded, sweeping her spear and sword at the assembled Atlanteans. "A generation of murdered Mer and Atlanteans to salve your grief? To build a new home on the bones of my people?"

Nestor did not flinch from her stare, his face hard as the stone at his feet. "You gave me no other choice."

Sisinyxa's rage smoldered deep, heating her to her very core. "There is *always* another choice."

Nestor looked down at the bodies strewn across the chamber, Mer and Atlantean. For just a moment, even across the dark chamber, she saw the man she had never liked but had once respected. Then he looked to the men on his left and the men on his right, and that grim obstinance settled over his face again.

"It is nearly finished." He muttered it, but Sisinyxa and the Mer heard him as clearly as though he'd shouted it.

"Advance!" he bellowed, and the Atlanteans complied.

Sisinyxa leapt behind the barricade, chased by spear and arrows, and called out to her warriors.

"Hold the line! Do not give an inch! For Okeanos, for your children—hold the line!"

Their voices rose into a beautiful, mournful song. Sisinyxa believed that many, if not all, might die that day, but they could do nothing else but face what was coming. Everything she loved lay behind; only darkness and extinction lay before. All they could do was stand and hold the line.

The first Atlanteans coming over the barricade died quickly, met by eager blades. But they kept coming, each time probing for weaknesses, each attack costing the Mer another citizen they could not afford to lose.

There was the rattle of chains and the sound of metal points being driven through stone and wood.

Sisinyxa was just finishing off a pair of Atlanteans who'd leapt screaming down at her when there was a sound like many dull, grunting voices sounding together. An entire section of the barricade groaned and tilted forward. Nearby Atlantean and Mer leapt clear as huge blocks of stone gave a grinding crash and tumbled down to the chamber floor or plunged into the pools with great splashes.

There were bare seconds of both sides gaping at the sudden opening before Atlantean and Mer warriors surged to fill the gap, stabbing and slashing as they came.

Sisinyxa leapt from enemy to enemy, dispatching each as quickly and efficiently as she could. She dodged or parried one attack only to run into another enemy, and killed that one only to find two more advancing. Her body burned with exertion. With each blow she struck or deflected, she was sure her weapons would be knocked from her numb hands. A hundred times she thought she'd given her last bit of strength, only to dredge up one more burst of energy.

Something collided with her back and she was thrown bodily into a pool. For a moment in that dark, cool place, where the screams and cries of the battle above were only muffled warbles, she felt a desire to let herself slowly sink down and sleep. Then a siren's scream stirred her from her stupor. At the far edge of the pool, two Atlanteans hemmed in a siren who was already bleeding from a wound on her shoulder.

Sisinyxa had lost her weapons in the fall, but her tail flexed powerfully and she fell on the two Atlanteans in a flurry of raking claws. The first fell without turning around, but the other managed to get the haft of his spear up between them and they wrestled with weapon as they fell back into the pool. She heard the strain and grunt of his voice through the water and then with a great heave he made to throw her off. Her whole body came up out of the water with the force of the shove, but she kept her grip on the spear. Using the momentum of her descent, she drove her body up over the haft at him where her talons found a home.

The injured siren had sunk deeper into the pool, and Sisinyxa could see her binding her wound with strips of leather from the dead Atlantean's clothing. Knowing she wasn't mortally injured, Sisinyxa took a moment to breathe. Exhausted as she was, she needed to get back into the fight.

She began to raise her head from the pool, hoping to steal a quick glimpse and avoid any stray blows, when a hard grip latched onto her hair. She cried out and reached back to gouge with her claws, but found no purchase. She was dragged, screaming, out of the water and thrown hard on the stone floor, clipping her head on the stones.

The world spun and wobbled, but she twisted and lashed out blindly. Rising to her knees, she bit and clawed at empty air as her vision began to clear. She was lying on the chamber floor surrounded by Nestor's retainers. She spun in a circle and saw Nestor standing over her, a bronze sword in his hands. She raised her claws to strike, but one of his retainers struck her a rattling blow across her back. Sisinyxa fell onto her hands and knees, and another blow cracked her ribs. Suddenly it became very hard to breathe.

Her vision swimming, she gasped and looked up at Nestor, his blade raised to plunge into her heart.

"I wish you had made the right choice," he said in a flat, cold voice. "This could have been avoided. This is your fault, Sovereign."

His lips pursed and twitched as he smiled grimly and Sisinyxa could read his expression clear as day—he'd had every intention of taking Okeanos from the Mer all along. He'd just been hoping to be let in where he could then slay them all in their sleep.

Sisinyxa glared up at him, defiant to the very end.

The entry pool exploded behind Nestor, sending Atlanteans spinning through the air to fall lifeless on the cavern floor. A single clear note hung in the air even as the last spray of water slapped to the stone.

"It is finished," she whispered, her voice craggy and raw.

Ajak and the tritons had finally arrived.

Tall, powerful figures leapt from the pool and surveyed the grim scene filling the broad cavern, bodies piled up at every entrance. For an instant, they shared a knowing look and then with bodies glistening with supple strength, they set to work. They loped forward with easy grace yet such speed that the Atlanteans could scarcely act before they were struck down. Some tritons had spears or blades that might have been taken from previous Atlantean victims, while others wielded tridents like their foes were mere fish. A few did not even bother with iron weapons, striking out with hands and feet which hit their targets like bone-crushing hammers.

Sisinyxa looked up into Nestor's face and saw his disbelief, and she might have laughed if it hadn't been such a struggle to breathe.

The armored retainers leapt to defend their master, but a pair of tritons, one with a trident and another wielding paired swords, made short work of them. Not even their armor was proof against a triton's frightening strength, and each fell as easily as the next.

Nestor rushed toward the trident-wielding triton as he made to tug his three-pronged spear from a corpse. Sisinyxa made to call out a warning, but the effort made her gasp and clutch at her side.

She needn't have bothered.

Ajak looked up and, quick as lighting, caught Nestor by the throat and wrist. With one hand, he lifted the fully-armored man as though he weighed nothing. With the other hand, he yanked the bronze sword from Nestor's grasp as though he was taking a toy from a naughty child.

Nestor squirmed and kicked in Ajak's grip, beating his free hand upon the arm that held him in the air. Ajak's dark eyes showed nothing but mild contempt as he reversed his grip on the sword and then drove it through Nestor's heart.

Sisinyxa was making to stand when Ajak strode over to her, his trident retrieved. Had he not been there, she would have collapsed back onto the floor, but he steadied her and for a moment she just leaned upon him, sucking in air.

"You are injured, my love." His fierce, handsome features were knotted with concern.

Her fingers tightened about his sinewy shoulder as she forced the words out. She pointed to the Mer still fighting with Atlanteans. "Help them."

He gave her one more concerned look, then nodded and began to call to his comrades who'd scattered to dispatch various stragglers.

He carried Sisinyxa to the edge of a pool free of bodies and lowered her into the cool water before then returning to join the others.

Together, the force of tritons turned toward the line of Atlanteans and unleashed the power of their voices.

It was not a scream because it was too low and powerful to be that, and too musical as well, but it tore through the air like one all the same. The gloomy air of the chamber rippled around the force of it, and when it struck the Atlanteans, they were either thrown upon the ground to clutch at their bleeding ears or they simply crumpled.

Sirens and *Foniádes* used that mysterious piece of extra flesh in front of their ears, as well as their hands, to protect their own eardrums from the sonic booms the tritons unleashed. From one end of the battle line to the other, the song of the tritons swept the chamber, leaving deaf and witless Atlanteans in its wake.

In the space of a few labored breaths, the battle to save Okeanos was over.

THIRTEEN

The images blurred yet again, and the breath whooshed out of me in a painful rush as I was released from Sisinyxa's memories. Now freed from my attachment to the mosaic, I fell and landed on my back on the stone floor. Breathing hard, my heart hammering in my chest and tears blurring my vision, I blinked up at the image of Sisinyxa.

The image gazed down at me, that same peaceful smile on her face, yet somehow it had become more knowing, more familiar. The image had chosen what to show me and I'd had to withstand the horror of it until she was finished.

There was no sign of Nike. I didn't know how long I had been lost in the visions, but apparently too long to keep her waiting.

Lifting a trembling hand to my eyes, I wiped the moisture from my eyes and the sweat from my brow as I sat up. My scalp was hot and damp from perspiration, like I'd been fighting that battle alongside my ancestor. Looking up at her again, fresh siren tears coursed down my cheeks and there was no stopping them.

"Now, you understand," came the familiar voice of Polly, her shadow darkening the door of the Hall.

I could not find the words to answer her. Disgust and shock still coursed through my veins. Disgust at the fighting and the blood, and shock at how different the Mer seemed at that time, how much things had changed.

"So many," I panted, my mouth parched, "tritons."

Footsteps on the stone preceded her and she knelt down beside me, a hand on my shoulder. She handed me a cup.

"Drink," she said, her whispered word sounding lost in the great cavern of memory.

Taking the cup with a shaking hand, I straightened and gulped back the cool, fresh water. Tears continued streaming down my face. "Why did you not tell me? Why did you not tell *us*?"

"You had to see it for yourself." She stroked my sweaty hair back from my forehead. "And these memories are for the Sovereign to bear; they are a burden your sirens should not have to carry. They trust you, and you must be worthy of that trust."

That Polly had not been asked into the Hall of Anamna by her Sovereign passed through my mind only fleetingly. In that moment, I felt like a little girl who wanted her mother's comfort. I was glad she was there.

"You see what our ancestors had, how they behaved?"

"Like mercenaries. They fought like soldiers, and the tritons..." My voice was still a dry rasp. I shook my head, wiping with futility at the continuous stream of tears running down my face and neck. "The tritons, they were so powerful, so beautiful. Where have all the tritons gone?"

Polly sat down on the stones next to me, something that I had never seen her do, even when I was young. Her dark eyes were heavy with sadness. "I don't know. They've been gone a very, very long time. But, Sybellen," she squeezed my shoulder with her hand, "if an attack like that came today..."

"That battle happened thousands of years ago, and we won. It was a different time, a different era. Different Atlanteans."

Polly drew back a little with surprise. "You saw how much they hate us. Just because they are weak now does not mean we should let down our guard."

But my mind was on the tritons, on their huge, muscular bodies glistening in the caves as they destroyed wave after wave of invading Atlantean. And those voices, the depth of sound they could produce. Such a being had never been imagined in all of my daydreaming.

"An entire gender of our species has disappeared, and I need to know why," I said, getting to my feet. My body felt tired and sore, as though I'd lived through the battle for Okeanos myself. I looked up at the image of Sisinyxa again and gave the mosaic a nod of gratitude. I rounded on Polly, who had also risen to her feet and now stood behind me. "The sirens of the Pacific, they must know something. Do you not think?"

Without waiting for an answer and caught up in my idea, I strode from the Hall of Anamna and called for the *Foniádes* to gather all of the sirens to the throne room.

"I will address the citizens of Okeanos within the hour, and I wish all who can come to attend."

Nodding, they scattered to make the call to my people.

"What are you going to do, Sybellen?" Polly asked as she took the steps down from the throne and came to stand in the center of the throne room.

"Either locate the tritons, or if there are none to be found, find out what happened to them. I'll use the Hall of

Anamna to learn what I can, but I want us searching the oceans as well."

"And the law about Atlanteans? You'll retract it?" A gleam came into her eye, hungry, but it did not make sense to me to give her what she wanted.

"You've become obsessed by your hatred of them. It makes no sense to hate today's Atlanteans for something their ancestors did almost five thousand years ago. By that logic, no single nation would peacefully interact with any other. You must forget your desire for vengeance. It is foolish."

Her face changed, her expression hardening. "They are diseased scum, a plague upon the oceans and a festering thorn in our side. It is your duty to cleanse the waters of the Atlantic of this scourge. Too long have we failed in our duty and I cannot fathom why any Sovereign before us has not already seen to this task. I would have accomplished it with a bit more time."

I rounded on her. "Because it's genocide! Yes, they were our enemy at one time. They lost their entire civilization, tens of thousands of their people. Their leader went about it the wrong way, but Nestor is dead, and Atlanteans of today are pitiful and sickly. All they wanted was a home."

"Yes, and they invaded ours, almost took it from us!"

"If Sisinyxa had made some kind of treaty with them, helped them find a new home, they never would have invaded in the first place. Treating them like the enemy is no way of moving forward. An eye for an eye is not our way."

Sirens began to appear in the stairwells and stream into the room.

Polly shut her mouth and stepped back, fuming privately. She would never have said what she had said to me in the presence of other sirens, and she'd only said this much because she felt that as my mother and previous Sovereign, she had a right to. But she'd given up her right to advise me the day she took the throne and opted out of being my caretaker.

Sirens streamed into the throne room, filling up the enormous cave with the sounds of their breathing and bare feet. I saw the blue head of Nike among the crowd as she wove her way closer to me.

"Something very important has been kept from you," I began, stepping up to be level with the throne but not sitting down. "You've been led to believe that there is no such thing as a male Mer, that they're impossible. But tritons once filled the halls and waters of Okeanos. They were brave, and beautiful. They were our defenders and our lovers. Male children born within these very halls were once common."

Murmurs filled the cave, sounds of wonder and surprise, and questions.

"Something happened to our tritons long ago and now we must mate with humans to maintain our species, and so every one of us must brave the curse. But it wasn't always this way. Once, we lived here in peace, never having to venture onto land unless we wanted to. Once, both sirens and tritons made up the Mer population, not sirens alone. I'm looking for volunteers. Brave sirens who are willing to scour the oceans, both our own and the remote Pacific. In all likelihood you'll be gone for years. We need to find the reason for this change, otherwise we'll always be slaves to the *Dyás*. I'll not force anyone, but I will ask. Anyone who wants to undergo such a search, please step forward."

Four sirens were already making their way to the front. By the time they were standing in front of me, expressions resolute, another two had joined. A few moments later, two more stepped into the line, flanking the others.

TARGA, Emun, and Antoni were staring at me, shock reflected in their eyes. A light sheen of sweat glistened from Emun's brow and he wiped it away with his sleeve.

"That was intense just to listen to," Emun said. "I cannot imagine what the experience of that memory was like."

"It must have been horrible," Targa said with a shudder.

Antoni, who'd been standing by the window, crossed to her and sat beside her, putting his arm over the back of the couch behind her again.

Targa continued, "But now I understand what you said about me recording your story with my phone. The Hall of Anamna was like a secret archive just for you."

"What did you do with the volunteers?" Antoni asked.

"I sent the eight sirens on a mission to find out what happened to the tritons, or better yet, find proof that they still existed," I explained. My gaze slid to Emun. "One hundred and fifty years later, the proof came to me...in the form of my own son."

Emun's eyes were shining, full of emotion. I wondered how it felt to him to be possibly the very last of his kind.

Sliding forward on my seat, I stretched my back and glanced at the window where it had grown dark. Sera would be calling us for dinner soon.

"It was clear to me through Sisinyxa's memories," I continued, "that sirens and tritons once mated with each other, resulting in offspring of both genders. But at some point in history, the tritons died out with no apparent cause.

I divided the sirens willing to go into pairs and sent two to the North Atlantic, two to the South Atlantic, two to the Pacific by way of the Indian Ocean, and two to the North Pacific. These eight returned with no news, so every twenty years or so I sent out another group. But later groups failed to return."

Targa's eyes widened. "They didn't come back ever?"

I shook my head. "No, and it got worse than that. Many other sirens who left the borders of Okeanos, such as on a mating cycle, never came home, either. But before I get to that part, I have to tell you about Jozef."

Targa's eyes opened wide. "Finally! I've been dying to know why you wanted him here. Was he a past mate? And when did you know him from? He can't be that much over forty."

I smiled at my daughter. "He's *well over* forty, I can assure you."

FOURTEEN

Decades passed. It was a time of peace and prosperity for us. Sad-looking Atlanteans sometimes passed through our territory, and we allowed them to feed and rest there. I had sent the volunteers to search the world's oceans for evidence of tritons, knowing it was a massive job, and I did not expect to see any of those sirens for five years.

I spent time in the Hall of Anamna, digging in memories to pinpoint when tritons had gone extinct. But though the Hall of Anamna was a place full of memory and information, it did not give up its treasures on a whim. I could not go to a portrait and ask it to reveal to me answers I was seeking. Rather, the portraits gave to me what they chose to. At times, the eyes of a Sovereign would gleam and welcome me, invite me in. I would enter the memory and take from it what I could. But even though I moved forward in time sequentially, it was difficult identify the critical point. The Sovereigns of the time noticed the declining triton population, forcing sirens to range abroad and mate with human men to maintain their numbers. But the Mer did not know what to do about the problem. As generations came and went, eventually there were no tritons at all. Those who remembered the tritons eventually died and there were no sirens left who had known any in the flesh. Generations passed and new generations began to believe tritons were a myth. After all, there were no triton portraits immortalized in the Hall of Anamna. To those who had never seen a triton, and didn't know anyone who had seen a triton, it was not difficult to believe that the citizenry of Okeanos had always been entirely female. Sirens returned with daughters, and those sirens went on mating cycles and returned with daughters.

I was able to determine when the aquamarine gemstones appeared, and sirens began to wear them—a few hundred years after the Atlantean disaster—but I was not able to discern *why* it had happened.

The searchers returned with reports of no tritons to be found and I resolved to send out volunteers every twenty years or so. Frustrated in my quest for answers, I spent less and less time in the Hall of Anamna, and more and more time abroad in my territory, exploring, the way I had so enjoyed in my youth. As for why Sisinyxa had chosen to show me the battle for Okeanos—it gave me an understanding of why Atlanteans to this day were malnourished and sickly nomads without any organization or strong leader. Nestor had amassed the entire population of Atlanteans, and they'd been destroyed. The few stragglers who survived produced a line of poor wanderers who no longer had a home on land or at sea.

Sometime in the mid-nineteen-seventies, something happened that changed my perspective on modern Atlanteans.

I had taken it upon myself to swim the entire border of Okeanos because I thought the Sovereign should be well acquainted with the nature of these borders. Since I had first swum over the *apotreptikó* when I was young and entering Okeanos for the first time, I had been curious to learn whether this black wasteland of barren and jagged rocks actually circled the entire mountain range of Okeanos. I had always assumed it did, for how else had sirens of past generations decided where the border actually lay?

Swimming the territory slowly gave me a chance to observe and learn in a way that couldn't be done at high speed, so I took my time. One of the *Foniádes* would join me for a time, swimming along patiently at my side before leaving and sending another. I hadn't given them the order to do this for I didn't feel the need for company; they simply didn't know what else to do with themselves and the Sovereign was their priority. It was the times between their visits that I enjoyed the most, for it gave me the opportunity to interact with animals in a way that might seem strange to the *Foniádes*, who tended to see sea life mainly as food. I found such beauty in these creatures, and though I also ate fish, I found myself thanking the fish for sustaining me. This sentimentality or spirituality was not normal for a mermaid, as far as I knew. But then, sirens were as varied in character as humans, so who knew what went on in the hearts and minds of other mermaids.

During one of these solitary times, I heard unusual sounds coming through the water. Pausing to listen, I cocked my head, trying to identify what kind of animal might sound like what I was hearing. Shaking my head, I realized that it couldn't be an animal, it had to be a ship with humans on board because the sound was steady and grinding.

The sound stopped, and was followed by scratching and clicking. I began to swim toward it, leaving the kelp forest and venturing out into a broad and open plain. It was almost like a desert, but this desert was colored by bright coral and large, slow-moving purple and gray fish. Following the sounds over these rolling plains revealed a humanoid shape in the distance, very close to the ocean floor and nearly upside down. It was an Atlantean, but even from a distance there was something very different about this Atlantean.

Curious, I approached.

It was a male, a large one, and healthy. This alone gave cause to widen my eyes and make me pause. He had none of the gauntness I had come to attribute to the Atlantean species, and he was dressed in clothing and equipped with gear unfamiliar to me. He wore a strange, close-fitting black suit which ended just above the knee and elbow joints. His hair was brown and short, and his beard was trimmed quite close to the skin. This was in stark contrast to the Atlanteans I had seen previously. Those had long ropy hair and were infected with sea lice, the males smaller than me, spindly of limb and thick of beard.

This Atlantean wore a belt upon which were fastened odd looking tools. Against his back was a bright silver spear. I was not familiar with modern spearguns, but the shape of it mimicked some of the older weapons we'd found scattered on the seabed, so I knew what it was. His bare webbed feet kept him steady and there was a strange thing strapped to his face. I'd never seen goggles before, though I had seen old brass helmets with face plates, so I knew he was wearing the odd-looking thing on his face to protect his eyes.

He was working some tool, which was drilling into the ocean floor. Noticing the small transparent bag at his waist containing a notebook and pen, I could contain my curiosity no longer.

"What are you doing?"

He started violently, head jerking up and mouth opening wide in a silent scream. He yanked the goggles away from his eyes and put them on the top of his head.

"Good grief!" He took a few deep breaths, still floating upside down. "You might want to consider making some noise so you don't give anyone a heart attack," he said. His voice had a pleasant, gravelly quality.

He righted himself, leaving the tool he'd been working stuck in the rock, to look at me properly. His dark eyes studied me intently.

"Hello," he said, finally, a friendly but cautious smile lingering at the corners of his mouth. "I'm Jozef. Who are you?"

"I'm Bel," I replied, moving closer.

He drifted backward as I drifted forward and I could feel a low hum of tension in the water around him. He wasn't sure what to think of me. My eyes drifted down to the strange tool sticking into the ground and back up to him, skimming over his person and his clothing and equipment.

"You're healthy," I said, noting the color of his skin—golden brown from the sun. Atlantean skin was more like human skin than ours, reacting to the sun's rays by darkening in color.

He gave a bemused laugh. "Thank you? I'm well fed."

He took a few breaths before adding, like he felt it was what he was supposed to say but he wasn't quite certain it was right under the circumstances, "You're healthy, too."

"What are you doing?" I gestured to the tool.

"Taking samples," he replied. "I'm an oceanographer."

I must have expressed a look of puzzlement because he went on to explain.

"It's the study of all things to do with the ocean. Right now, I'm studying the theory of plate tectonics, gathering data and samples to take back to my lab."

"Your lab?"

"Laboratory, where I...study...things," he paused between words, still watching me as intently as I was watching him.

"Forgive me," he said. "I've never been this close to a mermaid before. It's a bit overwhelming. I apologize for staring."

The tension emanating from him was easing, and I could hear his heartbeat as it slowed to a more relaxed rhythm. The scent he left in the water now was no longer of anxiety, and he smelled surprisingly pleasant.

"Show me?" I asked.

"Certainly!" He showed me how he was using a boring drill to penetrate deep into the rock and retrieve a cylindrical sample of whatever was below the surface of the ocean floor. "Ten years ago," he explained while he was showing me how the drill worked, "a professor at Princeton University in America presented a theory that layers deep in the earth move very slowly with respect to one another. This movement is why the continents broke apart, new land masses formed. and new oceanic basins appeared. By taking some samples, I may be able to help determine where these various plates might be."

"Why do you care?"

His dark eyebrows shot up. "Because if we know where these plates overlap, we might be able to determine where the most disruption might happen in the future."

He explained more about his science. From the bright expression on his face, it was clear he was enthusiastic about his studies.

"But where is your lab?" I asked, still trying to understand where this healthy and obviously very well educated Atlantean had come from. Did he also have some territory inside a mountain range or cave system? Why was he so different from others of his kind?

"I live in Gibraltar. My lab and work is there, along with my family. Where do you live?"

"Okeanos, of course," I replied, now floating beside him as he retrieved his sample and put it into a small bag tied to his belt with several others.

"My father has spoken of it," he admitted, "but frankly I never paid much attention. I wasn't entirely sure it was real."

"Of course it's real! You're not far from our mountains," I pointed back the way I had come.

"I see." He seemed to consider this rather seriously. I could hardly believe I had come across an Atlantean who did not know anything about Okeanos, but I supposed the Atlanteans had no organized way of passing knowledge down to their children. After all, they were homeless. They were poor, ignorant scavengers. Weren't they?

"So, you live on land? Gibraltar is above the water, is it not?"

"That's right. It's a kind of peninsula. It's not far from here." He looked at me with what I thought seemed a hopeful expression. "Would you like to see it? I realize my invitation might be inconvenient, for I'm sure you were on your way to somewhere, but you are welcome to visit my home. You seem the curious type." He was talking a little more quickly now, and his nervousness was back. "I'm curious myself, especially since I've never actually spoken with a siren. I mean, I have seen them in the distance but they never approach and I never want to bother them. This is the first time..."

"I would like to see where you live," I interrupted. In fact, at that particular moment in time, there was nothing else I wanted to see more than where Jozef lived. I was overcome by curiosity about this well-mannered, even cultured, and handsome Atlantean. "How far is Gibraltar?"

"Half-a-day's swim at forty kilometers per hour."

I hadn't heard of speed referred to in this way, and didn't know how big a kilometer was, so I replied, "You set the pace, then."

So he did, and while Jozef was fast, he was not as efficient in the water as I was with my tail. We conversed, but speaking came easier to me than to him.

Time passed, but I barely noticed, as I was engrossed in Jozef's commentary about the sea floor passing beneath us. I saw things in a way I hadn't seen them before, noticing how rock jutted up in places as though it had collided with other rocks, how there were cracks and deep narrow gullies carving their way between mounds of coral.

The ocean grew shallower and the terrain beneath us rockier and less hospitable. The number of broken bits of hull, jagged broken masts, and fishing nets documented how treacherous this part of the ocean was. The sun's rays were bright and penetrating here, shining down into the water like beams, refracting off white pebbles scattered between black rocks. Seaweed and small, brightly colored fish glimmered in the light, and the snaps and crackles of happy sea life grew loud as the depth of the water lessened.

Jozef ascended to the surface and I followed. When our

heads broke through and I inhaled, Jozef said, "That's the tip of Gibraltar, just there. Can you see?"

I nodded, but I could hardly focus on how Gibraltar looked in the distance because the sound of his voice in the open air seemed to penetrate to my very heart and soul and pluck it like the strings of a harp.

FIFTEEN

Startled by the feeling I had not felt in a very long time, I was momentarily struck dumb. Not wanting to alarm Jozef, I hid my emotions behind silence and a deadpan expression. I was thankful that he was happy to talk as we got closer and closer to his home on Gibraltar, and relieved that he didn't seem to expect me to converse.

My hand found the aquamarine at my throat, thinking with a flash of panic that it had fallen from my neck without me noticing. Feeling the small cool stone under my fingers calmed the panic, but not the surprise. I had always believed a siren incapable of having romantic feelings while carrying a stone, but the warmth in my belly and heart continued to grow with the sound of Jozef's voice.

What did this mean? I made a study of my feelings, dissecting them like a scientist dissects a specimen. Jozef's voice was having a perceptible effect on me. It was a similar experience to how I'd felt toward Mattis, but there were differences. My consciousness had not relegated my life in Okeanos to the dark corners of my memory the way it did when I was in a mating cycle. There was less urgency, less single-mindedness, less obsession in this feeling. Was this because I was Sovereign? Was that why it was happening? And it was happening with an Atlantean, not a human, which was probably even more shocking.

"...built just for the purpose..." Jozef was saying, as we approached the shore.

Jutting out into the water was a small boathouse, exquisitely made with details in the woodwork of the eaves and frames around the windows and door that was unusual to see in such a utilitarian structure. I set human feet on the rocks below the boathouse then crawled up the ladder after Jozef and stood up inside, looking around.

Jozef pointedly kept his eyes averted from my nakedness and I bit my cheeks against a smile. So, some Atlanteans shared the embarrassment of being uncovered with humans.

"I haven't got any women's clothing for you, I'm afraid," he said, rifling through a wooden trunk and pulling out some articles of clothing. "But these should work. We wouldn't want to give anyone in the house a startle."

Jozef's webbed hands and flipper-feet had transformed to human. His gills had closed up and his pupils had retracted to a normal size. Looking at him now, if I had seen him while on land, I would not have been able to tell he was Atlantean at all.

I took the button-up shirt and the cotton shorts he handed me and pulled them on over my damp body. While I dressed, Jozef stepped behind a shelf loaded with metal boxes to put on dry clothing. When he stepped out again, he was wearing plain clothing—a simple knit sweater with no fastenings up the front or back, and gray-blue trousers with wide bottoms. This was my first exposure to the fashion of the seventies. Many things had changed.

My hair was so long by this time that it hung to the backs of my knees. Twisting it into a large bun at the nape of my neck, I used a thinner tendril from the nape of my neck to tie it in place so it was off my back and didn't entirely soak the clothing Jozef had given me.

"Are you all right?" Jozef was looking at me intently. "You haven't said anything for a while. Do you feel anxious? I can assure you, you're quite safe with me."

That voice. It caressed me like a silk scarf, wrapping itself around my waist, my belly, my chest.

I smiled at him genuinely and with some humor, for he'd said this as though he wasn't aware of what a siren was capable. There was no one I feared, least of all the man whose voice could incite the feelings his had.

"I'm fine, thank you. It's just been a while since I was on land."

He gave a nod and smiled back. "Good. This way, then." A nervous energy was rolling off him in waves, whether it was at the opportunity to share his work with someone, or it was more personal than that, I couldn't tell.

"What was that black thing you were wearing in the water?" I asked, recalling its strange texture and thickness.

"It's called neoprene. You are not aware of it?"

I shook my head.

"When *was* the last time you were on land?"

"I don't know," I answered. "It would take some work to pinpoint a year, let alone a date." This wasn't entirely true, I knew that I had left Poland in the spring of 1869, but that was the last human life I'd had. I'd been on land since then, but not to mate, just for curiosity's sake. I enjoyed catching glimpses of humanity's progress—the development of electrical light, fuel-powered ships, and the growth of their coastal cities.

For some reason, I felt the need to keep things vague until I got to know Jozef better, even if I felt attracted to him. He was Atlantean after all, a potential rival, though it appeared that he was completely unaware of this rivalry, and certainly unaware of my status.

We left the boathouse and took a rocky pathway away from the shore and up to an impressive structure sitting among boulders and rock-gardens the way a bird sits in a nest.

"You live in a cathedral!" I cried when I looked up and fully took in the sharp features on the roofline of Jozef's home, the stained-glass windows, the stone gargoyles.

Jozef chuckled. "Not quite. Drakief Manor is over three-hundred years old, but it was never a cathedral. The architect was inspired by things he saw on a visit to France, but the Manor doesn't have the feel of a religious building, I can assure you."

"You really do not make your home in the ocean then," I wondered aloud.

Jozef looked back at me, the dark slashes of his eyebrows arched, his thickly-lashed eyes wide. "Certainly not. Life on land is much more preferable, especially for someone in my line of work. There are no universities or laboratories underwater."

"But you could live there, if you wished. Many of your kind do. In fact, all that I have ever met."

Jozef looked sad at this. "Those are the lost ones," he said. "The ones who fell through the cracks. Atlanteans who live underwater are subject to illness, I'm afraid. Our immune systems are much stronger on land."

The rock path became steps and the steps became a white gravel walkway which wound its way through a lush green garden buzzing with insects and fluttering with birds.

My breath caught in my throat at the beauty of the grounds and I could understand why Jozef would prefer to live here, along the ocean instead of within it.

"Your family has wealth," I said, further bewildered.

Jozef's cheeks flushed with pink, visible even beneath his tanned skin. I realized I'd said something a human with tact would not have said.

Leading me to a small side entrance on the ground floor of the house, rather than up the wide front steps to the columned porch, Jozef stepped into a cool stone space he referred to as a 'mud-room.'

A short, round woman with a smiling face and pink cheeks and wearing a black and white dress bustled up to Jozef. When her bright eyes fell on me, she smiled and said something in Spanish.

"Yes, this is Bel." Jozef introduced me.

The woman made a strange bobbing motion with her head, bending her knees and lowering her eyes for a second. The gesture triggered a memory; the staff in Poland used to do that. She was an employee, then.

"This is Gabriela," Jozef said to me before turning back to the woman and telling her she could use English with me.

"Very good," she said in accented English. "Would you like to take tea in the library, or the parlor, perhaps?"

Jozef looked at me, his dark gaze full of questions, his damp hair curling around his ears and at the nape of his neck. I had to take a steadying breath when he turned those eyes on me like that. "You're welcome to stay for supper, if you like. I know this is a long detour from your planned route."

I didn't know how to answer this. 'Detour' was an understatement. I took a little too long to answer and Jozef, feeling the need to fill the empty air perhaps, went on to say, "Or just stay for tea and some of Gabriela's delicious scones?"

I was not unaware of Gabriela's eyes wandering my person, the odd clothing Jozef had given me, and my huge mass of hair tied at the nape of my neck.

"Just tea," I began, and then added, "Thank you."

Gabriela bobbed again and disappeared up a set of wide white stone steps.

"Does she know what I am?" I asked, then added, "Does she know what *you* are?"

"No to the first, yes to the second." Jozef smiled.

"She's human?"

"Yes, she's from a small village near Barcelona. My growing up years were done when she came to us, but some women will care for anyone in their path, as she's done for me. My father is an investor and isn't home a lot. I'm thankful for Gabriela's company."

"And your mother?" I followed Jozef down a long narrow hallway until he opened a door and ascended a set of wooden steps not nearly so grand as the ones Gabriela had taken.

"I never knew my mother," Jozef explained, "but Gabriela has enough maternal instinct for three women. She still refers to me as Master Jozef, even though I asked her not to many times. I can't disabuse her of it, and so I suppose she'll call me that until she dies."

"Until *she* dies," I echoed. "Do you say it this way because she is older than you and you presume she'll go first, or do you say this because you would easily outlive any human?"

Jozef didn't answer at first, and he was ahead of me on the steps so I couldn't see his expression. He paused on a step, right near a candelabra on the wall which, I noted, was not lit with a flame but with an electric light. The yellow glow lit his features, highlighting the shadow under his cheekbone, the softness of his lips. Looking down at me, the line of shadow from his eyelashes making a dart on his cheek, I abruptly forgot what I had asked him.

"You're very blunt," he said, his voice soft and his expression full of curiosity. "Are all of your kind like you?"

"No," I said instinctively, and then laughed. "And yes."

He made a sound in the back of his throat. I wasn't sure if it was a sound of thoughtfulness, or laughter, but I wanted to learn to discern that sound.

"Of course, we do live long lives, this is the truth of the matter. It is sad, when we are attached to those who do not live so long. I feel the same way toward my pets. We love them like family, and in the end, they break our hearts when they go, whether they be animal or human." He took a breath and his eyes looked faraway. "I don't know if you can understand..."

"I understand," I answered. "I know of exactly the kind of heartbreak you speak."

His gaze sharpened on me then and an understanding passed between us. We'd both loved and lost humans, and that was the first of many things which bound Jozef and me together.

SIXTEEN

Jozef led me up the stairway, across a wide stone hall blanketed with ancient looking carpet, walls adorned with mirrors and sconces, and through a set of double doors. The library which we entered next took my breath away, even filled with dark shadows the way it was.

Jozef flicked a switch and a warm amber glow emanated from multiple wall-mounted lamps which looked something like the kerosene versions I'd known when I was young, only these were electric. The soft light illuminated seemingly endless bookshelves filled with spines of all colors. A wooden staircase led to two more levels of bookcases and on each floor were desks adorned with green lamps.

In the center of the library was a cluster of comfortable looking couches, enough to seat two dozen people easily. Coffee tables were neatly stacked with magazines, newspapers, and colorful publications. A fireplace, currently dormant, stretched to the ceiling, and wrapped around the stone wall above it was an octopus sculpture wrought in black iron.

The books, furniture, and lighting were one thing, but

the art gave another dimension to the space and I felt a longing to stay in this place forever, reading and admiring the atmosphere.

Drawn to a set of three colorful drawings, framed and mounted side by side on the wooden paneling between bookcases, I stopped and stared. The first was done in yellow ink, and was an artful image of a tropical fish. The second was of a seahorse rendered in red ink, and the last was a blue squid, its tentacles curved and flowing in beautiful lines. Each drawing was labeled in tiny handwriting, each body part noted in Latin and English. I knew very little about art, but I could tell these were not prints and that they'd been done by a loving hand.

"Who did these?" I couldn't find a signature or a name plate anywhere on the work.

"I did," Jozef said from behind me, sounding self-conscious. "I did them at boarding school when I was fourteen or fifteen."

I tore my eyes from the drawings to stare at him. "So young?"

He smiled. "I have always loved the ocean and everything in it for as long as I could remember. I have many more drawings like these, hidden in notebooks in my old school things. But these are the ones Gabriela loved most and so she had them framed as a gift."

He gazed at the drawings with affection, more for the human who'd had them mounted than the art done by his own hand.

He turned and gestured widely to the room. "In fact, all of the art is mine, except for a few pieces, like the wrought-iron octopus over the fireplace. That one was a gift from my father."

"It's so beautiful."

My gaze drifted to the other framed pieces and for a time, Jozef let me wander the room and take them in. All of Jozef's work was of sea creatures or the ocean itself. The renderings of the ocean were not seascapes like those of artists I'd seen in Europe—huge, frothing waves, and ships fighting to right themselves in an angry sea. Jozef's work was scientific. He drew in fine, colored ink, the flowing pattern of water as it hit a structure on the ocean floor and reacted above by throwing up the huge barrel of a wave. Some of these waves were labeled. Jaws, Maui. Mavericks, California. Shipsterns, Tasmania.

"These waves have names?" I blinked at him, feeling my mind stretch. The idea of naming an oceanic feature such as a wave had never occurred to me. "Did you name them?"

Jozef laughed and came to stand near me where I stared at a wall full of the small scientific drawings. "No, I didn't name them. I just studied them. What you've found here are the world's sexiest waves," he said. "These waves are known worldwide by surfers and I'm not entirely sure who named them. Probably the locals did, and it caught on."

"Surfers?"

His brown eyes found mine. "You don't know surfing?"

I listened intently as Jozef described how humans had taken to riding the waves close to the beach on top of a thin piece of wood made just for the purpose. Amazed at the ingenuity this took, I had a difficult time picturing the activity until Jozef took me over to a coffee table and found color photographs of people surfing.

"Do you surf?" I asked.

He showed his teeth in a boyish grin that warmed my heart. "I have tried it and it's enjoyable, but for someone like me, well, let's say I'm more interested in what goes on under the surface. When it comes to the ocean, I see hours of study, not so much the play."

He led me to another wall where there was another collection of wave drawings, much simpler than the surfing waves. Here he'd drawn a diagram which I wouldn't have known was a wave if he hadn't been there to explain it to me.

An oscillating line across the width of the page in blue, drawings of circles in green placed along the first line, and red arrows shooting out from each circle did not resemble any wave I had ever seen.

"Trochoidal Wave or Gerstner Wave," I read aloud from the label beneath the drawing. "František Josef Gerstner."

"That's who I was named after, in case you're wondering. Franz was a physicist and engineer. He published a book called *Theory of Waves* in 1804." Jozef pointed to another drawing, this one much simpler. "This one, the Stokes Wave, was named for Irishman George Gabriel Stokes..."

Jozef went on to show me numerous wave styles, some which looked more like quilt patterns than wave-action, which he'd studied at school and rendered lovingly into a science-based art form. Then we moved to another wall where there were more drawings of animals, and another of plants. Jozef's love for the ocean shone through his eyes, resonated in his voice, and vibrated outward from his heart like heat from a fire. All the while, his voice plucked at me the way a harpist plucks her instrument, making my heart sing.

Jozef paused in his commentating about a drawing of a starfish and looked at me suddenly and with a tinge of alarm. "Am I boring you?"

"You couldn't," I said quickly, and could not have meant it more.

He had one arm up and resting on the wall beside the drawing. We'd both been looking up as he talked, but suddenly, when he looked down, I realized how close we were standing.

For a breathless moment, we simply looked at one another and Jozef blinked slowly. Between the shutters of his eyelid coming down and going up again, his expression changed. His eye color seemed to darken, his thoughts seemed to flicker between one thing and another. His gaze dropped to my lips.

I wondered if my heartbeat was as loud to him as it was to me. I listened for his but couldn't hear it. Then I realized that yes, I could. It was just that it was beating in sync with mine.

Abruptly, he tore his gaze away and dropped his arm. "I fear I am being very self-absorbed," he said, his cheeks growing pink underneath his tanned skin. "Believe me, it isn't my habit to drone on endlessly about myself and my studies. I just don't often have such an interested audience."

A knock at the double doors made us turn as Gabriela came bustling in, carrying a tray. The room filled with the mouth-watering scent of hot bread. My stomach gurgled noisily and I realized I was ravenous. It had been a long time since I had tasted baking. Suddenly, I wanted nothing more than to taste bread and jam again, to sip hot tea and milk the way I had in London when I was very little, and in Gdansk, much later.

"Just a spot of Earl Grey," Gabriela said in her charming accent as she set the tray down on the largest coffee table in the center of the room, and moved bits of china about. "And some freshly baked scones with clotted cream and strawberry preserve. It's my mother's recipe."

She prattled on as Jozef and I moved over to the couches and sat across from one another.

"You're a wonder," Jozef told Gabriela, and she flushed crimson to the roots of her graying hair.

He kissed the back of her hand and she bobbed a curtsy, sending me a smile, but her attention was almost solely for Jozef. She adored him and it was obvious. She backed out of the room and closed the doors, leaving us to devour the scones and wash them down with the tea.

We hardly spoke as we ate, until Jozef looked at me bashfully, a spot of cream at the corner of his mouth. He licked it away. "I didn't realize how hungry I was."

"Me neither," I said through a mouthful of scone. Whatever Gabriela was, an accomplished baker was among her talents.

When we'd finished eating, I asked Jozef what had been nagging at me since I first met him out in the ocean.

"I have met with a few Atlanteans here and there throughout my life," I said, "but none of them were like you."

"No?" He sat back against the couch and settled his tea cup and saucer on one knee. "What were they like?"

"They were pitiful creatures, malnourished, many of them looked ill and infested with parasites of one kind or another."

A look of understanding crossed Jozef's face. "I can assure you, the Atlanteans in my circle share very little in common with the ones you crossed paths with in the deep." His dark eyes were sad. "The wanderers are afraid of me," he explained, "so though I've made attempts to talk with them on the rare occasion that I run across them during my observations, they tend to avoid me.

My brows shot up in surprise at this. An Atlantean avoiding a fellow Atlantean?

"It's something that used to bother me a lot in my youth, but now..." he shrugged a shoulder, "it's how they choose to live. Even if it doesn't make sense to me, it's their decision. They don't realize that they would suffer less if they spent more time on land. It's the sunlight. We need it for immunity."

This was not the case for sirens. I surmised that Atlanteans had to be closer to humans genetically. Humans needed sunlight to be healthy, too.

Jozef's expression was far away. "They remind me a little of some of the homeless people in the big cities. Most of them approach to ask for food or money, but some of them have nothing but fear in their eyes, and stay away. Even if you try to help them, they will not allow you to get close enough to offer it."

Jozef made it sound as though he'd lived the life of a human more than an ocean creature.

"But you were born in the ocean, correct?" I asked.

His eyes cut back to mine and he smiled, a dimple cratering in his left cheek. "Of course not," he said softly. "No Atlantean that I know was born in the wild."

Once again, my sense of reality was fractured. Jozef was unusual enough when held against the standards Atlanteans had set in my experience, but now he was telling me that he was not actually that unusual among his kind.

"I was born on the island of Sardinia, because at the time, my father believed he might find the ruins of Atlantis there. While my obsession has been to study the ocean and all of its mysteries, my father continued the work of my grandfather, and his grandfather before that—to find Atlantis. This search dictated much of the movement of my early life, and led to the separation of my mother and father." Jozef took a deep breath and I detected some pain in him on this subject. "When my father could not interest me in picking up the task after him, he sent me to boarding school in Pennsylvania where I could prepare to pursue a university degree in oceanography."

He spread one hand and shrugged up a shoulder as if to say, *and here I am.*

"My father has his faults," he continued, "but he did his best to give me what I wanted. He had me tutored in many languages, the ones he wanted me to know, but also the ones I wanted to know. He wanted me prepared from a young age to be equipped to enter the search for Atlantis. So though I studied oceanography, he ensured I took courses in classical languages, ancient history, anthropology. My life has been spent with my face in a book, or in a lab, or in the ocean itself–always learning."

I nodded, and could relate to his thirst for knowledge. "I love learning, too."

"I believe it. Your curiosity is apparent." He flashed a set of strong white teeth.

"Next year I have promised myself I will study the art and science of salvaging again, because there have been leaps and bounds of technological improvements made since the last time I studied it." He swallowed his remaining tea and leaned forward to set the cup and saucer on the table. "But that is more than enough about me, I have been talking about myself nonstop since we met and know nothing about you." He shook a friendly finger in my direction. "Don't think I'll let you get away from here without telling me more about yourself."

Suddenly, I felt the twangs of anxiety linking me to my people. I thought about the *Foniádes* who would have looked for me as their shift changed. While I'd been languishing in the sound of Jozef's voice and letting my imagination be carried away by his stories and art, those in Okeanos were wondering what had happened to their Sovereign. A form of panic rose in my chest.

I stood up and nearly spilled the rest of my tea. Setting it on the coffee table, I turned to go.

"I'm late," I said, my breath coming quickly now and my heart rate ramping up. As a siren, I could go anywhere I wished and do as I pleased. No one would care if I disappeared for years, but as Sovereign, I had responsibilities.

Jozef got to his feet, eyes troubled and expression disappointed. "Just like that, you're going to go?"

I made my way to the double doors and pushed through them, heading back the way we came. The sound of his voice pulled at me; he was genuinely disappointed that I had to leave, and knowing that sirens were not the best at mimicking the human social graces Jozef would have been brought up with, I stopped and turned back toward him suddenly.

He halted midstride as I faced him, our faces mere inches from one another. Without thinking, I stood on tiptoe and pressed my lips to his cheek.

His eyes widened and the tips of his fingers touched my elbows reactively.

"I am sorry." I looked him straight in the eye. "I do have to go. I forgot myself. Thank you, for the tea, and... everything."

I turned away and flew down the stairs, heading for the back door. I heard Jozef on the steps behind me, following me out the door and down the gravel path. It took him a long time to say anything, but he finally spoke when we reached the boathouse.

"But...will I see you again?" His voice cracked and he sounded distraught. The sound reverberated inside me as well and I paused in stripping off the clothes he'd given me.

Straightening to face him, the shirt he'd given me falling off one shoulder and the shorts already a puddle on the wooden floor of the boathouse, I took his face between my palms and wanted nothing more than to see that face every day.

"Yes," I said fiercely, and his brown eyes flooded with relief. "Yes, you will see me again."

With one last kiss, quick and chaste, on his lips, I left his clothing in a heap on the floor of the boathouse and slipped into the water.

SEVENTEEN

Once I had spent those first few hours with Jozef, it was impossible to get him out of my head and my heart. I continued the task I'd set for myself, to understand the boundaries of Okeanos. During my alone time, I slipped off to meet with Jozef, sometimes joining him on his underwater data-gathering missions, and other times going all the way to Gibraltar to spend only a few hours with him. At first, my journey around Okeanos allowed me to visit easily, but as I progressed around our borders, the space between me and Gibraltar became too far to traverse reasonably. So, I told my *Foniádes* to give me more time between shift changes to allow me to spend a few days, and then even weeks with Jozef. The chemistry between us continued to grow, and I became accustomed to the idea of wealthy and educated Atlanteans making their homes on land and living like humans.

It took me nearly two years to swim the perimeter of Okeanos. I learned that the *apotreptikó* did not surround us completely, but rather lay in patches, which altogether might total less than half of our borders. In retrospect, I learned more about the surrounding ocean from Jozef than I had from my own discovery project. I learned that disastrous earthquakes many thousands of years ago helped to form the oceanic crust and that these large-scale events happened in cycles, changing the terrain both above and below water, and even altering the climate. Learning these things humbled me, and left me with a continuous amazement of the natural world.

The day I returned to Califas, Nike greeted me on the stairs leading to the freshwater pools, where I longed to take a cleansing soak. She touched the space between my collarbones in deference and then threw her arms around me in a hug.

"You've been missed, Sovereign." Her body seemed to tremble against mine she held me so tightly.

Hugging her back, I frowned, picking up low-level anxiety coming off her in waves. "Are you all right?"

She released me and nodded, but her gray eyes were troubled. "May I join you at the pools? I assume that's where you're going."

"Of course."

It wasn't until after Nike and I had spent an hour soaking in the mentally clarifying freshwater that she opened herself to me.

"Our numbers are dwindling," she said, leaning against the soft curves of a blue moss-covered stone. "Sirens who left on mating cycles over ten years ago have not returned."

"Sirens can take that long and longer, Nike," I chided, "you know that. Have you spoken to Lia about your concern?"

Agliaia was an older siren who'd taken on (at my request) the job of marking down the names of every Okeanos citizen on a wall in one of the caves. Young sirens coming in for the first time were marked when their mothers brought them back. Sometimes the mother would know her daughter's precise birth date, other times she had only a season and a year. Sirens were not nearly so orderly and precise about putting events into writing for posterity as humans were. When it came to this task, a rough idea of ages and timelines were considered 'good enough.' It was an improvement, as far as I could tell, for in the Hall of Anamna only the names of the Sovereigns had been immortalized in the tile. The current Sovereign had to guess the date of their reign by observing clothing, customs, technologies of the time, languages, and other markers when visiting a memory. We were, after all, sea-creatures—only partially human. And as such we were only partially driven by human ambitions. The rest of our makeup was entirely primal—to survive and procreate without giving away our secret was our standard of success.

Nike was nodding. "I visited her, and she confirmed that few have returned from their mating cycles."

"Was she concerned?"

Nike gave me a withering look. "Lia isn't concerned about anything. She's got the metabolism of a manatee and the personality to match."

"So, why do *you* think that sirens are staying away so long?"

Nike's brows furrowed and she didn't answer for a long time, until finally, she gave the anti-climactic, "I don't know."

"But you don't think it's a coincidence. Otherwise you wouldn't have brought it up."

"No, I would not be concerned if it were only a few sirens, but according to Lia's records, of the fifty sirens who have left for a mating-cycle in the last fifteen years, only four have returned."

This statistic set my alarm bells ringing. I sat upright in the water. "Four out of fifty?"

Nike sighed and gazed at me lovingly. "Finally, I got through to you. Do you see now, why I am concerned?"

"I do. Why didn't you say so sooner?"

"You haven't been around lately." Her voice was laced with curiosity, and a little reproach. "Are you going to tell me where you've been?"

"I was swimming our perimeter, you know that. I told everyone it was something I wanted to do."

"Yes, but even dawdling at the speed of a turtle wouldn't have taken you two years to swim the entire thing."

"How do you know?" I replied, slyly. "Have you ever done it?"

"Well, no...but," she eyed me suspiciously, "there is more to it, isn't there?"

I let out a long breath and settled back against the stone again. There was no reason to keep my relationship a secret, even if it was unusual. I was Sovereign, and I could do what I liked. If one of my people came to me and said they'd mated with an Atlantean, I would have been surprised, but I wouldn't have forbidden it. In fact, some cross-breeding of our two nations might be just the thing to start fostering some peace between us.

"I met someone interesting," I explained. "An Atlantean."

"Really. You found an *Atlantean* interesting?"

"Why wouldn't I?"

"Because, according to your mother, they're the scourge

of the seas. Diseased and unintelligent, poachers and scavengers."

"I'm not my mother. And you don't think that about them, either."

"Maybe not all of them, but generally, they've not shown to be a desirable lot."

"This one is," I said a little too dreamily for Nike's liking. "Very desirable. He's healthy and beautiful, and so intelligent. He's nothing like the others of his species who make their homes underwater. He says it's because Atlanteans need more direct sunlight."

Nike's lips parted in surprise, her eyes glued to my face. She skipped right over the sunlight comment and went straight to the crux of the matter. "Have you *fallen* for this Atlantean? I can't believe it."

"Haven't you ever thought that an alliance might be a good thing between our people?"

Nike scoffed derisively. "A good thing? For them, yes. For us, no. We're the ones with all the resources. We own the richest, most valuable terrain in the Atlantic. How could we benefit from breeding with them?"

She shuddered and it shook her entire torso, it had come from so deep within her. She made a sound of disgust.

"I'm not so sure." I was thinking of Jozef's incredible intelligence, his love of the ocean, his desire to understand it better, his love for all things within it, and the ease with which he lived on land in harmony with humans.

"There are things we might learn from them... some of them," I added hastily. "I understand your point of view, Nike, but you're basing it on the vagabonds. The only Atlanteans you've ever seen, that most sirens have ever seen, are the wanderers. Even Jozef cannot relate to them."

"Jozef," she echoed, gazing at me. "The way you say his

name..." She halted that line of thinking and set her shoulders. Her chin tilted up. "I'm happy you've made a friend, but I don't think you should trust him."

"If you knew him, you wouldn't say that." I trusted Jozef entirely, and I had almost from the beginning. It wasn't something I could explain, but I could feel his innate *goodness*. I had nothing to fear from Jozef and I believed that with all of my being.

"Maybe so," Nike said, "but until we figure out why our sirens are not returning, I still think you should be cautious. And don't go giving away our secrets."

Nike quickly closed her mouth and colored. Perhaps she'd realized just how admonishing she sounded, and to her Sovereign at that.

I smiled at her. I liked that she didn't treat me any differently from how she had before I'd taken the throne.

"Well, do you have any magic that can help us determine why the sirens are spending so much time away?" I asked.

Her face went thoughtful, but after a few moments, she shook her head.

"I don't think so." Her gaze sharpened on me. "You are the one who should have the capabilities of finding out more about this problem, not me."

"I am?"

"Of course, you're Sovereign. We're all attached to you, and you to us. It's why no one can overthrow you unless the Salt deems them worthy. You have the power of the Sovereign. It's Salt-given, and it comes with great benefits."

I thought about the ability I had to go back into the memories of any Sovereign before me. Apollyona had lost that ability the moment I had become Sovereign. And what Nike had said about being tethered to my sirens was true.

When a siren was coming home, I could feel her, somehow. It wasn't an overt feeling, but there was a sensitivity in me to sirens coming home. I was never surprised by their appearance. I was never out swimming when they arrived in the caves of Califas, because I needed to give them their gem immediately.

I must have somehow known not to expect any sirens home for two full years, otherwise I wouldn't have taken on the swimming of our borders. I would never knowingly make a siren wait. But these things were not conscious; I did them without realizing that I was tuning in to some network between me and my people. If I was gone for too long from Okeanos, my anxiety levels began to eke upward and could be assuaged only by going home.

I thought about this carefully over the next few days. I sat in quiet places in Okeanos, both within the caves and underwater. I noted a few of the names Lia had listed as having left over a decade ago. I held their names in my mind, closed my eyes, and tried to consciously tune in to them. To call them to me.

I received no response, felt no connection to these sirens. Whether it meant they were too far away, or were on land, or were dead, I didn't know. But it troubled me increasingly as time passed.

JOZEF TAUGHT me much about the creatures and cycles of the ocean over the next couple of years. He taught me about sea animals that I'd seen but had no name for. Sirens hadn't much use for academia. Our interactions with humans were solely centered around finding a mate, and we didn't generally need to prove intelligence of the scholastic kind in order to do that. Even if we wanted a human male who happened to be more cerebral, if he wasn't attracted to a siren's personality, she could force the issue using her voice.

The attraction between Jozef and me was different from any I'd experienced before and I assumed that was thanks to the gem that sat at my neck. I was falling in love with him, and he with me, but our love had none of the urgency or desperation that I'd felt with previous mates. I enjoyed spending time with Jozef without thinking about an 'end game.' There was no active cycle within me, urging me to mate with him and produce a siren. We became friends first, then later, lovers.

I could have lived this way forever. I was happy. My only nagging concern—which Nike now increasingly brought up—was our decreasing population. I understood more intimately now how the sirens of centuries past felt when they realized that their numbers of tritons were dwindling. At a loss for what to do about it, I used my time with Jozef to escape the daily life of the Sovereign, although I never told Jozef who I was to the citizens of Okeanos. I was, for the majority, at peace.

Then I met his father.

Jozef and I were poring over his discoveries of life in the deepest parts of the ocean. We knew less, he said, about the depths of the world's oceans than we did about the surface of the moon. He took out folders full of sketches of the creatures he'd seen, but explained that he'd seen the deep-sea species from a submersible.

"You haven't swum with these creatures yourself?" I asked him, surprised because every other specimen he'd drawn had been produced as a result of an in-the-flesh encounter with the subject.

He turned his head to gaze at me, shaking his head.

We were sitting side by side in front of the largest coffee table in his library with a large leather portfolio open in front of us. The drawings were not much more than sketches—Jozef had yet to render them into full scientific drawings. These were the latest in his collection of sea art.

"Atlanteans are well suited to a life underwater," he explained, "given our gills, our webbing, and the fact that we repel sharks."

"You do?"

"As do you, Bel. You didn't know?"

"They don't attack us, but I never thought it was because we actually *repel* them. How do we do that?"

He smiled. "It probably seems like a big mystery, but it's simply a matter of taste. Sharks don't like the taste of iron-rich blood. Atlanteans, humans, and Mer all have blood high in iron content. We're not their natural food source. They much prefer the taste of copper-rich blood, which is what fish and other aquatic creatures have. We have all these features, but we cannot withstand the incredible pressures of the depths at which these creatures live." He paused, finely arched eyebrows up. "Can you?"

"Yes, sirens have no problem at any depth," I told him. "We even sometimes hibernate at great depths for years."

His lips parted in shock. "Really? You stay down there for years? With these creatures?" He waved a hand over the drawing of the deep-sea angler fish open in front of us.

The angler fish was a creature of nightmares, with transparent, bulging eyes and teeth so enormous the creature couldn't even close its own mouth.

I laughed. "I suppose humans would find these creatures grotesque, but I don't. I find everything that lives in the ocean beautiful in its own way. Don't you?"

Jozef chuckled. "Beautiful is a stretch, but certainly fascinating." He flipped over the drawing to the next one, a long parasite with dangling tentacles.

He made a funny gurgle of disgust and I laughed at him.

"We used to think that life could not survive this far down," he continued with a grin. "So far from sunlight, photosynthesis wasn't possible." He turned the page again, revealing a drawing of a bizarre-looking eel with very small eyes and an absolutely enormous triangular mouth. "It's exciting. Advancements in technology are allowing us to learn just how wrong our assumptions were."

"Perhaps I could help you in some way," I suggested, "given that I have the ability to go down there. I could bring back samples, or if you have some kind of device that can take photos underwater, I could try and get images of them."

I looked up into a pair of shining eyes. He put a knuckle under my chin and tilted my face up to his. "You're a wonder. You know that?"

He kissed my lips and then my cheeks and wrapped an arm around my neck to pull me close, burying his nose in my hair. He took a deep breath, inhaling my scent.

There was the sudden and loud sound of someone coughing to clear his throat. Jozef jumped and stood up, then began to laugh.

"Father," he said, putting a hand over his chest. "You startled me."

"I can see that," said the man standing in the doorway.

Jozef's father was as tall as Jozef, but much broader in the shoulder than his son, as well as a little rounder in the belly. He wore a navy jacket done up with two rows of brass buttons. His wool trousers were neatly pressed with a perfectly straight crease running down the front. His shoes were perfectly polished black leather. There was something vaguely nautical about his clothing and I wondered if he was a sea captain. An Atlantean as the captain of a human ship? It was another jarring thought which loosened the last of my prejudiced ideas about who and what Atlanteans were. His hair was white and clipped short, and he had a short white beard and brows, also neatly kept.

"I see you have a visitor," Jozef's father said, crossing the room to stand before us within the circle of furniture. His voice was good-natured, almost jovial. "When were you going to introduce us?"

"I didn't know you were arriving home today," Jozef replied, still standing. "Gabriela never told me. Welcome home."

I stood as he introduced me, smiling at the father of the man I loved.

"This is Bel." Jozef looked down at me and said, "Bel, this is my father, Claudius Drakief."

Claudius dropped his chin in a respectful nod and I reached out a hand, recalling that humans greeted one another this way, so perhaps Atlanteans who lived like humans did as well.

He took my hand in his, his flesh was soft and cool.

"Pleasure to meet you, Bel..." He raised a gray eyebrow and his gaze darted from me to his son. "Does the young lady not have a last name?"

"You could use Novak, if you like," I replied, offering him the last human surname I'd used.

Claudius looked at me again, quizzically this time. His gaze dropped to the aquamarine at my throat. The pleasant smile on his face slowly dissolved as his eyes lingered there, then rose to scrutinize my features. He made a study of my skin, my bright blue eyes, my hair—currently piled on top of my head in a top-knot to keep my neck cool, but obviously a great amount of hair.

His gaze found the gem at my throat again and his eyes grew hard. They cut back to my face, now expressing something completely anathema to welcome.

"Ah..." Claudius said, and let the sound draw long from his throat in a deep rumble that sounded like a realization, one he wasn't all that happy to have made. He dropped my hand and glanced at Jozef, his brown eyes glittering with anger. His reaction was instantaneous, and I felt the change in his temperament, for it was so swift and visceral that it seemed to suck all the air from the room.

Jozef however, appeared not to notice; either that or he chose to ignore it.

"Bel and I will be working together, we've just decided," Jozef went on.

My guts had begun to slowly curdle as Claudius stepped back from us, his mouth a line of disdain. The tiniest lift at his upper lip made him look like he was suppressing a snarl.

"Since she can visit places in the ocean that we can't..." Jozef's words slowed down as his father continued to back away. "Are you all right, Father?"

"Might I speak with you alone, Jozef?" Claudius asked, but his glittering eyes were on me. "Now."

"Certainly," Jozef replied, and his tone finally betrayed some level of doubt. With an apologetic smile sent my way, Jozef followed his father out the library doors.

My mind whirled. Why such a strong negative reaction to me?

Seconds ticked by and I sat on the couch again, too concerned to go back to the drawings. Seconds turned into minutes: ten, then fifteen. Still Jozef did not return. Unable to stand waiting any longer, I got off the couch and went to the door, straining my siren ears for some clue as to where the two men had gone and what they were discussing.

Distantly, I heard the drone of male voices having an argument they were making an attempt to keep hushed. Words hissed out on sharp breaths and high-pressured whispers.

"... made a mistake," the deeper, more guttural voice which belonged to Claudius was saying, "protecting you all these years from the knowledge our people have. I was trying to give you a good life, allow you to pursue the things you had a passion for. I never forced you to join us, and in fact sent you away so you could be free to live like the human you so obviously prefer to be."

"What are you saying..." Jozef's whispered reply began, only to be cut off.

"It's not your fault," his father said, with a tone that said he believed otherwise. "But I never thought I'd come home to this, to you..." there was a pregnant pause where Claudius searched for the right word, "fraternizing with a... a... one of *them*."

There was a long pause before Claudius continued, "It's time I give you a proper Atlantean education, the one you should have had when you were just a boy, the one I so foolishly thought to protect you from..."

I didn't wait to hear any more. The problem was clear enough. Claudius might walk on land and dress like a sea captain, but in his heart, he was all Atlantean. He had the prejudice that I expected most Atlanteans to have, and could I blame him? My mother had killed his people, no one would fully know how many perhaps, except for the *Foniádes* who'd executed her will.

It was clear I was not welcome in this house anymore, and my heart began to bleed with sadness. With the loving of Jozef, a hope had taken root in my heart, one I had nurtured in my quiet moments. The intensity of that hope was not fully known even to me until Claudius had come in and dashed it.

What if—my heart had asked—an Atlantean and a siren could make a life together? What if they could have a family? What if they could share the precious resources of Okeanos, and Atlanteans who wanted to live a life underwater could do so if they wished, and sirens who wanted to mate for life could do so as well? No more broken-hearted human males left in our wake, no more human boys abandoned by mothers who were simply unable to stay on land?

With the appearance of Claudius, a cold, dark shadow drained the color from this dream that I had just begun to lovingly nurture.

Unsure of what to do and not wanting to cause more difficulty for Jozef, I slipped out of the library, down the path to the ocean, and beneath the waves.

EIGHTEEN

My mind buzzed with concern as I entered the halls of Califas. I went straight to the freshwater pools, craving clearer thinking. But my muddled thoughts and emotions were not due to salt, and pulling sweet water through my gills did not help.

Claudius had displayed an obvious prejudice against me and my kind. I couldn't blame him for this, given what Apollyona had done during her reign. But it was surprising because Jozef, his own son, displayed such a marked lack of that same prejudice. Jozef spent time in the water for his work, but otherwise he lived as any human would enjoy living—with plenty of comfort, personal property, wealth, and enjoyable social relationships. Jozef had reaped the benefits of a generous education from his father. I knew that he was part of an extensive network of scientists, historians, and a multiplicity of other experts. He was respected, ahead of his time (naturally, given his abilities), and well established in his chosen career. How could a man with attitudes like Claudius have raised a man like Jozef?

I lay in the freshwater pool for a long time, gazing up at

the ceiling, completely unseeing and unappreciative of the multitude of glowworms and bioluminescent algae on the cave walls and ceilings. I was distraught for personal reasons, as well.

It was likely Claudius had already forbidden his son to see me again. I played the details of the scene and the snippets I'd heard of their conversation over and over in my mind, torturing myself with it.

By the time Nike found me, I had tears pouring down my face, leeching the salt from my system and sending it into the freshwater pool.

"You're back! I've been looking for you every..." She didn't finish when she saw my face. "Sybellen?"

When I didn't respond, she sat on the edge of the pool, her forehead wrinkling with concern.

"What's the matter?" Her tone hardened as her imagination fed her some guess. "What's happened? What did he do?"

I laughed in spite of the tears flowing freely down my face. "Jozef is not to blame, Nike." Sitting up straighter, I brushed my palms across my face. "You've been looking for me?"

"Yes, I hope you noticed just how empty and hollow our caves and valleys are as you made your way home." Nike lowered her chin and pinned me with a meaningful gaze. She was very concerned, to say the least.

In truth, I'd been too lost in my own thoughts to have noticed, but now that she mentioned it, I hadn't seen many sirens swimming about Okeanos as I might have expected.

"I noticed," I lied.

"Well?" Nike put a hand on her hip in an amusing display of ire.

"I am not sure what you want me to say, Nike. What

would you have me do? Send our remaining sirens out to look for the ones who have not yet returned? I tried calling them, I told you that. I got nothing but dead water."

Nike made an angry harrumphing noise in the back of her throat. "We can't just do nothing! Something is going wrong."

Pressing the heels of my hands into my eyes, I took a few deep breaths. Sovereignty meant I had to put aside my personal problems for the greater good of my people. "I'll go back to the Hall of Anamna," I said, lifting my hands away from my eyes. "Maybe something like this has happened before. If there is something in the past that might help us, then there's a chance I'll be led to it."

Nike closed her mouth and gave me a curt nod. "Thank you."

"You don't need to thank me, Nike." I said, standing and stepping out of the pool. "I should have done it before, I've been distracted lately."

"Sybellen?" A voice from one of the cave's smaller entrances interrupted us, and we looked over to see a *Foniádes* approaching on silent feet. "We've detained an Atlantean."

Alarm straightened my spine. "I thought I was clear that we were not to—"

"He passed your designated perimeter, Sovereign," she added hastily, "otherwise we would not have done so."

Jozef. My heart writhed nauseatingly in my chest like a fish impaled on the end of a spear.

"We tried to escort him peacefully to the perimeter, but he's insistent on seeing you. He won't go back without a fight." The *Foniádes* paused then, her lips parted in amusement. "He's a lot stronger than other Atlanteans we've had to deal with. Not to mention better looking."

"Bring him to me."

Nike's eyes opened wide with shock, but the *Foniádes* didn't hesitate. "Yes, Sovereign." She turned and hastily left the cave.

"Are you certain that is wise?" Nike whispered. In case there were ears within hearing distance.

"It's Jozef," I replied. "We love each other. He's as welcome here as any siren would be."

Nike clamped her mouth shut and did not give away her thoughts on this. Instead, she said, "May I be here when he comes? I would very much like to meet this mysterious Atlantean of yours."

I hesitated, then kicked myself when I realized why I was hesitating, and that I'd realized it too late to add a condition to the *Foniádes* escorting Jozef here. I made a frustrated noise in the back of my throat as I picked up the simple robe I had left draped over the stone. I shrugged into it and belted it a little too violently.

"What's wrong?"

"I should have told the *Foniádes* that I would meet him somewhere else."

"Why?" Nike cocked her head quizzically for a moment, but then understanding dawned on her features. "Oh, you don't want him to know you're the Sovereign."

I gave her a look that said she was right.

"I won't give it away," she said, "but you've said he's very intelligent. I'm sure he knows by this point. Having the *Foniádes* report his presence to you isn't something any soldiers of any realm, past or present, would do for an average citizen."

"I know." She was right. It was too late, but at least I could minimize the impact. "I'll go out and meet him..."

"Too late for that." Nike's gaze went to one of the

higher, larger entrances to the cave of freshwater pools, and I whirled to see Jozef striding between four *Foniádes*.

His expression was completely neutral, but the moment I saw him, I could sense his apprehension and his eagerness. His eyes brightened when he saw me, but he didn't say anything, and he wouldn't while locked between four intimidating sirens, three of whom were considerably larger than he was.

I dismissed the *Foniádes*, thanking them for escorting him. Jozef stood before me, his hazel eyes locked on mine, until the *Foniádes* had left the cave.

"Why didn't you tell me?" His words might have been accusing, but his tone was soft and genuine. And hurt.

"I'm sorry," I replied.

"You don't trust me?"

"Of course I do." I was moving my arm to reach for him when Nike made a coughing sound. I'd forgotten she was still there.

Stepping back a little, I introduced the two of them. "Jozef, this is Nike."

Unwillingly, he tore his eyes from me to settle on Nike. It took a moment for him to register her unusual features, then his gaze locked on her with more interest and curiosity. He took in her blue hair, light gray eyes, and dark skin. He didn't say anything about her unusual features, and instead he reached for her hand.

Nike glanced at me over his head, startled, as he bowed to kiss the back of her hand.

"How wonderful to meet you, Nike," Jozef said, standing upright. "It's marvelous to finally meet a friend of Bel's."

Her lips curved in a smile that Jozef would have taken as a warm greeting, but I knew she was smiling at his use of my human name. No siren would ever call me by that name again unless I lost Sovereignty.

"It's marvelous to meet you too," Nike said, enunciating the word 'marvelous,' as it was not one from her normal vocabulary. "You're the Atlantean oceanographer I have been so wanting to meet."

It was Jozef's turn to glance at me with surprise. "It appears she's told you about me, but has not told me about you. How interesting."

"It's clear the two of you have much to talk about. I'll leave you." She caught my eye and held it. "Do not forget what you promised to do."

"I won't forget."

Waiting until Nike had left the room to speak, Jozef reached for me. I relaxed into his hug.

"I'm sorry," he said into my wet hair. "I am terribly embarrassed."

"Don't be," I replied, pulling back and holding his face between my hands. My heart warmed, then melted like a jellyfish on a hot rock at the sincerity and concern in his voice.

"I am nothing like my father," he went on, stating the obvious. "I'm at a loss to explain his hostility, though I'm resolved to get to the bottom of it."

His brow pinched with anger, and it was a strange expression on his face. He'd only ever been happy and relaxed when we were together.

"I can help you get to the bottom of it," I said, then smiled at the idiom. "Funny how this saying suggests that we'll find the answers we seek at the 'bottom.' The bottom of what?"

He took my hands in his and squeezed them. "In this case—the ocean." His gaze clung to mine. "You do have answers, don't you, Bel? I've always felt that, from the moment I met you. Not only did I believe you had answers about the ocean, but I believe you're the answer for me personally."

My breath caught in my throat at these words.

"I was terrified when I returned to the library and you were missing. Terrified that you'd run away in anger or offense, terrified that I'd never see you again. And I realized in one awful moment that I couldn't allow that to happen. I need you in my life, Bel."

"But, your father—"

"Let me worry about my father. I did come here to apologize to you about his behavior, but I also came to ask you to attend a party with me."

"What?" This startled me more than any admission preceding it.

"I want to introduce you to my family and friends, as my partner," he added, touching my cheek, "if you'll allow it. If you'll agree. If you'll take me."

My shoulders dropped at these words—both at the joy I felt upon hearing them, but also under the weight of everything that already was and the complication I imagined would result from our union.

"I understand why you might hesitate," he said, looking around the cave, "even more so now that I've been in your home. This place is incredible beyond belief, and I'm astounded at how the world does not know it exists. But that is not our present concern. Please, just say you'll come to the party with me, just say that much. The rest we have time to figure out, and I know things will work out. I just know it."

"That is not a scientist talking," I said with a smile.

"No, it's a man in love."

An Atlantean in love, my mind clarified. And I was a siren in love. For the first time, I was in love while not under the influence of the Salt, and that was worth something.

That was worth everything.

A WEEK BEFORE THE EVENT, Gabriela met me in Drakief Manor's grand foyer. The petite, pink-cheeked woman was practically overflowing with excitement at the task Jozef had assigned her—make me look like a lady.

"Not just any lady," she said in her strongly accented English as I followed her up several broad staircases to the top floor of the house. She pushed through a set of white double doors and into a large bedroom. "The grandest, most beautiful lady at the party."

The room was furnished all in white. There was a white wooden four-poster bed, a white vanity with a huge oval mirror, four large white wardrobes, a white trunk at the foot of the bed, and even the bedspread and carpet were white, though the pillowcases had tiny red roses embroidered at the hems.

"I can see why you picked this room for such a task." I moved into the room, gawking at the expansive space of floor and noticing two more wide double doors leading to a washroom. "It is furnished for a lady."

"Yes, this room was furnished with our lady guests in mind," Gabriela said as she disappeared into the washroom. The sound of squeaky wheels echoed from within, and she reappeared pushing a rolling metal rack of clothes.

"Do you need help?" I asked.

"There's another one of these, if you'd like to fetch it,"

Gabriela said, wheezing a little as the wheels caught on the carpet and resisted.

Entering the washroom found me in a room full of mirrors. I grabbed the clothes rack Gabriela requested and pulled it out into the room. Each rack had been hung with gowns, all lined up in a rainbow of colors. I realized with a jolt that they'd been assembled for me—I could be rather slow sometimes when it came to human habits.

"Are all these for me?"

"Who else? The Queen of Sheba?" Gabriela laughed.

"Where did all these dresses come from?"

She settled one rack against the wall nearest the door, and the other one diagonal to it, so that they bracketed a full-length mirror framed in—what else?—white wood. She began to rifle through the dresses, touching and fussing, feeling and smelling.

"Some of them I found in Gibraltar," she said, "and some of them I had sent from Lisbon or Barcelona." She poked her head out from between two dresses, a fuchsia taffeta concoction and a sunflower yellow silk one which appeared to have swallowed her alive. "On loan only, you understand."

"Of course."

"Jozef has directed that you can keep the dress you choose for the party, though." She disappeared between two more gowns, her voice muffled. She reappeared carrying a white satin concoction with glitter along the hem, holding it up and assessing it. "Too much bride," she mumbled, and put it back.

She turned to me for a moment, inspecting my face.

"Such a pale beauty, and those eyes," she murmured. "And all that hair, that will be a task."

She arrowed for the other rack, closing in on the blues

and greens. Retrieving a bright teal gown with a skirt that looked like an upside-down cupcake, she held it up, looked at me, then back at the dress. She frowned. "Too fussy."

Drawn to a simple, dark indigo dress, I pulled it off the rack. It slipped through my fingers, soft and silky.

"This one seems comfortable," I said, smiling hopefully at Gabriela.

She frowned initially, then approached and touched the fabric.

"Understated. A beautiful woman like you could wear whatever you wanted. You're tall, slender, striking. There is nothing on this dress to set you apart in a crowd." Her brown eyes jumped to my hair, my face, trailed down my neck. "Then again, you would stand apart in a crowd even in a flour sack."

I laughed at the joke before realizing that she'd said it in all seriousness.

She tilted her chin down and peered at me through her eyebrows, as though to emphasis that this was a serious decision, probably one that would affect the rest of my life. "You like this one?"

"I like it."

"Try it on then, no harm in that." She handed it to me and shooed me toward the washroom.

Shedding my clothes, I slid down the side zipper and stepped into the many-layered dress. I shimmied it up over my hips and tried to pull the shoulders up until I realized it was cut to sit straight across and off the shoulder.

"Well, now, this is a surprise," Gabriela said as she bustled into the room. She zipped up the dress for me and stood back, her expression admiring. "You have excellent instincts."

Layers of indigo silk clung to my shape like a soft hug.

The color deepened the blue of my eyes and made my black hair look like someone had put in subtle, dark blue highlights.

"It's perfect," Gabriela said smartly. "Do you agree?"

I nodded and my reflection nodded back, my gaze skimming my appearance from head to toe.

"Now we have to figure out what to do about that hair," Gabriela muttered as she pulled the white stool out from under the vanity and set it behind me. "Sit please."

Taking a seat on the stool, I allowed Gabriela to lift my hair up, twist it this way and that, pile it up on the top of my head or bunch it into a ball at the nape of my neck. Her forehead began to gleam and her cheeks were tinged with pink by the time she let it fall and stepped back, almost puffing.

"There is nothing for it. I will have to cut it. It's too much. You will have a headache before you even sit down to dinner."

"We could leave it down," I suggested, opting for the easiest route.

"And cover your elegant neck and collarbones? Not a chance. This dress was made for an updo, trust me."

I trusted her. What did I know about how humans dressed in this decade, let alone for a party? The last time I'd lived on land, the dresses had been heavy, scratchy, and trailed on the ground, soaking up mud and getting caught underfoot. The corsets had been a nightmare. By comparison, this gown was as comfortable as underwear.

"And jewelry," Gabriela muttered, eyeballing my small and simple aquamarine gem.

"I'm happy with this," I said quickly, putting a hand protectively over my necklace.

"It is very plain," she said. "We can do much better. Pearls perhaps? Or an indigo velvet choker with a cameo?"

"I'd really rather prefer to wear my own; it means a lot to me." My voice softened and deepened as I said this, edging over into musical.

"All right." Gabriela smiled. "Like I said, you could wear a sack and still be beautiful."

I smiled back in the mirror.

"But this." She grabbed my thick, heavy hair in a fist and picked it up, shaking it in the mirror like she was threatening to punch me with it. "This *has* to go."

I agreed, and after changing out of the dress, Gabriela cut enough hair off to sell to a wig-maker for a small fortune, leaving me feeling much lighter. She elected to twist my hair back into a bun at the nape of my neck, pull a few wisps free to frame my face, and attached a white orchid just under and behind my right ear. The effect was lovely.

"What about makeup?" she asked as I was admiring the contrast of the white orchid against my black hair in the mirror.

"What's makeup?" I asked absently, mesmerized by the way the orchid petals reflected the light.

Gabriela, who'd been bent over a spread of colorful items on the vanity that I hadn't taken a good look at yet, straightened rather suddenly. Her voice was shot through with surprise. "*What's makeup?*"

I realized from the look of near horror on her face that I'd said something odd.

Gabriela's serious expression quirked into a smile. "Are you making a joke?"

I shook my head, my eyes falling to the array of items on the vanity behind her, finally curious about them.

"*This* is makeup." Gabriela spread her hands over the

colorful pots and trays, the brushes and colored pencils. "We use it to paint your face, highlight your features, make you look even more beautiful than you do now."

It was my turn to look horrified. Back in Poland, the only women who went around with paint on their faces were the ones who were shunned by other women in the community for tearing apart marriages.

"Don't look so shocked," Gabriela chided. "I won't make you look like a lady of the night, if that's what you're afraid of."

It was like she could read my mind.

"I was going to ask you if you wanted to do your own, but now I realize what a mistake that would be." She put her hands on my shoulders and bent over to peer closely at my face. "Amazing skin. You don't even appear to be human, sometimes. You know that?"

Her statement jarred me, but she turned away and began picking up and putting down items from the vanity, making a selection.

I sat still and allowed Gabriela to have her way with my face. She rubbed strange-smelling creams into my skin, dusted me with powder, plucked stray hairs from my brows, drew lines on my eyes, painted on my eyelids with colored powders, and used a fine brush to apply color to my lips.

When she moved away from in front of the mirror, my breath caught in my throat. I barely recognized myself. My eyes looked absolutely enormous, and so deeply colored they appeared violet. My eyelashes were a dark thicket framing each eye, my normally pale cheeks were tinted with pink, and my lips reflected the light like they were wet.

"Do you like it?" Gabriela fiddled with one of the eye pencils nervously. "I can tone down the eyeshadow if you want. Actually, blue eyeshadow is the color most ladies are wearing these days, but with your skin tone, I think it'll just make you look bruised, so I went for brown and neutral hues. What do you think?"

Staring at the woman in the mirror who couldn't possibly be me, I didn't know what to say. For a long time, I just looked at her, taking in features of her face I hadn't even known were there before. Were my lips really so fat? Were my eyelashes really that thick? Were my cheekbones really so prominent?

No. I decided they weren't. Whatever magic Gabriela had done with her paints had created a different kind of face. I was a portrait of myself, almost a caricature. Swallowing, I glanced up at Gabriela where she was standing nervously at my elbow, looking into the mirror at her handiwork. Maybe it was okay that I didn't look like myself. After all, no one at the party would know my true identity except for Jozef. I would be the only siren in the room, disguised as a human, or maybe an Atlantean. I didn't know how many of each would be in attendance, but most certainly I would be the only mermaid.

I swallowed down any doubts I had about wearing paint and accepted that for the night of the party, I could pretend to be someone else. I could pretend to be human. It wasn't like I hadn't done it before.

"It's perfect," I said.

NINETEEN

Jozef had called the event his family was hosting a party, but as we walked through the massive double doors leading to the ballroom, I realized that it would have been more accurate to call it a ball. We'd just finished our elaborate dinner, served in a room next to the ballroom at four very long tables. The number of people seemed even larger as they milled about and stood in small groups on the parquet floor.

The silk-covered walls were decorated with ornately framed mirrors, many of which looked to be gilded with gold leaf. Chandeliers and oil paintings and portraits of aristocratic men and women added more ambience and wealth. A grand piano in one corner murmured soft classical background music, the pianist barely visible—just the balding wisps of gray hair could be seen over the sheet music. A small orchestra was arranged around the grand piano but none of the musicians were playing yet. I didn't think anyone felt like dancing, not with such full stomachs.

Jozef bent to whisper in my ear, pointing out the aristocrats and politicians in the group and making me laugh with his cheeky gossip.

"That's Mrs. Emily Pierre van Ermengem," he said, not pointing but clearly indicating with his eyes the woman in a short, snow-white cape trimmed with ermine over a red satin gown. "Notice how her face doesn't move?"

I had been looking at the red jewels encrusting the hem of her spectacular dress, but at Jozef's words my gaze shot up to the woman's equally spectacular face. She was a honey blonde, with a long neck and dark doe-eyes lined with thick lashes. Her petal-pink lips were a perfect heart shape, and her eyebrows were thick and dark, arching over those huge dark orbs. She was listening to the man at her side, their heads tilted close together. He said something funny and she burst out laughing, displaying perfect white teeth. Though she'd laughed, her eyes did not crinkle, her brow did not wrinkle, and her cheeks remained perfectly smooth—like a mask.

It was true, her face did not have any folds or shadows, though I wouldn't have noticed it if he hadn't pointed her out. "You're right, why doesn't it move?"

She was very beautiful, but now that Jozef had brought her lack of facial movement to my attention, I couldn't stop staring and for the wrong reason. Now she seemed like something at an exhibition.

"Her son isolated a crystal toxin from a bacterium called *Clostridium botulinum*, which can cause a paralytic illness." Jozef stood just behind me and spoke quietly into my ear, one hand at my waist. "He was able to isolate it and now uses it privately to freeze the muscles in the face which lead to wrinkles forming in the skin. Emily was one of his first patients."

"She voluntarily has bacteria injected into her face?" I was sure Jozef must be tricking me.

"Just the toxin, not the bacteria. She is nearly one hundred years old. When they finally get permission to go public with it, she'll be an excellent spokesperson. Don't you think?"

I just nodded my head. How much the world had changed, and yet, in some ways, not at all. Women had always gone to great lengths to preserve their beauty; it was just the first time I'd heard of anyone injecting something into their face to achieve this end.

"Is that her husband?" My gaze drifted to the man who was making her laugh.

"Oh no, her husband is over there." Jozef directed me to look to where an elderly gentleman was seated on a velvet chair, perched on the end. He seemed in deep and serious discussion with another younger man. "The man she's talking with is a chemist named Schlatter who is working on an artificial sweetener that he discovered by accident during an experiment."

Jozef continued to point out people and describe their considerable accomplishments, most of which involved developing a new technology or inventing something obscure but life-changing such as something called an ATM where people could withdraw money from a hole in the wall. My mind was buzzing. The things people had invented, the changes that had been made since the last time I'd been part of human society, were too incredible to be believed.

"Why are there so many inventors here?" I asked, taking a sip of my own champagne.

"They're friends of my father's, mostly," Jozef explained, pulling me close to him as a group of people passed by us. "My father gets all the periodicals and white papers from the best universities, laboratories, and think tanks in the world."

"Think *tanks*?" I blinked in surprise.

"Not actual tanks," Jozef chuckled. "It just means a body of experts. He likes to know what everyone is working on and when he finds someone with something he thinks is promising, he funds them." Jozef bobbed his head in a way that indicated there were strings attached to the funding. "For a percentage of the profits, naturally. My great-grandfather was very good at nosing out opportunities. He passed his knowledge on to my grandfather, and my grandfather passed it on to my father."

"And you? Will you be next?"

Jozef shifted his shoulders inside his dinner jacket, a little uncomfortable. "The investing nose passed to my sister, who is even now on a plane to London to meet with some researchers. I'm more interested in the natural world."

The sheer number of intelligent minds and accomplished inventors assembled in the ballroom kept me engaged and amazed for hours that evening. Then I realized I hadn't yet seen Claudius. My stomach did a nervous turn at the thought. Jozef had told me I had nothing to worry about, but how could I not be apprehensive when it came to Jozef's father?

I really hadn't cared much what the families of my previous mates thought of me because I'd been under the power of the siren mating cycle. I had one powerful biological need driving my actions—find a mate and have offspring. If my mate's family didn't like the union, that was their problem.

With Jozef, things were different. My love for him was not driven by a desire to make children with him, but by a genuine desire to be with him and near him. He made me laugh, made me feel good, and most importantly of all, I liked who I was when I was with him. If Jozef's father didn't like me, it made me sad for Jozef, who I knew would suffer emotionally because two people he cared about weren't getting along. The idea of being caught in the middle wasn't a nice one.

"Where is your father?" I turned to Jozef, my indigo gown swishing against my bare legs.

"He always arrives late to these things," Jozef answered. "Sometimes he doesn't come at all. He throws them as a sign of appreciation, and to ensure his network of high-functioning brains meets one another. I'm sure he'll be along." Jozef's eyes cut to me, filling with concern. "I told you not to worry about him, Bel. He'll be a perfect gentleman."

"The youngest Drakief, what a pleasure," said a smooth and oily voice from behind me.

Turning, I saw a tall, slender man in a top hat and a long coat with tails. He must have recently come in from the outdoors, as small beads of rain had gathered on the shoulders of his jacket. He leaned heavily on a cane of dark wood topped with a silver knob.

"Hello, Professor," said Jozef, taking the man's outstretched hand. "You sneaked in through the back again, did you?"

"I am rather lazy that way." The professor doffed his top hat in one silky motion and set it on the head of a passing waiter carrying a tray of drinks. Upon feeling the hat, the waiter stopped and waited patiently for the man to take off his outer wear, shifting the cane from one hand to the other. The professor lay his wet coat over the waiter's shoulder and patted it.

"Thank you, my good man," he said. Then he turned to me and reached for my hand. "And who might this vision of loveliness be?"

"This is Bel Novak," Jozef said. "Bel, this is Loukas Vasilakis."

"Let me guess, another brilliant inventor," I said as he took my hand and bent low over it.

Loukas let out a belly laugh which sounded a bit forced to my ears. "More of a researcher, my dear." As he straightened, his gaze fell on my aquamarine and his face seemed to freeze. His eyes locked on my gem for several moments before his eyes slid up my neck, over my lips, and on my eyes. My stomach sank and the sensation of déjà vu chilled my skin.

"My, what an interesting piece of jewelry you have there," Loukas drawled.

To my horror, Loukas lifted a thin-fingered hand and reached for my necklace. It was all I could do not to step away, but the sudden and warm presence of Jozef's hand on the small of my back stilled me.

Loukas picked up the gem, brushing my skin with his fingertips, then turned his hand open and let the aquamarine sit on his palm.

"Such a simple but elegant stone. It brings out the blue of your eyes so fetchingly. How funny it was your chosen adornment for this evening," Loukas said, his voice crawled over me like a pair of ghostly fingers.

I kept my face neutral but it took effort.

"It's become so interesting to me, this particular rock." He looked me in the eye again. "Perhaps we have some tastes in common. Perhaps we are," he tilted his head and his eyes narrowed just a little, "kindred spirits."

The way he was looking at me made me feel we were

anything but kindred. I could not stand him handling my property any longer and my hand went to my throat of its own accord, pulling the gem from his grasp by the chain. My own gaze felt flinty. "How beautiful this world would be," I replied, "if we could find a way to be kindred."

His eyes became hooded as he let his hand fall to his side.

I became aware of more than a few glances in our direction, and a few people were whispering behind their hands.

"I look forward to getting better acquainted with you, Miss Novak," Loukas said, though his tone suggested that an acquaintance with him wouldn't at all be to *my* liking. With a last look that promised this interaction was not likely to be our last, Loukas moved laboriously away into the crowd. The sound of his cane on the floor was a sharp retort with every step.

"Jozef?" My hand reached for his though my eyes felt locked on Loukas's back before he disappeared into a cloud of colored taffeta and tiaras.

"I'm here," he said, quietly.

"How many of your father's friends are human," I turned my eyes up to his, "and how many are Atlantean?"

Jozef looked surprised that I would ask. "We are nearly all Atlantean, Bel. There are only a few humans in my father's circle." He let out a slow sigh and I felt his fingers tighten around mine. "I feel I should apologize for my father's prejudice; it's one I find childish. Even after you explained about the war between us all those millennia ago, I find it so ridiculous that I can't really believe the ancient war and his feelings are associated. I'm very sorry, Bel. Please take some comfort in knowing that I do not share these feelings."

"No need to apologize," I whispered, squeezing his fingers back.

A cocktail of apprehension and anxiety had filled my belly, in spite of Jozef's comforting words. On land, I couldn't tell an Atlantean from a human, but it was clear that if an Atlantean was really paying attention, they could figure out I was Mer without too much effort—even under the layers of Gabriela's make-up.

More and more gazes were being directed my way. The interaction with Loukas made me feel that those looks were tinged with hostility, but was I imagining it? Looking back at those who put cold eyes on me, I realized that they weren't eyeing *me* in a mistrustful manner. Their gazes were directed at my gemstone. Some of them appeared to be squinting, or discreetly moving to afford themselves a better view.

My hands drifted up of their own accord, and found the clasp of my chain at the back of my neck. Taking the aquamarine off, I slipped it into my clutch and out of sight. I was bound to mingle with many more of Claudius's friends as the ball wore on, and I didn't want the gemstone to become a liability. I wanted these people to talk to me like I was one of them. How else could I broker peace between our nations unless I could get to know them as they were among themselves? But my gem made that impossible.

"Are you all right?" Jozef asked, after he'd watched me take off my necklace and hide it.

"I'm fine. Just wondering why my stone makes people so twitchy."

Jozef's face relaxed into something like regret. "There are prejudices that run deep all over the world. It can't be entirely unexpected, silly though it may seem. Look at how colonization of North America two hundred years ago has left a legacy of tension."

I had no idea what he was talking about, but I took comfort in the fact that I had time to learn. It was clear that I had an overwhelming amount of history to catch up on. The world had changed while I'd been living peacefully in the sleepy waters of Okeanos.

WHEN CLAUDIUS finally joined the party, the way he was heralded made him seem like royalty. In fact, part of me wondered if that's what Claudius was, among his own kind.

Jozef and I were waltzing when the band suddenly stopped playing the waltz, got to their feet, and began to play an anthem heavily dominated by the brass instruments. It was loud, pompous, and formal. Everyone who had been dancing stopped and began to clap, straining to see over the crowd as Claudius's presence was announced.

"Claudius Araneus Heracleon Drakief, Lord Commander, Savior and Knight of the great nation of Atlantis," the doorman bellowed, teeth bared and sparkling. He looked fit to have a heart attack from happiness and launched into a spasm of energetic applause.

I blinked at this ponderous title. Jozef looked down at me and winked as he clapped. Leaning over he whispered, "I know, it's a bit much."

"Savior and Knight? Lord Commander?" I whispered back. "What does that make you?"

"A little weak at the knees under the weight of expectation," he replied through the side of his mouth, then laughed.

"Do they really have expectations that you'll 'pick up

your father's mantle' and all that? I mean, you're not even in the same line of work."

"As he reminds me on a regular basis." Jozef's words might have sounded bitter except that I already knew Claudius had paved the way for Jozef's chosen career in oceanography.

The icy blast I received as Claudius's gaze found his son and then me standing beside him was completely personal. He loved his son dearly, that much was apparent. I supposed I should have been thankful that Jozef and I didn't have to meet secretively, but it was difficult to feel gratitude when I felt like all Claudius wanted was to gouge my eyeballs out, and for no reason other than a centuries-old conflict that neither of us had anything to do with.

I suddenly realized, as we stood there applauding Claudius, that if I could help Jozef's father to see that peace was possible between our people, then I would win all of his people, too. A man who was this popular, this well respected, and seen somehow as a savior and Lord Commander—he'd be the perfect place to start.

Claudius addressed the crowd briefly, welcoming everyone to his home and thanking them for their friendship. He was genial and comfortable in the limelight, but he didn't bore the crowd with a long-winded speech. Rather, he signaled to the band to take up their waltz and to the crowd to continue dancing and making merry.

Jozef took me in his arms as the waltz began and we commenced whirling around the room.

A familiar face passed by—a smiling woman whose features seemed familiar. As Jozef spoke in my ear about his ambitions for his work and his latest discoveries, I kept an eye out for a glimpse of this face.

I saw her again, smiling up into the face of her partner.

Thick dark curls nested at her neck and a green feather fixed in her hair arched gracefully up over her head and swayed as they danced. Once I'd seen the feather, I couldn't lose her.

Frowning, I was loathing to tear my eyes from her face, but had to as Jozef and I whirled about.

"You seem distracted, my love," Jozef said. "Shall I get you a glass of champagne? Perhaps time for a rest?"

I sent him a smile. "Thank you, that sounds good. I'll wait just here." I gestured to one of the red velvet chairs against the wall and stepped out of the milling crowd. Jozef kissed my hand and headed for the bar.

Now able to look for the woman in earnest, I found the green feather and homed in on her face. She was tantalizingly familiar, but evaded being identified, no matter how much I watched. The way her lips moved when she spoke, just a little crookedly. She was lovely. Older, with laugh lines and a few streaks of gray in her brunette hair.

By chance, she looked over her partner's shoulder to see me staring and the two of us locked eyes.

I smiled and waved, hoping she would come over and introduce herself—putting me out of my misery.

Her smile slowly dissolved as her brown eyes stayed glued to mine. Her partner said something to her and she didn't answer at first, so intent she was on me, and I on her.

Suddenly, she whispered something in her partner's ear, gave him a smile, and left him standing on the dance floor alone. She turned her back to me and made her way toward one of the many sets of open doors leading onto the terrace and gardens.

I went after her, not too quickly, but I didn't want to lose her. Dodging dancing couples, I watched as she disappeared through one of the doorways, green feather bobbing and waving.

Moments later, I emerged on the terrace. Couples and small groups stood about chatting, laughing, and swaying to the music. I scanned the heads for the green feather, but I didn't see it anywhere.

Several sets of stairs led down one level to the gardens—a huge patch of land relegated to a maze of rose bushes and other growing delights. The evening air was rich with perfume, both from the party attendees and the night blossoms.

The woman with the green feather was nowhere to be seen, and as much as I wanted to pinpoint who she was, and talk to her, I wasn't about to go running out into the garden to track her down and leave Jozef to wonder where I was.

Frowning, I turned back to the party and almost ran into Jozef. He handed me a glass of champagne.

"Good idea to catch a breath of fresh air. It's bloody hot in there, even with the doors open," he said, hooking a finger into his collar and pulling it away from his throat. He noticed my expression then. "Anything the matter?"

"There was a woman with a green feather in her hair. I had the strangest feeling that I knew her, but I couldn't remember where I'd met her."

"A green feather..." Jozef's expression went faraway as he thought about this. "A young woman?"

"Not a maid. A mature woman. Her features, though..." I put my fingertips to my forehead and wracked my brains. "She was so familiar. I'm certain I know her, but it just won't come. My memory is not very good at the best of times."

Jozef smiled. "I'm sorry, I don't recall seeing a woman in a green feather. There are a lot of..." he glanced at the women on the terrace, dressed like cupcakes and princesses, "feathers around. It'll come to you."

I nodded and smiled. "I'm sure it will."

But when it finally did come to me, it was too little, too late.

TWENTY

The day after the party, I just had entered Okeanos's inner ring and was making my way to Mount Califas when I caught a glimpse of the *Foniádes*. They appeared to be holding a struggling creature between them. Drawing near enough to make out the details, I realized with horror that it was a mermaid. This was not the way we handled our own kind, especially within our own borders, so why were they hanging on to her so tightly. And more importantly, was why she was struggling so hard to get away?

It was only when I got much closer that I realized the answer—this siren was salt-flush and she was trying to escape them because that is what any wild creature of the ocean would do. The *Foniádes* were taking her to the fresh-water pools under Mount Califas to bring her reason back.

"Wait," I called out, catching up to them. I unclasped the aquamarine from my neck. "This will make your job much easier, will it not?"

The question was a rhetorical one, and actually a kind way of reprimanding them. Sirens were reluctant to part with their gems, and for good reason, but there was no risk to a *Foniádes* if she parted from her gem for a few hours. It annoyed me that they were so hesitant to remove their gems from their bodies that none would loan hers to a salt-flush sister to end her primal state and make it easier to get her to safety.

Reaching for the salt-flush siren's hand, I uncurled her fingers and tucked my gemstone into her palm. Reflexively, and almost spasmodically, her fist closed around the gem and her body stiffened as her mind was returned. She relaxed then, but her gills were still working hard and I could hear her heart pounding rhythmically in her chest.

Only then did I recognize her. She was one of the last batch of volunteers that I had sent out searching for tritons. She was the first one to have returned home, though clearly, she had not been in control of her travels.

The *Foniádes*, with chastened expressions, released her and backed up to give her room to breathe.

"Better now?" I asked.

She nodded, clutching the gem. Her big, dark eyes made contact with mine and her shoulders dropped away from her ears as the relief settled in.

"Thank you, Sovereign." She held the gem out to me, but her reluctance to release it was obvious in the way her fingers curled around the stone.

"Keep it," I replied. "I'll get another."

The *Foniádes* shared a look at this. It made me realize that the gems were being thought of as a personal possession of the siren who had received it. Her gem belonged to her as much as her hair color or eye color did. Sirens often commissioned custom jewelry to set off their gem. But any of our stones would cure and protect any siren from the Salt Curse—so I wasn't particularly attached to mine. As Sovereign, I guarded Okeanos's supply of aquamarines.

They were kept in the Hall of Anamna and they were plentiful.

"How did you come to find her?" I asked the *Foniádes*, who drifted quietly in the background now.

"I discovered her just beyond the northern border, saw her in the distance, luckily. She came just close enough to be spotted but was swimming away from us, so lucky for her I caught a glimpse of her and recognized by her behavior that she'd gone flush." The *Foniádes* who was speaking had long dark hair tied at the top of her head into a tail and the sides of her head were shaved. "I had trouble bringing her in. She's stronger than she looks."

"I heard Ama calling and came to help," said a redheaded *Foniádes* with short, jagged hair. "First time I've ever seen a salt-flush siren so close to home. If Ama hadn't spotted her, she'd be headed into the North Atlantic. Who knows how long she was in that state?"

"Your name is Toni, right?" I asked, proud that after so many years gone, I could remember.

She nodded, looking pleased as well that I'd remembered.

"Welcome home, Toni," I said. "I'm sorry for your suffering. Why don't we get you into the sweet water under the mountain and then we can talk? I think, from your look, you have quite a story to tell."

AFTER TONI HAD BATHED in the freshwater pools and drunk her fill, she came to find me at the base of Mount Califas. I sat on a moss-covered stone at the edge of a deep lagoon filled with flashing fish and watched as Nike and Toni picked their way over to me. I had retrieved a new aquamarine and wore it on a silver chain snug around my throat.

Word spread quickly that a missing siren had returned home, but she'd done so without a gem and she'd needed to be rescued.

Toni was wearing a simple, knee-length robe belted at the waist, the kind we had multiples of near the freshwater pools for any who wished to wear one. Nike was in her chosen state whether she was in siren form or human form—naked, and skin glistening with damp. They each chose a stone and settled down.

The sun was journeying toward the horizon and had turned the sky into a rainbow of colors. Toni closed her eyes as the light of the evening sun touched her face, basking in the feeling of the warmth and energy she hadn't felt in too long.

She opened her eyes and looked at me. "What I have to say will alarm you, Sovereign." Her eyes were not nearly so dark as they'd appeared underwater, but a verdant green and full of worry. "If you would like this information to stay secret, I recommend we talk alone."

Her eyes darted to Nike and back at me. Toni had the natural hesitance that all of the sirens of Okeanos had for the blue-haired sorceress who was the same but not the same.

"It's all right." I gave her what I hoped was a reassuring smile, for her words had set me on edge. "Nike is my closest confidante. Whatever you have to say can be said in front of her."

Toni nodded and swallowed. She stretched out long legs and set her feet in the pool.

"Before you begin," I asked, "do you know how long it's been since you left us?"

She nodded. "Lia told me. I've lost sixteen years to the Salt." She raised her eyes to meet mine again. "I was somewhere around the horn of Africa when I was attacked. There were three of them. I had no reason to fear them, based on my experience with those in our waters. But they didn't look much like the ones I'd seen before. I was curious, and they looked friendly."

"Who did?" Nike asked before I could.

Without taking her gaze from mine, she answered, "Atlanteans."

A cold feeling swept my forearms, raising hair and gooseflesh. "You were attacked by Atlanteans?"

"I know it's hard to imagine any siren, even a thin one like me, being overtaken by any Atlantean. But like I said, they weren't like the ones I had seen before. These were strong, fit, muscular. Their expressions were intelligent, but also calculating. They were talking and laughing while giving the appearance of traveling. They had weapons and strange clothing."

"Giving the appearance of fishing?" I echoed. "You think they lured you? That it was a trap?"

"I know it was."

"The clothing," I shifted forward on my rock seat and look into Toni's face. "What did it look like?"

"Almost all black and skin-tight. One of them had stripes down the sides of his legs, and another had them down his arms. The stripes were such a bright color, like the most vivid tropical fish you could imagine. The last one wore all black, simple and uninteresting. The clothing was fastened with a long zipper. If I hadn't already known it was modern from the texture of it, the zipper would have confirmed it for me. I remember the first time I ever found a zipper. It was on clothing caught in the coral. I played with it for hours."

"And the weapons?" Nike's brows were drawn with worry.

"They were like spear-fishing guns, like the rusted ones we have in the cave closest to the grotto. I was here the day someone brought it in so I knew what they looked like. Still," she shook her head, "I did not fear them. I know we're natural enemies, but I had never heard of an Atlantean attacking a siren, and we were nowhere near Okeanos so I had no reason to have a quarrel with them."

"Go on."

"They were laughing and seemed friendly. When they saw me in the distance, they waved at me and one of them beckoned me over."

At this, Nike tore her eyes away from Toni to look at me. The alarm in her expression had only grown, and it matched the quiver of apprehension growing in my own gut. I was thinking of Jozef and the other Atlanteans—healthy and fit Atlanteans. But the ones Toni was speaking of were so far from Okeanos, we had no idea who they were or where they were from.

"When I drew close, they attacked. Two of them held my arms while the other"—Toni took a shuddering breath—"the other took my pendant. I felt helpless not just from their strength, but also from pure shock. It was over so quickly. Suddenly, they had my gem and they were gone. They turned tail and disappeared into the blue, in three different directions.

"I took off after one of them," Toni said, rubbing her hands over her face and pushing her hair back from her forehead. "I chased him for a long time, but he was always just out of reach, and he was..."

She paused and her eyes seemed to glaze over and she appeared to be looking at something far away.

"What?" I nudged her gently.

"He was laughing." Her gaze snapped back to me and anger darkened them. Her eye teeth extended a little, caught the light of the sunset, and gleamed. "Like it was a game for him."

She shook her head, her anger palpable. "I never caught him, and even if I had, there was only a one in three chance that he had my gem. At first, I hoped it was a joke, that they were just playing with me. But when none of them came to find me and give back my gemstone, I realized it was intentional, what they'd done."

"Why would they do something like that unless they understood what it meant?" Nike asked, quietly, thoughtfully. She looked from Toni to me. "It's like they *wanted* her to go flush."

Toni nodded. "I continued to search for them, hoping to run across more Atlanteans—if not the three males themselves—so I could get my gem back. I didn't know what to do. By the time I turned tail and headed for home, I was already losing my mind."

Her lower chin quivered and she put her face in her hands as she remembered. "I don't know where I was in the world when I lost my ability to think rationally, but somehow, sixteen years later..."

Her voice broke and she looked up, her expression a hybrid of gratitude and profound sadness.

"By chance you came close enough to our borders to be found," Nike finished for her.

Toni nodded. She looked from me to Nike and back again, confusion etched on her brow. "Why would they do that to me? Was it just a cruel prank?"

Nike was nailing me with a glare.

"It was not personal to you, Toni," she said through a tight jaw. "You're just one of many sirens who have not returned home in many years. Our numbers are dwindling because mermaids who go out on mating cycles are staying away for longer than ever before."

"And the last group you sent out to look for tritons?" Toni queried, an alarm growing on her face. "Have any of them returned?"

Nike shook her head and I said, "No. Just you so far."

Toni's face crumpled. "But this is a disaster. It cannot be. Something is dreadfully wrong. What if I am not the only one this has happened to? What if my sisters are lost in the world's oceans, too? Stripped of their gems, we might never recover them! We have to do something!"

"We will." I tried to keep my voice soothing and calm. I was anything but calm, and my imagination was more than likely creating a worse scenario than what was actually happening. At least, I hoped it was. "I will make an investigation. There are a few people I can ask."

"People?" Toni cocked her head.

"Atlanteans," I explained. "In spite of what happened to you, we have been at peace with them. They are allowed within the ring of our outermost border, and they're allowed to fish there and forage for food. I've been getting to know some of them." I didn't say that I had really only had success getting to know one of them. I didn't want to make her feel worse.

Toni's eyes were growing wider and wider.

"You've just been through a traumatic event, perpetuated by what I'm hoping were rogue Atlanteans with a view to making mischief for a species they've never been at peace with until recently. We haven't had any problems with Atlanteans in the length of time you've been gone."

"Not that we were aware of, anyway," Nike murmured.

"You are the Sovereign," said Toni, eyes still wide, "so I trust that you know things the rest of us do not. The Salt chose you for a reason."

"Thank you." I reached over and put my palm on top of her hands where they still clenched her knees. "I will get to the bottom of it."

Toni nodded. "May I go back to the freshwater pools now? It's all I want at this moment."

"Of course."

She stood, then kissed her fingers and placed them at my throat in a gesture of respect.

As she turned to leave, I asked, "Did you ever find any tritons, before you had your gem taken from you?"

Toni looked over her shoulder with one foot on the edge of the pool. She shook her head, her eyes sad. "Not a one."

TWENTY-ONE

It was the evening of the following day when I arrived at Drakief Manor. The sun was just slipping below the choppy surface of a restless Atlantic. I had been through the Strait of Gibraltar enough times now to be acquainted with its predictable currents and wave patterns. When swimming from Okeanos to Gibraltar, I rode high in the Atlantic waters where the less salty majority continuously flowed east. When heading back to Okeanos, I would ride the deeper, saltier Mediterranean tidal flows which consistently ebbed west. These natural highways allowed me to get to and from Jozef's home much more quickly than the first few trips I had made on my own. Now that I'd figured it out, it was an easy commute.

Taking the steps up to the large wrap-around porch, my heart was heavy and my mind was buzzing like a beehive. A good measure of hope blossomed in my chest that Jozef might have some light to shed on things.

Gabriela opened the front door before I even had time to knock.

"Can I fetch you some tea?" she asked as the door creaked shut behind me.

"No, thank you, Gabriela. I'm here to see Jozef, and it's rather urgent. Where is he?"

She frowned, her forehead creasing. "I haven't seen him since early this morning, so I'm not sure. Please wait in the parlor while I find out."

"Sure, but do you mind if I wait in the library instead?"

"As you wish, Miss Bel." Gabriela bustled away, leaving me to find my own way to the room I thought Jozef was most likely to be in. As I pushed into the library, however, I was met only by the sound of the grandfather clock. No lights sent their usual soft glow over the spines and nooks of the library. The fireplace was cold, and long shadows sent their fingers across the floor.

I took a seat on one of the couches and waited for Gabriela.

In a matter of two or three minutes, footsteps in the hall preceded her entrance.

"I'm sorry, Miss Bel," she said, stepping inside the library but not approaching me. "Apparently, Jozef is out and won't be back for a couple of hours. You're welcome to wait here for him; I know he'd be put out with me if I let you leave."

I smiled at the woman. "Don't worry, I'll wait for him. I don't mind keeping occupied until he returns."

She nodded. "Can I bring you anything while you wait? Some tea?"

"No thank you," I declined a second time.

It seemed to me that Gabriela was nervous about something. Nervous and distracted.

"Don't let me keep you from your duties," I said. "I know this house wouldn't run without you."

She let out of a sigh of relief and gave me another smile. Then she gestured to the bell-pull beside the door. "Thank you, Miss Bel. Don't hesitate to ring if you change your mind."

I nodded my thanks.

Gabriela closed the door behind her and I was left alone. I tried to find something to read, but I couldn't concentrate. I looked at Jozef's artwork, but I'd seen it all many times before. I grew restless. The room was stuffy and smelled of dust.

Getting to my feet, I crossed the library to the rear exit, which I knew opened into a large courtyard that wound its angular way to the back yard. Opening the door, I slipped outside and took a deep breath.

The courtyard was drowsy with insects and blossoms closing up shop for the night. The air was clean and humid, and the songs of nightingales drifted softly on a gentle breeze. There was a sense of peace in the garden that I desperately needed. I walked the curling path, enjoying the scent of flowers and the sound of evening activity among the creatures who made their home in the manor's grounds.

Looking up, I noticed a light in the windows of an upper level. The faintest sound of trickling water reached my ears and I paused, listening. A shadow moved across the grass and I looked up to see the silhouette of a large man in one of the lighted windows. He was broader at the shoulder than Jozef and Claudius, and appeared to be looking down at me, but I couldn't tell for certain as his features were lost in darkness. He moved away from the window.

The sound of trickling water grew louder. I frowned and cocked my head, trying to discern its source. It sounded like a good amount of water; in fact, it sounded like some kind of serious leak. I thought it was coming from the rearmost wing of the Manor, a place I had never been, since the rooms Jozef used were near the front of the house.

Curious, and hoping there wasn't some broken pipe or other major problem, I moved toward the sound. I followed the narrow path down toward the rear wing, which I realized as I drew close, did not attach to the rest of the house. At least, it didn't attach by any visible link; there might have been an underground hallway. But to the outsider looking in, this outbuilding seemed isolated and not in use. The thick wooden shutters on all the windows were closed up. The building looked abandoned.

The sound of trickling water grew louder, but it was still muffled and seemed to be coming from below. The sound of the leak drew me to an exterior basement door. At the bottom of a good twenty steps into the ground, a wooden door sat on crooked hinges. The sound was definitely louder, and my curiosity to pinpoint the source was nearly overwhelming.

"Hello?" I called to the yard and building in general.

Taking the steps down to the door, I called out again. The only sound to answer was the incessant stream of water, which sounded bubbly now that I was closer.

Reaching for the old metal latch, I turned it and opened the door. Cold, dank air wafted out, smelling of must and seaweed and salt. I called out again, but without much hope for a reply. The place had the feel of emptiness.

There was an answer, just not one I was expecting. A dull thump met my ears. Soft but solid sounding, and definitely not my imagination.

"Anyone here?" I peered into the darkness, feeling for some reason that I should explain my presence in this basement.

"I hear a leak," I called, and felt kind of stupid afterward. I wasn't snooping, I was trying to be helpful. This was true, but I was also overcome with curiosity, the calling card of a siren. I knew that a human might have possessed some small amount of trepidation or fear in this circumstance. The place was spooky, there was no denying it. But I was not frightened, only inquisitive.

Thump, thump.

I frowned and stepped inside. Flicking the lone light switch beside the door flooded the room with white light from three bulbs hanging on bare wire from a low ceiling.

Letting the door drift shut behind me, I walked slowly into the room, taking in everything. Three long, metal tables lay in front of me, covered in paperwork, books, strange instruments, and what looked from a distance like sketches and maps. Two bookshelves filled with titles of all shapes and sizes bracketed a closed door.

The sound of running water was louder now, and it was coming from the other side of that door.

"Hello?" I called.

There was no answering thump this time. I crossed to the doorway and reached for the doorknob only to find the door was locked.

My eye fell on the spines of the books and I discovered that very few of them were in English, and many of them appeared to be in very old languages. I knew what classical Greek, Hebrew, and Latin looked like and there were titles in all of these languages as well as several other languages I didn't recognize.

Scanning the room, I took in some of the items on one of the metal tables. My heart gave an initial lurch as my gaze landed on a scientific sketch of something I could easily identify.

Pulling the drawing closer, I took a better look. The

sketch was very detailed, rendered in black ink on parchment. It was a cross-section of a set of gills. The inner workings of the gill had been carefully documented and reproduced here, obviously for scientific study.

The drawing reminded me a little of the kind Jozef did, but the hand which had produced this one was clearly not his. I had become well acquainted with Jozef's touch with a pen. This drawing had been done in thicker, harsher strokes. Also, I couldn't recall seeing any of the *insides* of a sea creature in Jozef's work, only the *outsides*.

Someone had to have dissected a fish bit by bit to make a drawing this detailed. I wasn't entirely surprised at having found such a drawing, though initially my body had a reaction to seeing a body part—a body part I was intimately familiar with—drawn in this way.

A jar on the far end of the table caught my eye and I took a closer look at it, now ignoring the sound of running water since it was behind a door I didn't yet have a key to. I made a note to ask Jozef about it when I saw him.

Picking up the jar, I peered at the contents. It was a jellyfish specimen, suspended in liquid and clearly dead and well preserved. A label on the bottom of the glass was written in a language I didn't recognize. I had seen this specimen alive in my travels many times, though only in very deep and dark water.

Another large drawing, just peeking out from underneath a pile of papers and books, caught my eye. The drawing was large and what I could see showed a beautifully done sketch of a fin. Brushing the books and papers aside to get a better look, I uncovered the full length of the work. The blood in my veins turned to ice as my eyes devoured the image.

It was a mermaid.

But it wasn't the fact that it was a drawing of a mermaid that made my body run cold and dread fill my stomach like lead. This mermaid had been cut open from breastbone to the base of her fin. The skin had been pulled aside to reveal her organs and the organs had been drawn and labeled while they were in place. Small arrows in red ink marked up every organ and major artery, small blue arrows followed her airways and lungs as well as to the sides of her neck where her gills were. She had no face, for the drawing stopped at the neck. The labeling of her innards above the pubic bone were numerous and written in both Latin and English, and many of them were labeled with the small notation, *identical*. Identical to what? To a human? To an Atlantean?

Small, hand-written text underlined with very straight lines leading from the various parts labeled the spinal cord, spleen, liver, gallbladder, ovaries, bladder, intestine, lateral line, and the list went on and on with parts I had never even heard of, like pyloric caeca, and olfactory bulb. From the ovaries and down had less labeling, and the striations and placement of the tail muscles were only partially drawn.

There was only one way anyone could have made this drawing, and it was the same way it had been achieved for every other species that had ever been studied.

Someone had captured, killed, and dissected a siren. And they'd done it in Jozef's house.

TWENTY-TWO

A small notebook near the drawing caught my eye. It was lying open and I spotted the word *mermaid*. I picked it up and studied the barely discernible scrawl on the pages.

Siren/triton cross equals Mer of either gender. Siren/human cross results in a human male, or a mermaid (always female). Triton/human cross results in Atlantean of either gender. Atlantean/Atlantean results in Atlantean of either gender. Atlantean/human results in either human or Atlantean of either gender. Atlantean/siren results in ?.

I read this over and over again, studying it through tight eyes and with a rising heart rate. Someone had to have made all of these hybrids to have this information, unless it was simply conjecture. My eyes were repeatedly drawn to: *Siren/triton = Mer of either gender*. So, whoever was responsible for all of this research knew that tritons existed at one time, and they knew that only the union of a mermaid and merman could result in a male Mer. So why couldn't we find any? Where *had* all the tritons gone? More imminently important, which one of the Drakief family friends or colleagues were responsible for these studies?

Memory took me back to the party where I had shaken the hand of the particularly cold and sordid Loukas. "*More of a researcher*," he'd said, leaning over his cane like a wilting tower.

I wished now I'd asked him more specifically about his research.

Thump.

The sound jarred me out of the shadow of horror that had swallowed me. I dropped the book and whirled to face the door. Rage rushed through me, heating my face as I guessed at what was likely making the sound. The trickling sound of the water on the other side of the locked door had become a menacing, insidious noise, and the dull thuds were a cry for help. My heart vaulted up my windpipe as I wondered if it was a triton.

Taking a deep breath, I lifted one foot, turned sideways to the door, and slammed my heel into the wood. My fury-fueled kick splintered the door off its hinges and broke it down the middle in one long jagged gash.

The ghastliness within the room was another blow that would have sent me wheeling physically back if I hadn't already been so enraged.

The trickling water fed an aquarium, and in the aquarium was not a triton but another siren—one of *my* sirens.

The rest of the room was lined with metal shelving covered with boxes and instruments. A large metal table with two gutters along the sides sat beside a tray laid out with menacing tools and instruments.

Running to the aquarium, I put my hand on the glass and peered at the pitiful creature inside. To my eyes, she was pitiful, but I supposed it was some small mercy that she was salt-flush. This was one of the sirens who had not come back from her mating cycle. I didn't know her name, but I knew her face.

She barely had room to turn around in the tank, and the thump against the glass confirmed the source of the sound. When she saw me, she backed away from me, her eyes darting back and forth and her gills moving, drawing oxygen from the bubbles fed by a tube into her cage. Her pupils were dilated and her expression vacant of intelligence. I wondered how long she'd been here.

The top of the aquarium was a thick metal lid locked into place at each corner with a padlock. I grabbed one of the padlocks and inspected it. I needed something I could use for leverage. Looking back at the table full of tools, I crossed to it and found a hooked pick with a thick metal handle. I didn't think it would hold. I put it down and scanned the room. The tools were too short and thin. I had the strength to bend some metals if I had enough leverage. What I needed was a long bar that was thin enough to go through the padlock loop and strong enough to break the lock.

I gave a cry of frustration when nothing could be found. A sense of urgency rose in my belly, cold and quivering. Jozef would be home soon, and how would I greet him with what I'd discovered? There was no way he knew about this; the very idea filled my whole body with adrenalin. I fully rejected that Jozef had any part in this.

I was taking this siren back to Okeanos with me and there would be nothing and no one to stop me short of a bullet. How long had she been here? Had they already tortured her in some way? How had they captured her?

Going back to the outer room, I frantically scanned the space again for something I could use. I let out a hiss of satisfaction when I found an emergency fire cabinet containing an extinguisher and an axe. Smashing the glass face with my elbow, I wrenched the axe from its holder and returned to the caged siren.

The thought occurred to smash the glass with the axe, but I took the risk of hurting the siren as she slid out and landed in all the broken shards. Instead, I used the sharp end to chop at the padlocks and break them. The sounds of my efforts echoed in the room like gunshots. Having broken the front two padlocks, I dropped the axe and pried the heavy metal lid upward. Grunting, I pushed the lid slowly up and up, inching along beside the aquarium to take the lid to fully open. It fell back against the wall behind it with a clang.

The siren inside wiggled and tried to dart around, but succeeded only in thumping the glass sides and probably bruising herself in multiple places in the process.

With shaking fingers, I reached behind my neck to unclasp the aquamarine at my neck. Lowering it into the water I dangled the gem from the chain and held my breath as it made contact with her skin.

There was a sound of a muffled scream and the siren's whole body spasmed. She twisted in the tank, sending a big wave of water over me and out the front of the aquarium. It splashed across the floor. Her hand darted to the gem and her fingers clutched it like it was a lifeline—which it was.

She thrashed and rolled over again. Pushing herself against the aquarium, she thrust herself upward and her torso shot toward me. A pair of cold wet arms wrapped themselves around my neck and she pressed her heart against mine and held on like it meant her very life if she let go. I wrapped my arms around her and just held her, my chin trembling at what she had suffered.

She was panting in my ear, her chest heaving, and I could feel her heart thumping wildly against my own.

I glanced down her glistening back to see that she'd already transformed into her human shape. I could see the knobs of her spine and the wasted curve of her buttocks. She was painfully thin.

"It's all right now," I said gently, and felt her arms tighten around me like she was afraid I was going to let her go. "I'm going to take you home. I won't let anyone else hurt you."

I let her cling to me until the urgency told me we couldn't afford to waste any more time.

"It's not safe here, we need to go." I patted her gently on the back. "I know you've been through a terrible ordeal."

I pulled on her arms, pulling her back enough that we could see one another's face.

"I need you to walk," I said. "Can you do that?"

She nodded. Her brown eyes were haunted and huge, her tawny skin tinged with yellow, and her nails had grown to a length that would make using her hands impossible.

"Let me put this on you." I touched her closed fist where the long nails pressed against the pad of her hand and her wrist. She opened her hand and I took the necklace. Her eyes never left it until they had to, as the gem settled under her chin and against her collarbones. She put a hand to it and looked up at me.

She spoke for the first time. "How did you know where to find me?"

"I found you by accident," I replied grimly.

She let me lift her from the tank and put her on the ground, where her legs buckled and I had to catch her.

"What is your name?" I asked as I grabbed one of the

sheets from a stack of them on the shelf below the metal dissection table.

"Fimia," she replied, her voice tremulous.

"Fimia," I repeated. "I'm Bel."

She gave a small smile and it warmed my heart. She was not so gone that she couldn't find a smile, which meant everything to me.

"I know who you are, Sybellen. I am not sure what astounds me the most," she said, articulating her words in a crisp way that made me wonder if she'd had an upper-class education somewhere, "the fact that I've been rescued, or the fact that it was done by our Sovereign."

I nodded. Of course she knew who I was.

The sound of men's voices in the distance made us both look towards the door. Putting my hands on her shoulders I said, "I need you to gather your strength. We might encounter some resistance to my taking you away from here."

I went to the tap, grabbed a glass jar sitting upside down in the dishrack, and filled it with freshwater. I tasted it to make sure it was clean. Returning to Fimia, I gave it to her and bade her drink. She swallowed the entire jar in a moment and asked for another, which I fetched her. The shaking in her legs seemed to lessen and she stood up a little straighter, under her own power.

She wrapped herself up in the sheet and we left the room and headed for the door. On the way out the door, I spotted a hat stand and a set of hooks with a few white lab coats on them. I grabbed the nearest one—with two pens clipped to the chest pocket—and gave it to her. She discarded the sheet and pulled the lab coat on, doing up a couple of the buttons. She crossed her arms over her waist. Hugging herself like that, she looked like a little girl.

I kept her behind me as we climbed the stairs and emerged from the basement into a dark but star-speckled sky. A partial moon glimmered overhead, half buried behind a swathe of choking clouds.

Taking her hand, I led her across the lawn in the direction of the water. We passed through a circle of light thrown by a garden lamp in the center of a rose garden. A fountain and pool encased in a round concrete reservoir reflected the lamplight.

"Hey, there! What are you doing?" called a strong and heavily accented male voice from the second-floor balcony.

"Run," I hissed at Fimia, pulling her in front of me and shoving her toward the water. "You can smell the ocean. Go!"

"What about you?" She clutched at the jacket with one hand and her other hand reached back for me.

"I'll be right behind you. Go! Now!"

"It doesn't have to be like this," she whispered, her eyes on the verge of panic. "Our voices, we can stop them."

There were sounds of pounding feet and slamming doors. More yelling. They were coming for us.

"No, we can't. They're Atlanteans. Now, run!"

As she made a courageous wobbling sprint in the direction of water, I saw three men running across the garden toward us. One veered to follow Fimia, and the other two came for me.

"Take them alive," called another, older voice from an upper window in the manor. Though I'd never heard him shout, I thought that voice sounded an awful lot like Loukas. "Do not let them get away!"

TWENTY-THREE

The two coming toward me slowed as they saw that I wasn't running like Fimia. I wasn't sure exactly what I was going to do, but I scooped up a fist-sized rock from the fountain feeding the knee-deep pools flanking the garden's main walk. The rough weight of the stone in my hand gave me a little more confidence, and that fed my angry fire.

I stole a glance at Fimia, running but still so weak, and my anger bloomed into something terrible and bright.

"Time to go back inside, little one," drawled the bigger of the two men, taking the time to roll up his sleeves as he sauntered forward. "We don't want to hurt you."

One look in his cold, dark eyes told me he didn't much care one way or another if he hurt me, and his shark-like grin only made me madder.

"But I want to hurt you," I growled, hefting the stone. My tone took on multiple pitches as my siren voice blossomed and bulged at the base of my throat. I couldn't have stopped it even if I'd wanted to. "Don't take another step or I'll show you how much."

The man just laughed, but to my surprise the other, a burly man in khakis with a dark beard, actually stopped dead in his tracks. I homed in on his face and realized from how blank his expression had gone that he was actually *human*. My heart tripped with hope.

I dared to ignore the other as he advanced, still smiling, and focused my words and attention on the bearded man.

"Help me." My siren voice pitched up, burgeoned and deepened. Leveling a finger at the other man, I commanded the human, "Stop him."

The Atlantean's shark-face had just enough time to register an 'oh shit' expression before the big bearded human tackled him from behind.

Both men hit the paving stones of the garden path hard and then they were grappling and rolling across the ground. The Atlantean would dominate, but he'd been caught off guard and the bearded man drove his meaty fists against his colleague like pistons. Win or lose, Sharky's smile was losing a few teeth.

There was a wounded grunt as Sharky threw an elbow into bearded man's face, and then the two of them tumbled into the pool beside the path. Water splashed everywhere and the two men became a single soaked, thrashing mess. In the precious moments I'd bought, I turned and bolted after Fimia.

"What are you two *doing*?" Loukas belted from the same door the men had emerged from. Looking over my shoulder, I saw another sturdy man in a madras shirt with oily blond hair. He squeezing past Loukas, his eyes fixed on me.

Loukas shouted while shaking his cane in the air and leaning on the doorjamb. "Stop them, you idiots!"

"Peter is a freakin' accountant!" the blond bellowed by way of explanation as he took off across the grass. He leapt a hedge while closing the gap between us much too quickly for comfort. A wild thought flitted through my mind at this strange statement. So, what? Atlanteans didn't like numbers, so they'd hired a human?

Ahead of me ripped a high, feminine scream. My head jerked up, scanning for her in the shadowy darkness. Fimia shrieked again, closer to me this time, angry and scared all at once. She'd been caught. I could make out her thin struggling form against a broad-shouldered hulk with his arms wrapped around her.

Spinning suddenly toward the Atlantean hot on my heels, I hurled my rock straight at his face. He gave a startled cry and tucked his head down. The rock cracked against the edge of his eye socket and his feet tangled underneath him. He went down. His hands were too busy with his face to catch his fall, but he twisted, skidding on his shoulder across the grass.

I skipped out of the way and sprinted in the direction of Fimia's struggling figure. Hurdling over more narrow pools and an iron bench, I skirted a thick and thorny rose bush.

"Release her," my siren voice boomed.

It was worth a shot, but the Atlantean did no such thing.

He was shorter than me, but his heavy, slab-muscled arms had no problem hauling Fimia around. He directed a chilling laugh at me as he dragged her back toward the abandoned wing with the lab in the basement. Fimia's overgrown nails feebly clawed toward his face, and her thin legs squirmed and kicked under the lab coat.

"Let go!" I roared as I threw my body into a charging

punch that took him across the ear. The shock of the blow radiated painfully up through my wrist and into my arm.

He let go of Fimia as he staggered backward, clutching at the side of his head and swearing bitterly.

Fimia fell flat on the grass. I rushed to her and reached down to haul her back to her feet.

"Run!" I gave her a little push that sent her stumbling toward the water again.

The large man recovered more quickly than I'd anticipated, and I caught a fleeting glimpse of his furious face before light and pain exploded across mine.

I didn't lose my footing from the blow, but it was all I could do to keep upright. I tasted blood in my mouth and spat to clear it.

My senses were clearing, and I gave a step or two as he began to advance on me. I felt the rose bush catch at the back of my arms.

The Atlantean glared at the bloody spittle on his fancy leather shoes. Then he gave an ugly snarl as he rushed at me. I gasped a quick breath and spun just as his outstretched paws made to grab at my face and neck. He barreled past me and I sent him on his way into the rosebush with a backward kick into his meaty posterior. His growling became a shriek of pain as he crashed into the thorns.

Looking into the gloom toward the rocky coastline, I made out Fimia picking her way over the jagged rocks. Waves pounded against the craggy shore, calling us both to the safety of the water.

I turned to see the man, still trapped in the thorns, glaring at me as he savagely ripped at the branches and creepers which entangled him.

Just past him was the iron bench.

I rushed toward him, my shoulder bent low. His feet bound together in the rose bush's thorny hold, as my shoulder check sent him tumbling backward. He crashed free of the rose bush and smashed face-first into bench. His head snapped backward as a metallic clang rattled the frame of the weighty bench. His body went as limp as a stringless marionette, his face still pitched up against the bench.

Hearing the slap of wet shoes on grass and angry shouts had me diving for the shadows. The mechanical sound of a pistol chambering a round galvanized me into action. I bolted, clearing the low wall in one leap and skittering over the rocks like a crab.

My siren hearing picked out Loukas's voice, now almost pleading. "I need both of them back! Both! Do you hear me? Once they're in the water you'll never catch them!"

Layers of skin came off my palms and knees as I scrambled over the rough terrain. Loukas may have wanted us alive, but the fact that a gun was out meant they might be too angry to follow orders. What do you do with a gun besides shoot it? And how many people were a good enough shot to intentionally shoot to maim? My own breath was a ripping sound in my ears, my heart a writhing, panicked muscle. The sound of that gun was like flames licking at the soles of my feet.

Clambering over the last of the big rocks, I spotted Fimia at the water's edge. The lab coat flapped around her body like soiled, ghostly sails. She was clearly torn, looking back and forth from the shore to the water and back again; she didn't want to leave me behind.

"Fimia," I hissed as loud as I dared, scuttling across the rock. "Go!"

Her eyes, huge with terror, found me as I thumped

down onto the pebbly sand only a dozen strides from her. The sound of footsteps was so close behind me that I was afraid to look back. My limbs shook with shock and exertion, my muscles burning.

"Go!" I called a little louder, glad to be off the exposed surface of the rocks. "I'm here now! Swim!"

Not looking back was a mistake.

Pain exploded across the back of my head. The blow sent me face-first into the pebbly sand. So there *was* something you could do with a gun besides shoot it.

The world reeled as colorful lights popped like New Year's crackers behind my eyes. Nothing I saw made sense. The sound of waves crashing seemed to come from everywhere. I tried to get up, but the world was crooked. I stumbled and fell, hitting the beach, which my confused mind thought was in the other direction. I expected the fiery, tearing pain of a bullet at any moment, but a fist took me hard in stomach instead, knocking the wind out of me. The world was a spinning blur of blacks and blues. I gasped for air.

"I got one!" a voice shouted above me, and a second later I heard that same voice give a shocked cry. There was the sound of something heavy splashing into the water.

Still dragging in wheezing breaths, my clearing eyes saw one of the Atlanteans standing over me with Fimia on his back, pounding her fist over and over into his face. The gun was nowhere to be seen. They yelled in unison.

As the siren raised her hand again, I saw the jagged end of a broken pen jutting from the bottom of her fist. The same hand holding the pen sported three ragged fingertips where her overgrown nails had broken off.

The pen-punctured Atlantean flailed his arms and managed to get a handful of Fimia's lank hair in his fist. He dragged her pathetically small frame off his back and threw her onto the ground. His cheek was a mess from the stabbing pen, but his eyes were wild with rage as he lunged. His hands closed tight around her thin neck, squeezing off Fimia's cries.

Reaching for something, anything, I took a fistful of sand and hurled it into his enraged eyes.

He snarled as his hands left Fimia's neck to paw at his face. She collapsed onto the beach. With whatever strength Fimia had left, she rolled over and scrambled toward the water.

I kicked out, driving my heel into the side of his knee. The Atlantean lost his balance and toppled, cracking his head on a boulder. He hit the ground like a sack of rocks and didn't move.

Still a little unsteady, I used the rocks for support and levered myself to my feet. My vision was finally clearing, my equilibrium returning. A dull ache spread across the back of my head and I reached up as I ran toward the crashing waves, wincing at the lump growing there.

Fimia glanced back one last time, saw I was behind her, and dove. Her bony back disappeared as she plunged into an oncoming wave. The crack of a pistol sounded behind me. I was already running when another bullet buzzed past me like a hornet from hell, disappearing into the rolling waves.

An instant later, I did the same.

THREE SETS of wide eyes stared at me. Targa clutched a pillow against her stomach, wrinkling the fabric with tense white fingers. A sheen of sweat glistened from Antoni's wide brow while one arm rested around Targa's shoulders, his hand gripping her upper arm tightly.

Several long moments later, Emun was the first to move, taking a sip of water from the glass on the table beside him.

"What if they'd caught you?" Targa wheezed on dry air, and at the sound, Antoni reached for a glass of water also and handed it to her. She drank, greedily.

"But they didn't," I replied. "We made it back to Okeanos alive and in one piece."

"Those maniacs," Emun ground out, "dissecting sirens." He rubbed a hand over his face as though trying to wipe away his repulsion. "It's sick in the head."

"Yes and no." Antoni replied.

Targa looked sideways at him, taken aback.

"Dissection is necessary for science," Antoni explained. "It's not that part I take exception to. It's the abduction, abuse and holding of a siren in a tank that's the crime."

"And the murder of the siren they made a diagram of," Targa added sharply.

"You don't know for certain that they murdered her," Antoni answered, keeping his voice neutral.

Targa shot him a withering look. "I know you've been trained not to make assumptions, and that's good. But consider that sirens live a very long time. Do you think it likely they captured one and she died of natural causes a short time later?"

Antoni let out a long breath. "No. It's not very likely," he said, quietly. "You are probably right."

"If you think that's bad then you're not going to like the rest of what I have to say," I said, reaching for my own glass of water. Just the exercise of going back into the details of my memory was enough to make my mouth and throat feel parched.

"It gets worse?" Targa choked out.

I took a gulp and set the now empty glass back on its coaster. Settling my back against the couch, I prepared to tell the last part of my story.

"It gets worse."

TWENTY-FOUR

My mind was racing the entire journey home; even the effects of the salt on my nervous system was not enough to soften all the questions or erase all the tender bruises. I pulled saltwater into my mouth and swished it around to soothe my swollen lips. We had to swim slower because of Fimia's condition, but the Mediterranean tidal flow helped us along.

I never had gotten to see Jozef. Was he really out, or was Claudius keeping us apart? Had I been told to wait as part of a trap? Gabriela had seemed nervous. Was it because she'd been told to lie to keep me there? What would have happened if I hadn't followed the sound of water? What was the end goal for Loukas? How long had he been studying sirens? Questions gnawed at my mind like rats.

I escorted Fimia to the freshwater pools and instructed her to drink and bathe while I asked another siren to bring her food, and then I went to the Hall of Anamna to think. I felt that somehow my predecessors might lend me some wisdom. My heart was filled with lead. I missed Jozef, and was greatly troubled by the events that had passed, which added a concerning dimension to the issue of our dwindling numbers—both the halls and valleys of Okeanos seemed empty.

"Sovereign," came an urgent cry from the direction of the throne room.

Running from the Hall, I emerged from behind the throne and took the steps down to where one of the *Foniádes* stood, her expression fraught.

"What is it?"

"Atlanteans," she whispered. "They've passed the inner border and they're headed this way. Straight to Mount Califas, like they know it's our very heart."

"Rally your sisters," I bade her. "We may have a confrontation on our hands."

She shook her head, her eyes misting.

"What?" This defeat was so unlike a siren, let alone one of the *Foniádes*, that I couldn't process it. "Speak."

Her voice trembled. "There are *so many*," she whispered.

I could only stare at her. It took me far too long to find my voice. Scenes from Sisinyxa's battle flashed through my mind, illuminated as though by lightning. But this was no longer the ancient world. Battles like that did not occur now. It was the twentieth century, and we were not warriors, trained the way our ancestors needed to be.

I swallowed down the irrational fear that history was about to repeat itself.

"Under or over the water?"

"Both," she replied.

I kissed her quickly on the cheek and then made for the stairway leading to one of the natural terraces on Mount Califas. The droning of distant engines reached my ears, carried on the wind and coming from the northeast.

My remaining sirens and *Foniádes* were scattered across the surfaces and bays of Mount Califas and the inlets beyond, watching. Seeing them all outside at once like this really hit home. So few?

Someone's upturned face caught my eye and she said something to the siren nearest her upon seeing me. A cry went up and every siren began to move, making her way toward Mount Califas's beaches beneath me.

Then I saw them, a collection of dark dots on the horizon, the sounds of their diesel engines growing louder by the moment. Their shapes and details began to clear. As I counted them roughly, the blood pumping through my heart turned icy cold. There were at least thirty of them, ships and vessels of all sizes, from small bright yellow inflatable zodiacs to sharp, fast, evil looking boats with what look like actual guns mounted on the front.

Sirens emerged from the waters below. They sprinted over the beaches and climbed the rough-hewn and worn stairs leading up to the various entry points of our underworld. My eyes scanned the sirens beneath me, climbing and running to get closer to their Sovereign, and then I moved.

Taking the steps and cliffs as fast as I could manage, I dropped to a lower point on the side of Califas, one that overlooked the beaches where the squadron of boats were headed. My sirens had begun to gather there.

No one said a word as I joined those remaining, probably less than one hundred sirens, from the thousands who had lived in Okeanos when I had arrived alongside Polly those many years ago—and the tens of thousands who had lived here when Sisinyxa ruled.

We watched as the lead boat closed the gap, now able to

hear its hull slapping the waves, and see the men and a single woman standing on the deck.

Claudius himself stood foremost, and I was reminded of the way Nestor had led his own attack all those thousands of years ago in these very waters, on these very beaches and spits of rock.

My sirens and I could not fight this force. To send my citizens to attack would be certain death. But if we stood, unflinching, prepared to talk in a reasonable manner, perhaps we could stave off violence. This became my goal—that if it were possible, every siren would survive the day.

Claudius gave a signal that the boats should slow, for now they approached dangerous territory for their hulls. The rocks and tides were treacherous here. The boats first slowed, then stopped, their engines droning as they awaited their orders.

I scanned every boat desperately, searching for Jozef, but he was not visible among them.

The woman beside Claudius handed him a small red megaphone, which he took, his eyes lifted to where we stood on the cliffside.

"We, the descendants of the survivors of Atlantis, led by me, Claudius Drakief, do not intend you harm. Should you do as I say, there will be no bloodshed today."

His amplified voice was lifted and carried on the breeze. Not a one of the sirens around me moved or shifted, save for their eyes, which darted from the scene below to me and back again, waiting for me to give an order, to tell them what to do.

"Where is your Sovereign?" Claudius demanded. "We bid you come forward, for the lives of your people. We have no wish to stain these beaches with your blood."

At these words, I moved toward the nearest steps leading down to the beach. A hand touched my forearm and gently closed over my wrist. I looked back into the face of one my *Foniádes*.

"It's all right," I said gently. "He just wants to talk."

"Those guns do not say he just wants to talk, Sovereign."

I put a hand against her cheek. "And what do you propose to do against guns?"

She had no response for that. Pulling gently from her grasp, I began to descend to the beach. Seagulls screamed and the wind whipped my hair around my face. Sometime between leaving the cliff and stepping onto the beach below, the boat engines were turned off, and only the sound of the waves and seabirds could be heard once again. If I closed my eyes, I could pretend everything was normal, and that there was not a squadron of armed Atlanteans on the shores of Okeanos.

As I picked my way through the rocks to the beach, Claudius was wading through the waves, a group of armed men following him, and still that single female.

I stopped on the sand and waited for them.

As Claudius closed the gap between us, his eyes took in my features and opened wide with recognition. His cheeks paled with shock.

"You," he said, his tone not unfriendly or even malevolent, only surprised. "You are Sovereign?"

He came to stand on the sand not far away from me, staring at me with disbelief. He opened out his palm and the men behind him stopped, pointing their weapons at the earth.

I glanced back to see with a little jolt that my sirens had followed me down, and were even now emerging from cave entrances as well as descending the steps on the face of Califas. Nike, her blue hair stirring in the breeze, had come to stand just behind and to the right of me.

"She is chosen by the Salt to rule this place, and you are unwelcome here," spat someone a hostile tone I didn't recognize at first.

I looked to my left and saw Polly emerging from the crowd to stand just behind me also, shoulder to shoulder with Nike.

I looked her in the eye and gave the slightest shake of my head.

She pinched her lips shut and clenched her hands into fists at her side.

"She might be chosen by the Salt," Claudius said with some mirth in his tone, "but this bit of geography has nothing to do with that. The world has changed, and you are a nation that has not kept up. Where are your fearsome tritons?"

There was an uncomfortable shifting on the sands around me, but I did not take my eyes from Claudius.

"Ah, I see that you still think they are a creature of myth. Perhaps we should make quick work of what nature intends for your species anyway."

At this there was the sound of metal clinking as some of the men bearing weapons made to bring the barrels of their guns upon us.

But Claudius put up his hand. "A joke, a joke. We have been planning this for a very long time, taken our time, to be sure that this could be done without violence." He cocked his head and put his hand down again. "You should be thanking us for our mercy."

At this, Polly spat on the sand. I could feel Nike's tension behind me, like a hot energy leaking from her very pores. Nike had magic, that much I knew, but her magic could not come between us and thousands of armed Atlanteans, could not send them away or make them disappear. And if she acted, they'd most certainly retaliate without the so-called mercy Claudius was bragging about.

"If I had known who you were all this time," Claudius said to me, still a little dazed that I was Sovereign, "I might have planned this differently. No matter. Here we are."

"Does Jozef know you're here?"

His heavy brows lifted and his forehead wrinkled. "Jozef? No. Rest assured my son did not betray you. As much as my son is dear to me, he does not possess the constitution needed for this."

"You mean he disagrees with you, and will be angry with you when he learns what you've done."

"He'll get over it," Claudius said, putting a hand over his chest. "Consider it a gift that I am admitting to you that my son really loves you. I can give you that much before you die."

A murmur of voices rose behind me as his words struck home among my sirens—Claudius meant to let them all go free, all but me, the Sovereign.

"Oh, it's nothing personal, I assure you," Claudius said in response to the unhappy muttering of the sirens. "As Sovereign, you hold the memories of your nation, you are the representative of every Sovereign before you and every decision ever made by and for your people."

A sea bird screamed in the space between his sentences, foreboding and mournful.

Claudius's expression darkened. "I am sure you know the particular decision to which I refer. We too have ways of remembering what has gone before."

"That was thousands of years ago," I said, nearly breathless at the indomitable stubbornness of the prejudice remaining between us. "You mean to tell me that the events of those days actually have bearing on what you are doing here today?"

"That, as well as the millions of tons of mountain copper beneath our feet, a precious metal the world has not seen in a very long time."

"I warned you of this," the woman said from among those behind Claudius. "Did I not tell you this would happen?"

Claudius put up his hand again with a disdainful expression. "I'm doing the talking."

But now that the woman had brought my attention to her, I could not look away. She was the woman with the green feather at the ball, and it fell into place suddenly who she was. She'd been the starving, parasite-infested Atlantean I had encountered when I'd left Okeanos for the mating cycle which led me to Mattis.

Atlantis will rise again, she'd said. *We will kill your unrighteous Sovereign and scatter your people to the dark places of the oceans.*

Somehow, she'd found her way to Claudius's care. And suddenly I could see it. All of the wandering unfortunates of Atlantean descent had been gathered to him. They'd been nurtured and provided for, made to feel a part of something, a part of Claudius's ultimate goal to own Okeanos and all its resources.

I closed my eyes against the awful consequence of the continued divide between our people. My efforts to mend the centuries-old rift between us had come far too late.

"So, it has come to this," I said, opening my eyes in despair. "You'll let my people go away unharmed, as long as I give myself over to you?"

Claudius nodded and said, "And one more thing. Each of you must leave your gemstone here."

The woman handed him an empty brown sack, which he took and threw onto the sand in front of us.

"Put them in this bag." He then barked an order to the armed men behind him and they formed two groups with a channel down the middle leading out into the ocean beyond. "Each of you will deposit your aquamarine, remove any clothing you're wearing, and drop any weapons you're carrying. Then, you're free to go." He gestured to the narrow passageway through which he intended every siren to walk. "Through there. You have one minute to decide."

I sucked in a breath and turned around to face my sirens. Polly, Nike, and the *Foniádes,* as well as several sirens, pressed in close to me.

"You must do as he says." I pitched my voice low.

"We will not hand our Sovereign over to that scum," Polly hissed. "I'd rather die."

All of the *Foniádes* and several of the sirens were nodding in agreement.

"I will not allow it." I glared at my mother and sent that same glare into every set of eyes. "I will not have you slaughtered. Go to the Pacific sirens and join them. Okeanos is lost. I command you to go."

The murmur of my command passed through the sirens and slowly, beginning with a few of the younger ones at the back, together with their mothers, they crossed the sand. Dropping anything they'd been wearing or carrying, and depositing their jewelry into the bag, they walked slowly, cautiously, down the aisle the Atlanteans had made for them.

Everybody was tense and watching, but the Atlanteans kept their guns down, and a stance of ease. They watched the humiliation of my people as one by one they walked this narrow passageway of shame. Of shame, but of life. And that was all I cared about—preserving life. If it had to come at the cost of my own, that was a small price to pay.

Soon all that remained of Okeanos's population were three *Foniádes*, myself, my mother, and Nike. Slowly, with a reluctance that was painful to watch, the rest of the *Foniádes* made their way through the channel, their expressions grim and broken-hearted.

Polly did not move. Neither did Nike.

"Take my life instead," Polly said, stepping in front of me and closer to Claudius.

"You are not the Sovereign," Claudius replied, coolly. "Don't miss your chance to escape."

"I was Sovereign before Sybellen," my mother said. "I have all of the memories she has. Take me as the symbol of all the Sovereigns before."

"No." I grabbed Polly by the shoulder. "What are you doing?"

Claudius narrowed his eyes, looking from me to my mother. "You have a look I do not like. I do not take kindly to lies and treachery, especially in the face of my mercy." He spat onto the sand, and eyed Polly again. "What is she to you?"

"She is my daughter."

My heart had begun to pound in earnest, as Claudius looked as though to be seriously considering her offer. My mind also spun at this unexpected display of care for me and tears sprang to my eyes. I brushed them away angrily, so furious in fact that I did not know what to say. Why wait until now to show her love for me, when she'd had ample opportunity throughout my entire youth?

Claudius made a grunting sound in the back of his

throat, like he and Polly had an understanding. "It will be torture for you to watch your daughter executed, but executed she must be."

"No, take me. Please!" Polly screamed, and went to her knees.

"Mother." I began to kneel beside her when the world slowed down.

Claudius's right shoulder lifted up in a shrug. His expression went from thoughtful to bored, if not almost weary of the drama playing out. He reached into his jacket and retrieved a pistol.

"No!" I screamed and made to dive in front of my mother where she knelt there on the sand with her hands out. Some force wrapped tentacles around my wrists, ankles, and waist and jerked me backward.

Claudius pulled the trigger.

Twice.

I was flying backward across the sand like I'd been shot from a cannon. Arching through the air, I went high above and saw my mother's body jerk twice with the impact of two bullets in the chest fired from only a few feet away. I screamed and clawed at the air, desperate to get to her, desperate to save her.

The Atlanteans behind Claudius lifted their eyes to follow my strange trajectory through the air, the whites of their eyes visible, their mouths open in shock. Guns were being raised, and Claudius's gaze lifted to find me.

My mother crumpled to the sand and lay still, just as I landed hard on the stones in front of the mouth of one of the many caves leading into the heart of Mount Califas.

The breath was knocked out of my lungs and it felt as though my insides had vacuumed together and I'd never be able to breathe again. There was yelling on the beach and the sound of splashing water and booted feet thumping on the hard-packed sand as the Atlanteans pursued me, running over Polly's body in the process.

Sucking futilely at the air, I thrashed to get up when that same invisible force yanked me backward into the cave. This time I did not hit the ground, but slipped neatly through the passageway, as though riding a cart set on rails.

"I'm sorry, my Sovereign," Nike's voice whispered and echoed through the caverns and passageways as the invisible tentacles pulled me deeper and deeper into Mount Califas.

Still struggling for air, my lungs finally opened and I sucked in an enormous breath. A scream emanated from my body unlike any I had ever loosed before. It came from the very bottom of my broken heart. Broken as I'd seen Polly's back blossom with red, broken as the choice to take the bullet intended for me had been stolen from me, broken at the sight of the beaches of Okeanos now emptied of sirens, broken at having lost the chance to see Jozef one more time, broken that Okeanos, after untold millennia, the home to our people, was no longer ours. The Atlanteans had won.

I landed in a cold pool of water and immediately and unconsciously transformed into my siren form, my gills now pulling oxygen though my chest was still heaving. The gripping tentacles released me and my head surfaced. Distant echoes of shouting from high above told me the Atlanteans had penetrated Mount Califas and they were coming.

"Let them take me," I seethed to Nike, though I could not yet see her.

The siren sorceress that everyone underestimated and no one really knew emerged from the pool behind me. She wrapped a forearm around my neck and across my collarbones.

"Don't let your mother's sacrifice be in vain," Nike hissed in my ear. "You stay alive. As long as you are alive, the memories remain. If you are killed, we'll lose the memories forever. You have a responsibility to survive!"

I could hardly understand what she was saying to me, the pain was so acute.

Nike pulled me back with an unbelievable power, and I could not have resisted her if I'd tried.

"You there," she called to a siren who had been hiding among the pools and whose head had just emerged, her eyes frightened and darting about. "Trina, isn't it?"

One of Apollyona's handmaidens during her reign, the bossy one.

The siren nodded and her jaw cleared the water, her lips parted, seeing who Nike had locked in her iron grasp.

"Sovereign," she whispered. "What is happening? What happened up there? Polly told me to stay inside."

Nike practically dragged me, kicking and struggling all the while, and threw me into one of the deeper pools that led to a deep and long underwater river and spat out any traveler far out in the North Atlantic.

"Nike, let go of me at once," I cried, humiliated that I had no strength against her. She was using her magic to detain me and it set my heart in a rage.

"I'm sorry, my Sovereign. But it is for the best, you'll see." She began to mutter an incantation under the water and I felt myself growing warm. One hand held me still while the other moved and flashed around and over my form.

A layer of milky film came over my vision. I tried to ask her what she was doing, but I found I couldn't move my jaw fast enough to speak. All of my movements had become heavy and sluggish, as though weighed down by rocks tied to my limbs.

"I'm entrusting her to you," I heard Nike say to Trina. "You'll find her easier and easier to carry. Don't stop until you reach the exit. This channel will take you to the far North. I will meet you there. Now listen carefully, for we must protect your identity as much as the Sovereign's, in case you are discovered before I can come to you..."

My ears felt as though they were closing in with cotton, and now I could barely see, my vision going white instead of black. A strange, viscous liquid seeped around me, growing thicker by the moment. It filled my eyes and ears, it coated me completely.

My consciousness faded.

The last thought I recall having was a flicker between Polly's face as she fell, to Jozef smiling a welcome and opening his arms to me.

After that, there was nothing.

TWENTY-FIVE

Targa was seated cross-legged in front of the fire, staring up at me with those big beautiful eyes. Her lips were parted and she seemed frozen, as though waiting for the story to continue. Emun was perched forward on the couch, his elbows on his knees and his fingers covering his mouth, his intense blue eyes peering at me from over his fingertips.

Antoni stood behind the couch, his arms crossed high over his chest as though he was cold, he pallor a little paler than normal.

"That's it? You don't remember any more?" Emun prompted.

"My next memory is of being tucked into a car seat as Trina—who I believed to be my mother—and Hal—who I believed to be my father, were loading the car for a camping vacation. I think I was three for I had not yet had my salt-birth."

"So, in order to protect you, Nike did to you what she'd done to that turtle...she reversed your age? All the way to infancy?"

I nodded. My stomach rumbled from emptiness, but the

last thing I felt like doing was eating. "I don't think she intended for me to reverse all the way to infancy, or for Trina to have to look after me for very long. Just long enough for Nike to save as many sirens as she could before coming to find me and return me to my former state."

"But that didn't happen," Targa added. "What do you *think* happened?"

"I think Nike knew there was a chance she might be killed when she defied Claudius and his Atlanteans. In case of that eventuality, she enchanted Trina to believe she was my mother, and to take me to land with her to raise her infant daughter. I believe she must have taken Trina's gem and promised to return it to her when she found us. But when she didn't find us..."

My voice went hoarse at the thought of Nike being murdered by those treacherous Atlanteans. I swallowed hard.

"Her emergency plan kicked in, leaving you to live a whole new life, with no memory whatsoever of who you were or what had happened," Emun finished for me. He fell back against the couch, sighing and shaking his head. "It was both brilliant and insane on her part."

Antoni had begun to pace. "So, all those years that your population was dwindling, it was because Claudius had bidden his people to take the gemstones of every siren they came across?"

"That big cylinder full of gems that we found, it was a collection years in the making..." Targa said, wonderingly. "And they hid it in Okeanos."

"I think so." I was nodding. "Because it is now Atlantean territory and has been since that day."

"Well that explains the crazy Atlantean in the bar," said Emun. "It seems like Atlanteans were indoctrinated, and are *still* taking gems from sirens. But when we were in Okeanos, it was abandoned, used only as a hiding place for the gems they'd taken."

"You don't understand how large Okeanos is," I explained, getting up to stretch my legs and add a few more logs to the fire. "You said there was rubble there, as though there had been a collapse, right?"

"Yes, and it looked like no one had been there in a very long time." Antoni picked up the iron poker and prodded at the now crackling fire.

"It was just one cavern of thousands," I said. "It doesn't mean that the Atlanteans are not using those caves anymore. If they're still stealing the gems from sirens, then they could still be adding to the stash."

Emun was frowning. "But there was some kind of magical dome protecting the gems, and the cylinder was chock full to bursting. It looked more like they'd finished collecting all the aquamarines and then locked them up so no one could take them."

"And we have them now," Targa said. "Enough gems to free all of the remaining sirens in the world from their mating cycles."

I looked at her, eyes shining. "And we have an elemental who can call them by name."

Targa slowly got to her feet. She came to stand by me and stare into the fire, which had now also captured my gaze. I needed something to look at that allowed the idea blossoming in my mind to flesh itself out.

"Even if I call only Aris, or your friend Lusi," she said, speaking to Antoni, "all they have to do is give me one more name, one more siren that they know. If every siren can remember even one, their mother or their daughter or a friend, then eventually..."

She raised her eyes to mine and we stood there, the firelight reflecting in our eyes and revealing that the same idea was growing in our minds.

I finished Targa's sentence. "We can call them all."

She nodded in agreement, her eyes taking on the glint of ambition. "Every. Siren. Alive."

EPILOGUE

The sun was disappearing into the Baltic, sending a spectacular array of pinks, yellows, and purples across the horizon. Targa, myself, Antoni, and Emun were seated at a picnic bench in the park nearest the manor, eating the cheese and meat Sera had packed for us and talking about how we should go about giving gems out to sirens.

"It'll take the sirens a long time to arrive," Targa was saying, "I mean, God knows how close the nearest one is. They could be anywhere. It could take weeks, even months for them to get here."

"And once they come, what do you plan to do with them? Just give them a gem and let them go on their merry way?" Antoni glanced at me from across the table, his expression wary. "Somehow, after all you've been through and all you've lost, I doubt you want your story to end that way."

"What are you suggesting?" I asked. "Taking back Okeanos?"

Antoni and Targa both paled.

"That sounds like war," Targa said, her voice cracked. She stared at me uncertainly.

"I haven't gotten as far as thinking about recovering Okeanos," I replied, and watched as Targa visibly relaxed. "To be honest, Jozef is my priority right now. Jozef, and freeing any sirens we can from the *Dyás*."

"What if there are sirens who react the way Targa did when we give them the gem?" Antoni asked. "Clearly, the gem isn't a solution for everyone."

Targa, Emun, and Antoni had told me all the events that had taken place in the caverns they'd followed the submersible into. I had no explanation for why the gems were poisonous to her. Our only conclusion was that she was an elemental and therefore different from other sirens, more powerful. But why should that mean that the gem would harm her? Nike was powerful, too, and she was never without her gem. But Nike was a sorceress, not an elemental. It was a puzzle for everyone, but especially me because I had the longest history and the most experience with the gem. I'd never seen a siren react that way to the stone.

Emun, who'd been munching quietly, finally spoke. "You said that you were able to pinpoint the time in your history when the Mer did not wear gems, and the time when they did. Right?"

I frowned. "Roughly. It's not like I have an exact date, or even an exact century, given that I had to fish through a bunch of very old memories to figure it out. It was some time after the fall of Atlantis, though, because while Sisinyxa didn't wear any gem, the Sovereign following her did."

"Curious," Emun said thoughtfully. "It seems to me that if our next move is to call all the sirens to us so we can give them freedom from the curse in the form of some jewelry, that we're ignoring the four-hundred-pound gorilla in the room."

"What would that be?" Targa asked, snagging another piece of cheese.

"Why you need the gems in the first place."

Emun's question hung in the air over the picnic table.

He continued. "It's a curse, right? A curse needs a creator, so who created it and why?"

Antoni frowned. "There were bits and pieces about some myth on the fragments those Winterthür guys made me interpret."

"About an angry sea deity, right?" Targa prompted.

I straightened, my heart rate elevating. "They mentioned the curse in those fragments? Why didn't you say so?"

Antoni looked sheepish. "There wasn't a good time! First we thought maybe you died, then all of a sudden you're back and you want Jozef, but I can't find him, and then you've got this crazy story to tell. It didn't seem important enough to interrupt you..."

I cut Antoni off in my eagerness. "Was there more on the tablet about the aquamarine?"

"It wasn't always in small pieces," Targa explained. "Antoni told me about it while you were resting. "It used to be one big piece, a cylinder."

Antoni nodded. "A six-sided columnar."

"When did it get broken up and who broke it?" Emun asked.

"I don't know," Antoni replied. "The tablet is locked. That's why I took it to a hacker, to see if he could get into it."

An electronic ringtone made all of us jump except for

Emun. Antoni's hand whipped to his pocket and he pulled out his cell phone.

"Is it Jozef?" My heart lurched with hope.

Antoni stared at the screen, frozen for a moment before shaking his head. He answered the phone in Polish. There was a rapid conversation during which Antoni didn't take his eyes from mine. A moment later, he said goodbye and ended the call.

"That was the hacker," he said. "The tablet's been unlocked."

SALT & THE SISTERS

AVAILABLE ON AMAZON

ALSO BY A.L. KNORR

The Elemental Origins Series

Born of Water

Born of Fire

Born of Earth

Born of Æther

Born of Air

The Elementals

Mira's Return Series

Returning

Falling

Surfacing

The Siren's Curse Series

Salt & Stone

Salt & the Sovereign

Salt & the Sisters

Elemental Novellas

Pyro, A Fire Novella

Heat, A Fire Novella

The Kacy Chronicles

Descendant

Ascendant

Combatant

Transcendent